Convalesced

Aella C Grey

The Book:

"There's not a single person in this world that doesn't have a price or a threshold where they'd give up their morality for something that benefits them or someone they care for."

Kilian Sterling is a medical researcher who's discovered a possible cure for cancer, all while battling a chronic illness that has slowly taken over her life. As clinical trials begin, Kilian finds herself desperate not only for a cure for herself, but also for her best friend, Aiden, after he volunteers in her clinical trial.

Desperate for relief from her illness and willing to try anything, she meets Stolas—a mysterious, beautiful, otherworldly figure who she believes to be her spirit guide. As she grows closer to him, she begins to question what he truly is, where he comes from, and what he wants from her.

As the trials spiral out of control and Kilian's health deteriorates rapidly, danger closes in from all sides. The more she uncovers about the trials and Stolas, the more she realizes the stakes are far higher than she could have imagined. Her body and mind are in a race against time as the truth about the trials—and the forces surrounding her—begin to unravel in terrifying ways.

Will Kilian survive long enough to finish the trials, or has she already run out of time? Find out in Convalesced, book three of the Prince of Hell series.

The Author:

Aella C Grey is an author hailing from Winnipeg, MB, Canada, currently residing in the sunny state of Florida. When she's not immersed in the world of writing, Aella indulges in her other passions, such as playing video games, diving into captivating books, and cherishing quality time with her beloved dog and supportive husband.

With a vivid imagination and a deep appreciation for storytelling, Aella brings her unique perspective to the realm of fiction. Her love for literature and interactive entertainment has fueled her creative endeavors, inspiring her to craft compelling narratives that transport readers to captivating worlds.

Aella's writing draws readers in with dynamic characters, intriguing plots, and a touch of magic. Whether she's exploring mystical realms or delving into the complexities of the human experience, her stories are infused with emotion, suspense, and a dash of the unexpected.

Stay connected with Aella C. Grey through her website to discover more about her upcoming works, behind-the-scenes insights, and to join her on thrilling literary adventures.

Convalesced

Prince of Hell III

by

Aella C Grey

Aella C Grey - Florida, USA

1. Edition, 2025

Aella C Grey - Florida, USA

Table of Contents

Important

Much like the Unbroken, the Prince of Hell series has ties to real world problems, which some readers may find uncomfortable. As with all fictional books, the relationships are special in their own way, with characters that have their own personalities and flaws. None of my writing is meant to diminish the seriousness of what individuals have gone through in their lives, nor is my writing meant to demean religion in any way, shape or form.

Since Convalesced jumps at times between meditation to waking moments, you'll find two images to help you follow along.

Eyes open: Kilian is awake

Eyes closed: Kilian is meditating or dreaming

Trigger warnings:

Anxiety, Alcohol, Attempted Assault, Blood, Cults, Chronic Illness, Death, Demons, Eating Disorder, Gore, Hospitalization, Kidnapping, Murder, Medical Malpractice, Needles, Profanity, Religion, Religious Trauma, Secret Society, Sexually Explicit Scenes, Violence

This one is for all the readers who look at themselves and don't real-
ize just how amazing they truly are.
The ones who pick themselves apart so that no one else can.
I love you, dear reader.
It's time for you to love yourself, too.

Glossary

There are multiple pronunciations for these words, especially given different dialects, so please see the phonetic pronunciation below as intended for this series.

Kilian (Kill-ian), Aiden (Ay-den), Stolas (Sto-l-ahs)
Arrenault (Arr-eh-n-alt), Merrick (Meh-rr-ick)
Vassago (Vah-sah-go), Greenberg (Gree-n-berg)
Daimōn (Dey-mohn), Godfrey (God-free), Barclay (Bar-clay)
Marianne (Mah-ree-ann), Janine (Jah-nee-n), Abbess (Ah-bess)
Qur'an (Qur-ahn), Ramayana (Rah-mah-yuh-nuh)
Mahabharata (Ma-hab-hara-ta), Puranas (Pu-rah-nuh)
Upanishads (Oo-pan-i-shads)
Bhagavad Gita (Buh-guh-vuh-d gee-ta)
Lemegeton (Le-meh-jeh-ton), Solomon (Sol-uh-muhn)
Grimoire (Grim-wah-r), Goetia (Go-eh-sha)
Theurgia (Thee-ur-jee-ah), Paulina (Paw-lee-nah)
Almadel (All-mah-del), Notoria (No-toh-ree-ah)
Bael (Bay-ehl), Asmodeus (Az-moe-dee-us), Purson (Per-son)
Vine (Vy-n), Beleth (Buh-leth), Paimon (Pay-mon)
Balam (Ba-lahm), Zagan (Zai-g-ahn), Belial (Bee-lie-all)
Agares (Ay-gar-es), Dantalion (Dan-tal-eon)
Amdusias (Am-do-see-as), Vapula (Vah-pool-ah)
Aym (Ay-m), Bathin (Bah-th-een), Zepar (Zeh-par)
Eligos (E-lee-gos), Gusion (Gu-sh-ion), Barbas (Bahr-bahs)
Valefor (Val-eh-four), Vepar (Veh-par), Astaroth (As-tuh-roth)
Berth (Behr-ith), and Buné (Boo-neh) Ipos (Eye-poh-s)
Sitri (Sih-t-ree), Gäap (Guh-ahp), Orobas (Oh-roh-bas)

Prologue

Cardiac glycosides, flavonoids, saponins.

To anyone else, these might just sound like three of the components found in oleander and a handful of other toxic flora, and that would be it. But for anyone here in Seraph BioMed, the small branch of researchers from the university here in Pennsylvania, these compounds could be the key to improving cancer treatment efficacy.

Glancing at the plaques on the wall, I go through the motions of extracting all three compounds from the plant. It took some getting used to, seeing my name beside a handful of researchers whom I respect more than anything makes my chest swell with pride.

Our work here is so important.

After graduating from university, I'd landed a position here after Ron, the guy who runs this place, read through a few pieces of the research I'd compiled during class.

Apparently it was good enough to be offered a position here, earn a decent starting wage, and I've spent the better part of the last year showing my appreciation by working myself to the bone every single day.

Distracted in my thoughts, I continue to work on extracting compounds from the samples, swabbing one Petri dish before sliding it onto the counter and working on the next.

Light peers in the front window, bathing me in the orange glow from the sunset as a crow lands just outside the window. Not bothering to look, I reach over for the solvent with a yawn.

Warmth from the direct rays of sun from the window contrast the chill from the cool air from the vents overhead, and I set the vials off to my left as the door opens behind me.

A quiet knock fills the air. "Kilian, you busy?"

I glance over at Jen's lean form standing a few feet away, and smile. "Never too busy for you. What's up?"

Her dark hair shifts as she tilts her head and grins. "That's what I like to hear." I turn to face her fully, and she steps closer to my desk, her cardigan loosely draped over her shoulders. "Did you get wind of that rumor yet?"

I frown. "Probably not. I live under a rock."

She covers her mouth with her hand and chuckles. "At least it's a nice rock..." She leans in closer. "Supposedly, Ethena Health's CEO is stepping down."

My eyes widen, and I rear back. "Thomas Rempson?"

She nods. "Apparently, he wants to focus more on family and let his son take over, but people are speculating that someone accused him of infidelity, and he is avoiding a PR nightmare."

Shaking my head, I reach over to grab the three vials that should have compounds isolated and let out a dry laugh. "Color me surprised another billionaire has a mistress."

As she walks over to stand off to my right, I continue to run absently through the process of isolation. "Well, think about it though. If he's stepping down, who is going to take over? What does that mean for us?"

My gaze flicks to her for a breath of a moment, and my pulse quickens. She's not wrong to be concerned. Ethena Health is one of our biggest sponsors right now since they fund the research that the university does. A few months ago, they'd requested for us to look into accelerants and enhancers for chemotherapy... but they could pull the rug out from under us at a moment's notice if they think we aren't producing results.

"It means we need to find a damn enhancement—" I whisper, grabbing a set of three vials for a separate set of in vitro tests. "And we need to find it soon."

She grumbles something beside me, crossing her arms over her chest as she sighs. "I should go see if Trinity is coming to karaoke tonight. You're gonna be there, right?"

I nod and walk over to the freezer while tugging on a protective set of gloves. "I wouldn't miss it for the world." The liquid nitrogen blows a cloud of fog as I open the door, and my chest tightens. Grabbing three different cultures, I carry them to the counter and Jen heads to the door.

"We'll meet you there then." She chimes as she disappears around the corner, and I lose myself in finishing the testing. My mind distracted, circling the realization that our entire department could lose funding as soon as Rempson steps down.

By the time I've cleaned up, it's been hours, and I go through the motions of my routine initial 2-D test of the cultures. Each Petri dish contains different cancer cells, and I'm really only looking for certain flags to exist in the initial review to show signs of efficacy.

To put it simply, if things look terribly wrong, as in, the cancer cells have grown or mutated, it's a wash. If things look slightly different in a neutral or slightly better way, we wait for twenty-four hours before doing another test.

Most of our tests have been inconclusive so far, and I review the first culture only to find much of the same. The second culture shows nearly no change, and I swap for the third, expecting the same. Sliding it under the microscope, it comes into focus and I freeze.

This can't be possible.

Leaning back for a breath of a moment, I return to the eye-piece with a sense of urgency. The dark spots and walls that were once unmistakable cancerous cells have shifted and changed. What was once a deadly disease capable of destroying the human body, ruining lives and families is... now nothing more than a protein?

My pulse rages in my ears, and the adrenaline that's pumping through my veins threatens to overwhelm my thoughts.

I imagine this is what every inventor and scientist who discovered new things felt, questioning their own vision and knowledge, but deep down, knowing that something huge is happening right before their eyes, and they're at the center.

The question is, what the hell do I do now?

My attention turns to the phone sitting on my desk, and I inhale a deep breath. Rolling my chair closer, my hands tremble as I dial Ron's extension.

"You're still here?" Ron's gruff voice fills the air through the speaker, and my mouth drops open to respond, but nothing comes out.

Do I just tell him? There's no way in hell that he'll believe me without seeing it.

A long moment passes, then two.

"Kilian?"

I need to tell him. He needs to see this.

Swallowing hard, I clear my throat, but my voice still comes out shaky. "Can you come to the lab? You're going to want to see this for yourself."

The line disconnects, and I'm left in utter silence, staring wide-eyed at the inverted microscope as if it'll magically disappear any second.

Part of me worries it might, and that I'm just dreaming.

Because how else could this be possible?

Footsteps echo in the hallway behind me before the door creaks open. "I'm here. What have you got for me?"

His footsteps slowly approach my side, but my gaze hasn't left the microscope.

"Take a look for yourself." I whisper, gesturing to it.

It takes all of forty-five seconds for Ron to walk up to the eyepiece and lean in to look before he rears back. "Why am I looking at proteins?"

I huff a dry laugh. "You mean dead cancer cells?"

A flash of surprise followed by denial crosses his expression. His bushy, grey brows pull together, deepening the crease in his forehead. "It's not April Fool's day, Kilian—"

"You think I'd joke about this?"

I hold his gaze for a long moment, and he glances at the other cultures. "It's only this one?"

Nodding, I swallow hard. "This was adenocarcinoma."

Ron rubs the stubble along his jaw, the movement making the light reflect even more off his shaved head. "How is this possible? What test was this for?"

I huff another dry laugh, crossing my legs and smoothing out my tights. "Adenium. I separated the non-toxic compounds and did the cell culture with a two-hour incubation."

Handing the paperwork to him, he frowns. "This has to be a mistake."

My eyebrow raises, but I say nothing as he scans over the paperwork. When he shakes his head, my heart sinks into my stomach. "Well, there is a mistake, but not what I was suspecting."

He hands the paperwork back over to me and points to the second box of the third page. My eyes follow his finger, and the bolt of dread settles in my gut like a bag of rocks.

The compounds used in this test were wrong.

My heart pounds in my chest, and I glance at the vials on the counter. "It wasn't Adenium, it was the Oleander compounds." I whisper and cover my mouth with my hands.

I'd mixed them up. *Holy shit.*

Ron curses, rubbing his palm over his shiny head. "The only way out of this is to pretend we did it on purpose."

My eyes widen, and a selfish wave of relief washes over me. "You mean you're not going to fire me?"

He just scoffs like that's the most ridiculous thing I've ever said. "Not a chance, but we're going to pretend we had intended for this to happen, and we're going to start another round of testing to make sure this wasn't a fluke."

I nod, gathering the cultures to store them for the night. By the time I close the door to the storage area, my lungs are tight, and I cough hard.

"Take the night, Kilian. But tell no one that you found this. When you come back in, we'll register for pre-clinical trials immediately. I expect to initiate clinical trials this year."

My heart thrashes, and a nervous excitement buzzes through my limbs as I nod. "Yes, sir."

Chapter 1

A few months later...

"Kilian Sterling?"

I glance up at the nurse in the doorway, donned in blue scrubs, holding a clipboard to her chest as her eyes scan the room. When I push to my feet, her green eyes snap to me, and she gestures through the open door.

"Room seven, straight ahead and to the left."

The wheezing in my lungs becomes more pronounced with each step, and by the time I'm in the exam room, I have to clear my throat to cover my cough.

"Can you confirm your date of birth, please?"

"June 14th, 1999."

She tucks a lock of blonde hair behind her ear and marks something off on her clipboard. "Great, and your full name?"

*... Didn't she **just** say my full name?*

"Kilian Sterling."

She blinks, and her eyes lock with mine as we both laugh quietly. "Right. I just said your name like two seconds ago. Long day." She shakes her head slightly, pulling a disposable gown from the cupboard before gesturing to the exam table in the middle of the room. "Please change into this. Doctor Newlin will be right in."

I frown as she aligns the papers on her clipboard. "I thought I was seeing Dr. Thompson."

Her expression becomes solemn, and she shakes her head. "I'm sorry, Dr. Thompson is no longer with us."

The way she says it implies that she doesn't just mean the practice, and I swallow. "Oh."

I'd only seen Dr. Thompson for six months, but it's exhausting to have to reiterate my symptoms and my history, only to get repeat tests completed.

Dr. Newlin will be the tenth I've seen in the past three years, and I'm not sure what more I could do to get better with how many times I've been set back in treatment.

Giving me a tight-lipped smile before stepping out the door, I'm left to put on the half-gown, wondering if I'll ever understand what the root cause of my asthma is.

For years, I've gone from doing okay to barely alive, and every time, the doctor's put me through rigorous testing while on a myriad of medications, all to have to start all over with a new doctor.

It's rage inducing.

There have been days when the medication does what it is supposed to, and others where it feels like each breath may be my last. Two weeks ago, my medications got low enough to be refilled, but work has been so busy, I stretched out my medications just long enough to get to my day off.

Hopefully, this Dr. Newlin knows what he's doing.

My phone vibrates, and I glance at the unknown number on the screen. It takes half a guilt-ridden thought to hit the red button, sending them to voicemail.

Number three for the day. They might be going for a record.

Granted, if I were a debt collector and someone owed me eighteen thousand dollars... I'd be calling multiple times per day, too.

In my defense, all of it comes from medical bills.

My health insurance repeatedly denied my claims for certain tests as not medically necessary; after weeks of testing, sick visits, constant diagnosis, and the procedure, they denied almost all my subsequent appeals.

Two knocks fill the air before the knob turns, and the door slowly creaks open.

"Ms. Sterling?" A man who looks to be in his late twenties with short brown hair steps inside, gesturing his hand between us as he offers a smile that doesn't seem to reach his honey-brown eyes.

Shaking his hand, he moves to the side of the exam table and sits down with his laptop, flipping it open.

"Nice to meet you."

He doesn't respond, his eyes scanning the screen as he scrolls through what I can only assume is my patient file.

"You're in today because of your asthma, correct?" He doesn't wait for my answer as he turns, seemingly done looking at my history. "Can I get you to lean forward for me, please?"

Going through the motions like every other appointment, I lean forward, feeling my back more exposed as the gown shifts with the movement.

The cold metallic piece on my back sends a chill through my body, and Dr. Newlin places his hand on my shoulder.

"Deep breath in."

I suck in as much air as I can through my nose, feeling the crunch-like wheezing as my lungs expand.

"Now exhale."

Blowing out my mouth, I get halfway through before I cough, and my chest constricts with each huff.

"Are you currently taking any medications?"

I nod my head, somewhat relieved that he's skipping past the testing phase of this, and I watch as he grabs a long swab from the cupboard.

"Doctor Thompson prescribed me some medication for my asthma attacks and my normal birth control."

"Open wide and stick your tongue out, please."

The swab scratches the back of my throat, and I gag as he withdraws it before moving to the cupboard once more. He grabs the otoscope from the wall and turns the light on, stepping to my side and checking my ear.

"It appears as though you have a minor upper respiratory infection. I'm going to prescribe you a round of antibiotics. Once we get that under control, I would like to get an x-ray of your chest to rule out pneumonia, and we'll go from there."

My heart drops. "Dr. Thompson already got an x-ray of my lungs."

He just nods, and his brow quirks as if already annoyed by my statement. "That was months ago, and they were inconclusive at the time. You can arrange the x-ray appointment with Kelly in reception, and we will send your script to the pharmacy on file."

He types into his laptop and leans over to his prescription pad, scribbling something down before ripping it over. Holding the paper between us, I swallow my nerves and nod.

"Great. Thank you, Dr. Newlin."

He gives me a curt nod before slipping out the door, and I sigh.

This is my fifth round of antibiotics this year alone.

It's been years of endless prescriptions to combat the infection that seems to tear through my lungs. Years of symptoms of chronic asthma attacks followed by diagnostic testing have been the constant pattern, but the worst part of it all is the medication.

When my inhaler doesn't cut it anymore—which has been happening more often than not recently—onto antibiotics I go.

By the end of the ten-day period, I feel like shit, and I'm already not looking forward to another round.

Tugging my leggings on, my lungs crackle with each exhale.

If only the antibiotics helped for longer than a couple of months.

Slipping my sweater overhead, I snag my purse from the chair and head toward the check-out counter.

Maybe this time will be different.

Chapter 2

Standing in line at the pharmacy, my eyes drop to my phone, scrolling through social media videos with the volume low as I wait my turn. The video playing shows a woman with a green screen behind her with the caption talking about newly unclassified documents from the government. She's animatedly talking with wide eyes, and I click the volume up button twice.

"... the mind and what it controls. Studies have shown in these classified documents that in the years of research completed, individuals reduced their illnesses or symptoms to near-zero without actually getting any medications. The control groups achieved better results than those receiving medication."

The line moves, and I take a step forward as the person in front of me goes to the counter.

"As a parallel test, scientists conducted multiple trials in which groups of individuals used meditation to holistically repair their bodies through intention, yielding faster results than the other two tests. Interestingly, only the subjects who met and interacted with their spirit guides during meditation ended with long-standing positive outcomes."

The person in front of me walks away from the counter, and I slide my phone into my purse as I take their place. The pharmacist, Heather, types something on her computer, not bothering to look in my direction.

"Name and date of birth?"

"Kilian Sterling, June 14th, 1999."

If she recognizes my voice from the countless times I've been here, she doesn't show it as I ease my debit card and ID through the small opening of the counter. She snags both and places them in front of her, typing into her system before stepping into the back. It's a long moment before she returns holding a bag in her hands.

She slides the cards back to me, along with my medications and the receipt. "Thank you, Ms. Sterling. Have a good day."

"You too, Heather." Walking away from the counter and stuffing the medication into my purse, I pause, glancing around for a moment and recounting mentally what's stocked in the kitchen.

I normally get pre-packaged meals delivered for lunches, but there's nothing I like more than a good evening snack before bed, and my feet automatically head toward the aisles that house all my favorites.

My lungs strain with each breath as I start with the chip section, grabbing a bag of pretzels and some jalapeño cheddar chips before snagging a package of white cheddar rice cakes. Turning around, I slam into a hard chest and gasp painfully as a carton of milk falls from his hand to the floor.

Recovering from my sudden gasp, a cough claws from my chest. "Oh, my god. I'm so sorry."

My head tilts to look up at the stranger, seeing a man with a short buzz-cut, and a hard look on his face. He says nothing, but looks nothing less than pissed off as he stares me down, and I slink away, shuffling to the side to get past him.

He still says nothing as I walk away, murmuring apologies until he's out of earshot. I continue absentmindedly to the vegetable section, and grab a couple apples before wandering to check out.

This should be more than enough for me for the rest of the week with the delivered meals, considering that I ordered food for most of my lunches last week even though I had meals prepped...

Whoops.

At least I froze them.

Well, most of them.

Thankfully, the clinical trials start up at work next week, and I've been foaming at the mouth to see the progression of our research on this new drug's effect on cancer cells. We spent an entire week laying out each stage's plan, and even did an exercise to predict what outcome we thought we might see. This week is where we gather participants, and determine eligibility, so safe to say I've been more than hyped for it.

By the time I've paid and grabbed my bag of groceries to leave, I'm lost in thought. It's as if I'm on autopilot as I head to my car and a shrill bird call that sounds like a warning fills the air from the trees that hang over the parking lot.

It gets louder, and I glance around for the source until my gaze lands on the man from the snack aisle not far away. He's already looking at me, and my heart lurches into my throat as I pick up my pace. Another shrill sound fills the air, and I fumble to press the button to unlock the car. Hurrying in the driver's door, I slam the door shut, and locking it with a click.

My lungs crackle as I wheeze, and the lack of movement around the car only makes me wonder if I over thought the entire situation as another vehicle drives past mine in the rearview.

I spot his short buzzed hair in the driver's seat before the vehicle disappears, and exhale a tense breath. He was probably going to his car, and I just freaked myself out for no reason.

Blowing out a shallow breath, I put it in reverse and drive home more rattled than I was to start. It's not until I'm pulling into the long driveway that my wheezing has finally calmed down, and the car shudders to a stop when I finally start to feel more relaxed.

I really need to take these antibiotics soon.

Outside of just wanting to feel normal again, I wouldn't stand a chance if anyone came after me.

I would be in big trouble.

Grabbing the groceries, it's only a handful of steps up the stairs before I'm at the door, and by the time I'm inside, I'm huffing strained breaths as I put the snacks into the cupboard.

Feeling lightheaded, I pause, focusing on my breathing for a few seconds as my heart pounds. The tactic seems to help, and I reach for the half-full water bottle with one hand before reaching into my purse for my medications with the other.

No better time than the present to kick whatever infection I have in the butt.

Swallowing the pill down with a couple gulps, my mind wanders back to the video I was watching at the pharmacy.

What if I give meditation a go?

It couldn't hurt, right?

I mean, look what focusing on my breathing did for a few seconds.

It's not like anything I've tried thus far has been effective.

Glancing at the clock, I nearly jump out of my skin when the doorbell rings, shattering the comfortable silence of the house.

It rings again, and I nearly roll my eyes. "Coming!"

Taking my time to get to the door, I actually roll my eyes this time as it rings again, and I tug the door open.

"Patience is a virtue, you know."

Aiden's disheveled brown hair is the first thing I notice out of place as he huffs and pushes past me. "Unfortunately for you, virtuousness and I are never in the same room."

A small laugh escapes me, and I shut the door behind him, following to the front room where he's dramatically thrown himself onto the couch, hugging a pillow to his chest.

"Do I need to ask what has you so worked up, or are you just going to tell me?"

He chews his bottom lip nervously, but the seriousness on his face is so out of character that my feet carry me to the couch, and I slide in next to him.

Aiden's been my best friend for years, starting in middle school when we shared a few classes together and ever since, we'd been inseparable. People thought we were dating for the longest time, but I'd known deep down that he wasn't interested in me, nor I him. Our souls just bonded instantly.

When he came out to me before anyone else in his life, it was an honor and a secret I knew I'd carry to the grave with me when he asked me to not tell anyone else. Still, rumors flew around us, and he never corrected anyone. Our false relationship throughout the school year built an impenetrable shield around him, so that when he was ready, and felt safe enough to tell people, he did.

That number of people who know is small, though.

Here in our small town, it's not well received when people stray from the norm, so I protect his secret like it's a treasure guarded close to my heart.

My head tilts as I lean toward the back of the couch, resting my arm on it.

The last time Aiden was like this, he flew to Italy with some guy named Ronaldo, thinking he'd found his soulmate. Three months later and a one-way flight back, I thought he'd learned his lesson.

Judging by the nervousness in his expression, though, clearly there's a chance he didn't.

"Aiden, come on."

He sighs, curling up into a tighter ball. "I need to confess something."

My brow raises slightly, and I feel my pulse spike. "Well, you came to the wrong place, then. I'm not even close to a priest. Literally or figuratively."

Jabbing his elbow into my arm, we both laugh for a brief second before he sucks in a breath. "I have cancer, Kil."

Staring at him for a moment, I question if I heard him right, and my mind grasps desperately at the hope that I didn't.

"I'm sorry, you—"

"Have cancer."

The bluntness to his tone and the tears in the corner of his eyes snaps me from disbelief and denial into full acceptance, and I clear my throat.

"What kind?"

He swallows, and he glances up at me as my heart feels like it could crawl out of my throat.

"Colon. My constipation wasn't just my diet, I guess." He chews the inside of his lip. "It's been a year of treatment and my markers aren't improving, so my oncologist wants to go over other options tomorrow."

Every memory of him being sick comes to the forefront of my mind, including the one from two days ago, where he had walked over from his house to get milk, looking like he's been up for days.

My heart fractures, and I reach over to grasp his hand. "I'm so sorry, Aiden... Why didn't you tell me?"

Guilt flickers across his face, and his large hand tightens around mine. "When I was diagnosed... I couldn't believe it. I didn't even tell Connor at first, but once I went for my first treatment, I knew I had to..."

Aiden's thumbs rub the back of my hand. "I went into denial for a bit, and a month later, I was so sick... I wanted to tell you that day you'd brought soup over, but it had already been so long that I couldn't bring myself to. Plus, your lab had just registered for pre-clinical trials at that point, and you were just so *happy*... I didn't want to ruin that."

My heart fractures more when I think back to all the days he'd been in bed with the flu, tired from a long day at work or sad. "I understand why you didn't, but I can't say I wish I would have known sooner."

He swallows, and his throat bobs. "I'm so sorry, Kil... It's not that I didn't want to... I just—" his breath hitches. "Telling you felt like it would make it real, and by the time I was going to, it felt like it was too late."

I nod, and he grabs the remote from the table with a shrug. "I just figured you should know, but it changes nothing."

My lips twitch slightly. "Yeah, cancer or not, you're still a pain in my ass."

He laughs. "Are you okay if I stay here for a while until Connor gets home?"

The look on his face is lighthearted, but I can see the concern behind his eyes as I nod. "Mi casa es su casa."

"Great." He breathes, clicking the television on and flicking through channels. "No better time to catch up on our show then."

A huff of laughter escapes me, and I snuggle in alongside him just as his arms encircle my shoulders. His head leans against mine, and a long moment passes as the show plays, but when I hear him swallow, I already know it's taking everything for him to hold himself together.

"We'll get through this, Aiden. You won't be alone."

I feel him nod with his cheek still pressed against my hair, and I don't know what more I can say to ease his mind. All I know is that he's my best friend, and I'll move mountains if it means being there for him.

Chapter 3

"Well, I better get going. Connor should be home any minute."

Yawning deeply, tears form in the corners of my eyes as we pace to the front door, and I cross my arms over my chest, watching him put his shoes on.

The chill from the evening seeps through the door, and I shiver. "Do you want to borrow a pair of gloves?"

Aiden grins and shakes his head before standing at his full height. "It's a literal two-minute walk to the house. I might be dramatic, but not enough to steal your gloves for **that** short of a walk."

My quiet laughter fills the air, and I open the door as the brisk air kisses my skin, making my hair stand on end. "Right, well I'll remember that days from now when you tell me how you have frostbite."

His eyes narrow, but he just grins because he knows I'm not wrong. "Alright, babe. I'll text you later."

Within seconds, he's halfway down the steps, and another cold gust of air has me shutting the door behind him, rubbing my palms together to bring the warmth back as I yawn. The cold air tightens my chest and I cough suddenly. It's as if a bowling ball is sitting on my lungs with each gulp of air.

A familiar sense of panic washes over me, and I hurry to the bedroom, stumbling to the dresser as air escapes my lungs in a wheeze.

If I can just get to my inhaler...

My breathing is labored, and each feels starved of oxygen as my head swims. The dark that shadows every corner of the room does nothing to help as I knock over several items, desperately feeling around for my inhaler.

Come on, come on. Where is it?!

Finally, my fingers brush the plastic cap, and I rip it off. It clatters to the ground as I bring the mouthpiece to my lips, pressing the top down before sucking in a drag of air.

The cold mist hits my lungs and I fight the cough tickling deep in my chest as I gulp down air. Each moment feels like an eternity as I count to thirty and repeat the action with my head spinning.

The room spins as I career to the side, and my hands slam to the wooden dresser with my inhaler clattering to the floor before the rest of my body leans into it for support.

My heart thrums loudly in my ears as I try to focus on my breathing, but with my balance being thrown off, it's nearly impossible to calm myself down.

Glancing over to my bed with desperation coating my veins, I stumble over to it, losing my balance with my last step and heaving onto the soft surface with a huff. My lungs wheeze with each breath and I roll to my back. Squeezing my eyes shut, I focus on calming myself down, but the panic won't settle at all.

It's not enough. I need something to help distract me.

Sliding my phone from my pocket, I type in a quick search for meditation, and click the first one I see, holding the volume button to turn it up with some last ditch effort to drown out my own thoughts.

The serene music fills the air, and within seconds a woman's voice joins it, sounding just as tranquil.

"Hello, and welcome to tonight's guided meditation practice."

The voice goes on, but I'm only half listening as I feel tingling in my toes, so I shift further onto the pillow, getting comfortable as the guide instructs me to take three clearing breaths.

"Let your mind and body surrender as you breathe. Draw your attention to the crown of your head and imagine a blue light beaming down to meet your crown."

My breathing evens out as the medication does its work.

"Allow this divine light in, and let it through your body, dissolving any tension it comes across. From your head to your shoulders, your chest, through your lungs, to your arms and down. Feel it flowing through your hips, down your legs and descending all the way to your toes. Envision your entire being enveloped by this light."

My breathing calms even more, and I exhale as the guide instructs to release all the tension. I picture the blue light pouring into me, filling every orifice of my body as I relax further, melting more into the mattress.

"...and continue to breathe normally, allow the light to ease from your feet, creating a beautiful marble staircase that will guide you where you will meet your guardian angel."

My head still spins as I remain still, but to my surprise, an image of solid blue stairs form on the back of my eyelids, and I picture myself taking a tentative step forward.

"Two. Take another step onto the exquisite staircase, feeling the stone beneath your feet. Ground to it as you steady yourself."

Breathe in. Breathe out.

"Three. Feel yourself become more relaxed with this step, allowing your mind to remain awake as your body falls deeper into a sleep-like state."

Breathe in. Breathe out.

"Four. Each step brings you closer to the level of enlightenment of your angel, where your energy and the divine remain in complete harmony."

Breathe in. Breathe out.

"Five. Further and further you go. Each step grounds you to the solid marble staircase, keeping you safe and sound."

Breathe in. Breathe out.

"Six. You are moving into another realm of reality with this step."

Breathe in.

"Seven. Exhale another centering breath, letting yourself take another step toward divinity."

Breathe out.

"Eight. Feel the state of calm within yourself, and open your mind to what you want to achieve. What questions you want to ask."

Breathe in.

"Nine. Allow each breath to come and go. Take another step further onto the marble staircase as your heart and chest open to the divine."

Breathe out.

"And ten. Take the last step off the staircase, see a large set of doors. Push the doors open."

The music quiets down as I push through the center of the doors, only to find myself surrounded by beautiful trees. Oak, pine, willows, birch.

Paths line the dense brush around the trees, with gorgeous flowers of varying kinds sprouting from them. There's a low hum emitted from each, and I glance up at the sky from between gaps in the foliage, revealing hundreds of thousands of stars.

"Breathtaking, isn't it?"

My head snaps to the source of the deep male voice, only to find no one there.

"Who are you?" A warm breeze glides across my skin, and I shiver.

"Who do you think me to be?" His voice sounds powerful and resonant, the baritone itches deep in my mind as I look for where he might be.

Thinking back to the guided meditation, my heart thumps steadily in my chest. "My spirit guide?"

There's a long moment before I hear his voice again, but it almost sounds as if he's amused. "You sound uncertain."

Blowing out a breath, I nod. "Well, this is kinda new to me. I don't even know what I'm doing, so I guess I am."

Another warm breeze sends a shiver down my spine. "You journeyed here on purpose, Kilian. You do yourself injustice by questioning your own desires."

I blink. "How did you—?"

Oh, right. Spirit guide. "What's your name?"

The tops of the trees rustle, and I glance up to see a star shooting in the sky, leaving a thin streak of light before dissipating into the glittering sky.

My chest tightens at the sight. It's been so long since I've seen such a beautiful sky without half of them being satellites and the other half being planes.

"My name is Stolas."

I blink, and my brows shoot up. "Nice to meet you, Stolas..."

"You came here for peace? Is that not correct?"

His voice sounds like it's coming from my right and I turn toward the sound, my eyes scanning the trees.

"Sort of. I needed to calm down until my medicine kicked in." A wave of unease comes over me, and I feel another breeze graze my skin.

"Come this way, Kilian." The breeze rustles the branches along one path from the direction of his voice, so I take confident strides forward.

Stolas is right. I came here of my own accord, so it's not like I have anything to worry about. This is a figment of what I wanted and where I must have desired to go.

"Stolas," I whisper. "Is there anyone else here?"

A wide break in the trees gives way to thick, soft moss that pillows out from the ground, and the moonlight brightens the area as I walk into the center, feeling my feet sink into the moss with each step. By the time I'm standing in the center of the opening, I scan at the tree-line, looking for where the path went with a frown.

Where do I go now?

"There could be others, but for now there is not. Look up."

My gaze turns to the sky, and I watch in awe as streaks of light line the stars. Meteors or maybe stars continue to fall, and I sink down to the ground, laying on my back as another warm breeze comes through.

"Beautiful, is it not?" The deep baritone voice sounds like it's all around me, and I nod, not daring to remove my eyes from the torrent of stars in the sky.

"I don't think beautiful properly describes it."

A tentative silence falls over the surrounding space, and I blink slowly at the sky, following each star before they burn into nothing, disappearing from my eyes.

"Where are we?" I ask, searching the area for where his voice comes from.

"A space between worlds where the soul can breathe." His words caress my ears and I shiver against the grass. "Inhale deeply, Kilian. Let this place soothe you like it does me."

I swallow. "Do you come here to relax, too?"

When his voice fills the surrounding space, I can almost hear the smile in his words. "While this place is beautiful, I do not come here often enough to enjoy it as you are."

A light streaks across the sky. "Maybe you should," I murmur, and he chuckles in response. "Everyone deserves a little rest."

Silence extends between us, and the smell of lavender fills the air as I sigh, melting further into the mossy ground. I'm not sure how long I laid there in silence, enjoying the scenery, but soon, my heavy eyelids slide shut, and sleep claims me.

Chapter 4

I yawn deeply, a bitter chill causing a shiver to run down my spine as my eyes open.

The sun creeps in from between the window shutters, and I stretch my arms far over my head. A slight throb sends pangs of pain into my skull, but it seems to dissipate as slide my legs off the bed.

My feet hit the floor, and I tilt my head left and right, hearing the crack that echoes into my ears as much as I feel it.

Frowning, I glance around the room.

How the heck did I fall asleep?

It takes a few minutes, but I finally recall the asthma attack through the fog in my mind, and I recount my decision to listen to a guided meditation, but after picturing the blue light travelling through my body, there's nothing else.

I can't help but feel exhausted though, even though I got a full night's rest.

Walking to the kitchen, I grab a yogurt from the fridge when a loud bird call outside blends with the whistles of the cardinals and the squawks of the blue jays.

I glance at the clock.

Oh, shoot.

It's already past my usual time to put food in the feeder.

More 'kraa' sounds fill the air and I frown.

I'm used to having crows around, but that's a weird call, even for them.

Carrying my yogurt to the back door, I place the spoon in my mouth, using my free hand to shovel a scoop of bird food before maneuvering the door open.

The cold air hits my lungs like a sack of bricks, and I brace for the cough as I take a couple of steps to the base of the patio. I get all the way to the feeder and pour the seed into it before it hits me.

No asthma attack yet.

A silent wave of excitement washes over me, but not wanting to push my luck, I hurry back inside, placing the scoop back in the bag as the birds continue to chirp loudly.

My stomach churns as I polish off my yogurt, grabbing the container of medications off the counter with a sigh. Shaking one into my palm, I sigh.

"Bottoms up."

Cracking open a bottle of water and gulping down two sips, I grimace, feeling the large pill make its way down my throat.

Some day we won't have to take horse pills for antibiotics.

Some day.

My phone vibrates, and I glance down at the debt collector's number across the screen. Sending them to voicemail with a grimace, anxiety swirls in my gut.

I'll deal with that later... much later.

The calls outside become louder and more chaotic, so I snag a few almonds before going outside to investigate. It wouldn't be out of the norm for squirrels to get into it with crows over food, but this just **sounds** different.

Slipping on my shoes, I only get a few steps down the patio when I hear the usual flutter of wings as birds take off from the feeder.

Movement to my right catches my eye, and I glance over at my other neighbor's yard. My gaze lands on the barrel of a gun first, and my eyes widen as I watch Paul take aim into a tree in my backward.

"What the hell are you—?"

A thunderous bang fills the air and my hands shoot to my ears. The sound sends all the birds in the area flying, and I barely hear their feathers rustle against the wind as they all take off.

What the fuck is he doing?!

The barrel of his gun drops to the ground, and I follow his line of aim to where an enormous crow lies on the ground, its wing straightened out with speckles of blood splattered around it.

"Stop!"

My voice is shrill, and I hurl myself down the steps as he steadies his aim. My heart thunders as I take the few last steps, putting myself between him and the crow.

"Get out of the way!" He waves his hand to the side, gesturing for me to move.

"Never shoot anything on my property again, Paul! I will call the police so fucking fast!"

Paul grumbles something about a stupid loud bird, but I'm not paying any attention to him as I gaze down at this giant crow staring right back at me.

No. Not a crow.

A raven.

It shifts slightly, and the movement presses its wing against a log as it gurgles in what I can only assume is disapproval.

"Shit."

From what I can see, the gunshot tore through a couple of feathers and grazed its wing, but there might be more damage than that.

Sliding my cardigan off, the enormous bird watches me intently, glancing behind me now and then as I remove the material from my arms.

Paul hasn't made a move, standing there with the barrel of his gun lowered as he glares at me and the raven.

The bitter air makes the tiny hairs along my arms stand upright, and I count a blessing or two for having more meat on my bones to help shield from the cold.

"Alright, easy now." Tentatively I lean in to cover the enormous bird with my cardigan, and it just blinks, tilting its head peculiarly as it watches.

My chest tightens, and I pick up speed, gently scooping the bird into my arms, hearing crows in the treetops above. The creature in my arms is so large that its enormous, curved beak brushes the exposed column of my throat, and I silently hope that it knows I'm here to help, not harm.

Each rush of air that leaves my lungs makes them crinkle, and I glance up at the crows lining the branches above, watching me as I climb the patio steps.

Each one jostles the bird, but if it's in pain, there's no sign, just the gentle swish of feathers as I bring the creature to the kitchen.

Delicately placing the bird on the counter, I remove the cardigan from its shoulders, and the creature bristles as the feathers around its neck form what looks like a thick, puffy scarf.

"Right. Well. I'm sorry you got shot, but I need to make sure you aren't going to die." My gaze drops to the counter, relieved to see there's no blood before settling on his extended, bloodied wing. "Good news is, it doesn't look like it, but we should still check."

Moving closer, I bend down to look up at the enormous creature's wing as it continues to watch me intently. I see damage to the feathers along its wing, with one or two missing completely. Just as I'm about to move closer, the bird jerks away, clicking its beak and tilting its head.

Chewing the inside of my lip, I lock eyes with the bird. "I need to check if it's still bleeding." A long moment passes as it blinks, and I move to check the spot again as it jerks back.

I release a sigh. "Please."

Tilting its head to the side again, it turns slightly, and I move to lift its wing.

"Stop."

My eyebrows shoot up at the raven's deep voice, and its feathers flatten down as it tilts its head in a very bird-like manner.

"Okay," I blow out a breath, and it clicks its beak again. "Well, if you won't let me check your wing, I'll have to bring you in somewhere to get checked out."

Pulling out my phone, I'm about to look up bird rehabilitation facilities near me when the raven bristles again.

"No." It steps over to my hand and I freeze as its beak mouths my finger before it pulls back, firmly repeating itself. "Stop."

I knew ravens were intelligent, but this one sounds like it's literally telling me it doesn't want me to look up a rehab facility. But if I don't, that means I'll have to take care of this bird with no knowledge of how, while someone's probably missing their pet raven.

This has to be someone's pet, right?

Taking a deep breath, I shake my head. "Right, well. Your funeral then, I suppose." I go to type rehabilitation in my search bar, and the bird nips at my hand as I gasp.

"Stop."

Pursing my lips, the creature and I stare at one another before I finally place my phone down with a huff. "Okay, okay." Glancing around the room, I realize that there's literally nothing for a bird to do.

What do ravens even like, anyway?

"Looks like we need to go buy–" I gesture my hands toward the bird with furrowed brows. "–whatever ravens need to survive."

Moving to walk to the door, a rustle of feathers and tapping claws has me whirling around to see the creature with outstretched wings as it frantically chases after me, and I stare at it with wide eyes.

"Okay, okay, calm down. It's fine. You, ah, you can come with me?" The bird's wingspan is impressive as it folds them inward again, and I note the way one wing still looks uncomfortably tucked against its body.

Grabbing a jacket from the hook next to me, I glance around the room, trying to figure out how the heck I'm going to sneak a raven into a pet store. When my big old purse comes to mind, and I grin, holding my palm out and backing away.

"Just... stay there, okay? I'm going to get something to transport you in."

It just blinks at me, tilting its head in a birdlike manner as I disappear down the hallway toward the bedroom. Mere seconds pass by before I hear more feathers whooshing, followed by a repetitive tapping sound, and I already know the raven followed me.

Is it normal for them to be this curious after being shot at?

Could this be some sort of trauma bond?

I know they're intelligent, but I didn't think they could pick up words or behave like this.

Swinging the closet door open, I kneel, rummaging around for my old purse, cursing every time I think I've found it, but it's another purse or bag I'd hoarded.

My fingers wrap around the thick handle and I tug it out from the back where it was, squeezed beneath a few smaller purses. "There it is!"

When I turn to the raven once more, it seems more curious about what's in my hands than scared, so I place the purse down in front of it and lean back on my heel.

It blinks and cocks its head as I gesture to the purse. "Well, go on. Take a look."

Feeling like a kid in a candy shop, I watch with a bated breath as the bird steps closer, inspecting the purse and casting cursory glances at me before peering inside.

The bottom of the large purse is solid, and the frame allows the purse to curve over its wings. Of course, I wouldn't be able to zip it up, but it's long enough that only its beak and head might stick out, and it wouldn't put pressure on its injury.

Before I can wonder how I'll get it into the purse, I watch with wide eyes as the enormous creature uses its sharp talons to climb into the bag. My mouth drops open as the bird ruffles its feathers before settling in, and the puffy look of its body becomes more sleek.

"I suppose that means you approve." Gently bringing the handles up and lifting the purse, the raven settles in even further, and my chest tightens as I pace to the front door.

Something about the trust this creature has in me without me even doing anything to earn it has me swallowing hard as I slip my shoes on and head out the door.

Maybe it's that my parents always told me that trust is harder earned than broken. Maybe it's because I have always had a soft spot for animals.

Hell, maybe it's both.

But all I know for sure right now is that there's no way in hell I'm going to break the trust it's placed in me anytime soon.

My eyes gravitate to the neighbor's yard, and thankfully there's no sign of Paul as I reach the car. The raven remains silent as I hoist him over the center console, placing the purse on the passenger seat before turning the key in the ignition.

"And it's off to the races we go."

Chapter 5

It's mid-afternoon, and I'm out three hundred dollars by the time I've left the pet store. Even though I had looked up what ravens need to thrive while we were shopping, I still feel entirely inadequate to care for one.

Placing the purse onto the counter, I widen the top so the bird can climb out before unloading the puzzles and other stimulating items while a rustle of feathers fills the air.

I glance over to see the creature teeter awkwardly before stumbling, and my heart drops.

Shit. I knew it was hurt.

Hurrying over to its side, I ignore its clicking beak as I look it over for any injuries, feeling the pit of dread only deepen at the large wound along its ribs where the wing folds in.

No wonder it wasn't sitting normally.

Damn. How could I be so careless?

The bird's beak nips dangerously close to my hand just as I let go. Tugging the door to the cabinet open, I quickly snatch the small safety kit under the sink.

When I turn around, the bird's already trying to follow me, with talons clattering against the tile. The raven sidesteps awkwardly again, and I hurry over with my heart in my throat before it collapses.

"God damn it. Why did I listen to a damn bird? I should have called the rehab center..."

Feeling entirely guilty, I spend the next few minutes putting pressure on the wound to stem the bleeding. By the time I've built up the gauze over it and wrapped the raven's body with some spare long sheets of cloth I'd had from my last major injury, the creature seems to be more lucid than before.

Looking over the dark blood that looks near-black splattered around the floor, I blow out a breath and scoop the bird into my arms, feeling it lean against my chest heavily.

It takes a few minutes to get cleaned up, still supporting the raven tucked into my chest, but I finally get the last bloodied cloth thrown into the laundry with a deep sigh.

My phone vibrates on the counter, and I walk over, feeling my chest tighten with each breath, which is arguably better than it's been with how much walking around I've done in the past hour.

Seeing an unknown number on the caller ID, I press the button to answer and hold the phone to my ear. "Hello?"

"Hi. Is this Ms. Sterling?"

"Uh, yes. This is."

"Good morning Ms. Sterling. My name is Ginny. I'm a patient advocate from Dr. Newlin's office. We wanted to call to let you know that your insurance denied the pre-authorization for your testing next month. You can still get the testing done, but it will have to be paid out of pocket unless you decide to appeal the decision. If we decide to appeal, we will need you to come back next weekend for some more lab-work to support our records."

My shoulders droop, but I can't say I'm surprised.

I sigh. "Yes, I'd like to appeal. I'm open next weekend to do more lab-work."

The sound of keystrokes fills the air as I put the phone on speaker and walk to the front room, easing myself and the raven down before turning the television on.

"Alright, looks like we have a seven o'clock, eight, and eight-thirty—"

"Seven is fine."

Ginny falls silent as she types some more. "Great, you're all set. Have a great night, Ms. Sterling."

"Thanks. You too."

The line disconnects as I toss my phone aside, blowing out a tense breath.

How long will I have to argue and fight just to live?

I've paid more into my health than any other facet of my life, and yet somehow I have nothing to show for it.

It's not like I've gotten any better. If anything, I've only gotten worse over the years, even with all the medications and testing. Something has to give.

Anything.

The raven shifts in place, cocking its head like it's fully lucid again.

"Finally back from the dead?"

Its feathers puff up, and it clicks its beak a few times before its deep voice fills the air. "Thanks."

My eyes widen. *It really picked up words I've said that quick?*

Unable to fight the urge, I reach over and run my fingers over its head, watching as it blinks slowly in response to my touch.

"Do you have a name, mister bird?"

It's a lengthy assumption that this raven is male, but judging by its sheer size, I think it's a fair one.

The raven looks at me for a long moment and cocks his head, but when he doesn't say anything, I huff a quiet laugh. He stands up and stretches his wings slightly, and his claws dig into my skin.

I hiss. "Ow, damn, those are sharp." The moment I say it, the raven's claws release my skin and I shake my head.

"That's it. Your name is officially Talon."

Talon's beak clicks a few times in what I can only hope is approval before he shakes, ruffling his feathers before settling in once more into my chest.

I struggle to not stare at him as he curls his head to the side, resting it along my arm. It takes everything I have to force my eyes on the television, but every few minutes I can help but glance down.

There's something special about a creature putting full faith or trust in me to take care of it, and that seems to tug at my heartstrings more than anything has before.

My phone vibrates again, and I reach over to grab it, waking Talon up in the process as I answer the call.

"Tell me you're hungry."

The demand in Aiden's tone is borderline pleading, and I laugh. "I haven't eaten since breakfast, so yeah, why?"

"Oh, thank god."

"What did Connor make too much of this time?"

I can hear the wind and birds chirping from his side of the line. "Birria tacos, and Kilian, these will knock your socks off."

I just laugh harder, wiggling my bare toes. "That'll be tough since I'm not wearing any, anyway."

"Well, consider yourself lucky then that I'm freezing my ass off for you, fingers, toes and all."

Footsteps thunder up the front porch as Talon's head jerks toward the sound. For a hint of a moment, I worry Talon won't receive Aiden as well as he has me when the front door opens and Aidan waltzes inside.

His steps echo into the kitchen, and a bag rustles as if he set it down in a hurry. "Food is on the counter, babe! I can't stay though, it's movie night tonight."

"Thank you!" I call out just as the front door shuts once more, and I glance down to Talon as he bristles. "Let's go get you some dinner, too. You need to get your strength up."

Pushing to my feet, my next inhale suddenly constricts my chest, and I cough hard while trying not to jostle Talon too much. Each tremor in my body jerks him slightly, sending a fresh wave of guilt through me.

Maybe we both need to get our strength up.

Setting Talon on the counter, I reach into the fridge and pull out some cut up watermelon, snagging the container of raw almonds from the cupboard as well, pouring a handful of each into a bowl, sliding it over to Talon.

Setting the bag aside, I'm opening the container of tacos when I feel eyes on me, and I look over to see Talon watching curiously.

My eyes travel to the untouched food in front of him. "You've never had watermelon or almonds, have you?"

He cocks his head to the side, and I reach into the bowl, taking a piece of watermelon and biting it in half. I'm still chewing when I offer the other half to him.

I don't know why I thought that would convince him, but he looks between me and the fruit for a moment before taking the piece and eating it in one go.

He steps forward and snags an almond, chomping his beak as I dip the taco in Connor's homemade consommé and take a bite. I only chew twice before I feel eyes on me again, and my gaze slides to look at Talon as his head cocks to the side.

Swallowing the bite, I hold it up between us. "This is a birria taco... and while good, I don't think this is raven-approved." I dunk it again and take another bite, hearing my phone vibrate on the table in the front room.

"Shit, I'll be back in a second."

I hurry over, feeling my chest tighten again and the crunchy wheeze resurfaces as I look at the message from my boss on my lock screen.

Ron: "We had a handful of applicants withdraw, we're extending the application period by another week."

Kilian: "Gosh. Alright. Do you still want me to start eligibility for those who already applied tomorrow?"

Ron: "Yeah, we should get ahead of it. Who knows what other roadblocks we'll get into next week."

Kilian: "Sounds good. See you tomorrow."

Chewing the inside of my cheek thoughtfully, the tickle in my lungs makes me cough heavily as I get into the kitchen, only to see Talon scarfing down the last bite of taco, and I gape at him.

"I said I didn't think ravens could eat birria. That didn't mean that you should eat it, anyway!"

He blinks and clicks his beak in what I can only assume is approval again as I sigh. The sudden exhale makes my lungs crunch but this time it's actually painful, forcing me to cough more violently. My hands brace against the counter as I lean forward with my lung that feel like they're seizing.

Shit.

Without a word and half in a panic, I head for the bedroom, feeling my heart in my throat with each step. By the time I'm at my dresser, I'm pressing my lips to the mouthpiece of my inhaler and taking a deep breath of medication that feels like ice in my lungs.

I count to sixty before taking another, and the feeling in my chest loosens ever so slightly.

Every time these attacks happen, I always think it'll be my last, but for some reason, this time feels different.

Maybe because I know I need to take care of Talon right now, or perhaps because I know he needs me. I just feel like I need to get better.

I hear a clatter behind and turn, seeing Talon in the hallway, observing me carefully as I give him a weak smile.

"Sorry, Talon. I didn't mean to scare you at all or leave you like that." He steps closer, and I bend down to scoop him into my arms. "I think I just need to relax a bit, and I'll be okay." Every exhale still crackles, and I clear my throat before snagging my silk housecoat and camisole from the chair.

If I can just calm down, I should be fine.

It's a short distance to the bathroom before I set the robe and camisole on the hangar, grabbing two towels. Placing one near the tub for myself, I fold the other one-handed before setting it on the long, cold countertop.

"This is for you to get comfy." I murmur, easing Talon onto the plush towel, and he ruffles his feathers before settling onto it. The way he just seems so curious and amiable makes me think he really is someone's lost pet, or maybe an escapee from a nearby rehabilitation center.

There's no way in hell that a wild raven would behave like this.

Walking over to the tub and cranking the hot water on full blast, I turn the cold water on halfway, pouring a couple scoops of aromatherapy oils into the water. The eucalyptus hits me first, and I nearly sigh in content, squirting some bubble bath under the rushing faucet before glancing at Talon again.

He turns his head, resting it against the towel as his eyes close, and something in my chest feels like it's squeezing, though I don't think it is my asthma this time.

I could have locked him in the bedroom, but I have no idea if that would stress him out, and with his wound finally under control, I'd rather not risk him reopening it.

At least he's able to get some rest.

Testing the water's temperature to make sure it's hot enough at just-below-hellfire, I strip off my clothes and climb into the water, turning off the faucets before fully submerging myself all the way to my neck.

The heat of the water soothes the tension in my muscles, and the water line glides up and down my chest with each crunchy breath I take. I think back to last night and chew the inside of my cheek.

Perhaps it couldn't hurt to try it again. I *did* feel slightly better after.

Replaying the guided meditation in my mind, I picture the blue light at my crown before relaxing and letting it wash through my entire being. Within a minute of focusing on my breathing, the blue light has turned into familiar blue marble stairs.

By the time I count to ten, I've pushed past doors that also look very familiar, though I can't seem to put my finger on why as I walk through the beautiful forested garden.

Each step I take is slow, like I'm purposefully delaying myself as I walk along a pathway of greenery, with flowers on either side in full bloom. My attention lingers on each, but I'm only half paying attention as I peer into the shrubbery.

For every second that I look at each plant, I spend three searching around it. It's like I'm looking for something or someone, judging by the odd sense of longing that's washed over me.

Like a sense of severe déjà vu, this place seems so remarkably familiar, yet I still feel as if I'm forgetting something.

"Hello?"

My voice carries along the wind as it blows past me to the tops of the trees, and I pause, smelling a light floral scent that reminds me of spring. It stands out, so much so that I turn in a full circle to find where the scent is the strongest, and then I follow it.

Chapter 6

It feels as if I've been walking forever when I finally find the source, and suddenly I realize why the scent struck a chord in me.

It's an oleander bush.

The deep cherry-red petals sway with the wind, and I can't help the small laugh that escapes me.

Oleander has the chemical component that our clinical trial is based on, so it makes sense why there'd be an oleander bush here. My fingers gingerly brush the green leaf, and I shudder, knowing how toxic this beautiful plant is.

My gaze shift to the leaves, and the knowledge that such a beautiful creation in this world could take someone out so easily makes me shudder.

"Back again so soon?"

My heart leaps into my throat at the deep voice that carries on the wind, and sounds like it's all around me. But even though my pulse rages, all I strangely feel is more excitement than fear.

"Couldn't stay away, I'm afraid."

A low chuckle fills the air, and I turn to follow the sound.

"Evidently so. Have you come for yet another night of peace and calm then, Kilian?"

I know I'm more than likely fabricating this all in my mind, but despite that, my heart rate spikes as if it's oblivious to the fact that this is a figment of my imagination.

"I have..." Clearly, I've forgotten a key part of what happened the last time I meditated, which explains the déjà vu.

What's his name?

Shit.

Without his voice guiding me, I glance between the path I'm currently on and the one running parallel mere feet away contemplatively.

"Very well, then." His voice sounds so close that it's hard for me to tell if I'm going in the right direction.

What if I should follow that path instead? What if there's a fork in the road ahead, and I'm not going the right way?

I spot a break in the dense underbrush between the two paths, and turn to walk through it when a hand suddenly wraps around my bicep.

My entire body freezes, and each heartbeat sends blood raging into my ears as I turn to look up at the person who has such a firm grip on my arm.

Even with the moonlight illuminating it, his dark brunette hair is a breath shy of black, framing his high cheekbones and chiseled jawline, but it's the colors of his eyes locked onto mine that pull me into his orbit.

Patches of forest green surrounded by an ocean of bright, sky blue, as if two globes with pupils are gazing back at me from beneath thick, dark lashes, but it's the humor painted across his features that has me clearing my throat and breaking eye contact.

Though, looking at the rest of him is arguably a worse decision.

His black polo is half-buttoned, exposing his collar and part of his chest, with the white cuffs of his sleeves folded just below his elbows. My gaze flicks from his forearm to his white, perfectly form-fitting dress pants as I swallow. Not trusting myself to not stare, I quickly bring my attention to his face once more.

"Who are you? What are you doing here?" My voice comes out more of an accusation than kind, and I cringe internally at letting my nerves get the best of me.

"At this very current moment, I'm stopping you from having an uncomfortable time tonight. That's stinging nettle right there." He just smirks, gesturing with his free hand to the bushes behind me. "This place is definitely beautiful, but beauty will always find a way to bite."

My mouth drops open to ask him who he is again, as if the baritone, velvety voice isn't sign enough that he's the visual embodiment of the voice I'd been hearing, but I still need to know his name.

"And as I said last night, my name is Stolas." The voice rumbles all around, sounding like whoever it belongs to has a grin on his face.

"Last night..." I trail off as my brows pinch together. Once again, I'm struck by a case of déjà vu as I try to reconcile why he sounds so familiar to me.

He chuckles, but I'm still caught up in the realization that I've met someone here in the recesses of my mind, and that I've met this individual twice but somehow don't remember the first time.

It's like having a dream you don't remember once you wake up, and then you dream about it all over again. The memories of it are elusive and hidden, but I can *feel* them there.

"Are you real?"

My question must take him off guard, because he tilts his head and his dark brows furrow slightly. Seconds later, his large hand slides down my forearm, and his palm gently encircles my wrist as he guides my hand to his chest.

I swallow hard, staring at my hand with wide eyes as the warmth of his body graces my palm through the soft fabric of his shirt. My finger presses against the hard button of his polo while two others brush the soft skin that peers out from under his shirt. The steady thrum of his heart pulses beneath my palm as his chest rises and falls, breathing some reassurance into me.

"Any other questions about the nature of my existence?"

"You're my guardian angel?"

My gaze rises to his. When his grasp on my wrist disappears, I slowly drop my hand to my side.

He searches my face for a moment thoughtfully. "Not quite—"

"Oh, right. That's probably silly to ask, isn't it? I just thought, you know, with the whole meditating thing..."

I don't know why I'm rambling on or asking such a ridiculous question, but whoever Stolas is, he doesn't seem to mind. At least not outwardly.

"Some might have once called me an angel, but, a guardian, I am definitely not." My mouth drops open but he continues. "There are many who have different ideologies on what I would be called, but some titles are better than others."

I nod, even though I don't fully understand what he means. "Well, I guess to me, you're just Stolas, then. Nothing more and nothing less."

His lips twitch upward, and he inclines his head, but it's his eye contact that draws me in more intensely than anything I've ever experienced in my life.

If eyes are the window to the soul, I would like to look at his for a long, long time.

For science, of course.

"I would like that very much, Kilian." The soft expression he wears makes my chest tighten, and I take a breath to center myself.

Is it normal for spirit guides, angels, or whoever else to be so... ethereal? Attractive? Intimidating? I thought most of the time people connected with animals of some sort.

What are the odds that mine is very human looking?

Do they just hang out here and wait for people to show up or is this some sort of shared plane of existence?

I mentally file away all my questions, hoping that I'll remember when I wake up so that I can look it up.

"I'd like to show you something," Stolas says quietly, taking a step down the path, and I follow his slow pace, torn between watching his movements and looking at the scenery.

The way he carries himself is a calm sort of confidence; like he knows every inch of this green, flower filled forest. Still, something tells me that this might be as new and out of place to him, seeing someone else here as it is for me.

"Is there anyone else here?"

Hearing a huff of laughter, he glances at me, and I wince. "I asked you that yesterday, didn't I?" He nods, I can't help the laugh that escapes me. "Well, if nothing else, I'm consistent, I guess."

Stolas grins and gestures to a small path. "Right this way. And to answer your question once more, sometimes there can be others here, but as of right now, there is only us."

I nod as we break through the treeline, and I freeze, feeling Stolas' presence at my side as I gaze at a pond with crystal clear waters. In fact, the water is so clear that with the arcs of moonlight shining through, that I can see every crevice, plant and rock beneath the surface that looks so calm, as if it's made of glass.

"This is incredible." I breathe, taking another step closer and pausing, feeling as if my intruding presence dares to disturb the tranquility.

"I thought you might like it." Stolas' voice sounds quieter than before, and as I stare at the pond, part of me wants to just lie down and look at it for all eternity. "Kilian, you need to wake up. Now." His rushed words are strained, and when I turn to look at him, a loud noise jolts me awake.

Chapter 7

Sitting upright, I sputter a cough as water sluices down my face, and look around wildly. My gaze lands on a panicked Talon on the side of the cupboard, clicking his beak and bristling. My heart pounds, and I go to inhale once more before coughing painfully, feeling like I have mucus or water in my lungs.

My fit continues, and I'm nearly certain that I'm having an asthma attack when I realize my surroundings. The brisk air on my soaked face, with the way my hair sticks to my skin, tells me I very well may have fallen asleep in the tub and nearly drowned.

Talon gargles, and I'm sure he's cursing me in his own bird language as I calm myself down, taking deep breaths to clear my lungs.

That was close.

Far too close.

Opening the drain, the water makes a sudden suction noise as it whirls downward, and I cough again. "Note to self: no meditating while bathing."

Talon squawks in what I can only assume is agreement, and I stand up, feeling water sluicing down my skin as I gather my hair in front of my chest to strain it out.

Stepping out of the nearly empty bathtub, I move to the shower and turn the faucet, coughing some more as I wait for the temperature to warm. The cough becomes violent, and I turn to the counter, bracing on it to remain upright as I catch my breath. It still feels as if there's fluid in my lungs, and I'm silently cursing myself for being so thoughtless.

Was meditating even worth it at that point? I did it to calm down, and that was anything but calm.

My mind reflects on it, and I strain to remember anything. Once I relaxed into the water and counted to ten again, I remember going through the doors and finding the oleander, but that's it.

At least I remember more than last time.

Maybe it's like a muscle that needs to be worked out in order to recall what happens.

Finally, my coughing fit ends, and I blow out a breath before turning to step into the shower.

My mind continues to wander aimlessly as I scrub the bubble bath from my skin and wash my hair. I go from recounting what I remember to the oleander bush, and the clinical trials that start soon.

If everything goes well, and judging by the pre-trial testing we did, it should—by all intents and purposes—go well, then we could be looking at a cure for one of the more prominent forms of cancer that the world has ever seen.

When my gaze flicks to Talon silently watching me from the counter, I realize that I'm back in the office tomorrow.

Shit.

Will he even be able to stay here by himself? I guess he hasn't destroyed anything yet.

Well, other than my taco.

But he seems to have some kind of attachment to me; I just hope it's not one of those, destroy the entire house from separation anxiety.

My focus remains absently fixed on the raven as I finish showering, and by the time I'm done, I've decided that whatever damage he causes while I'm away is inevitable, but there's a small part of me that hopes he'll just sleep while I'm gone.

I guess we'll cross that bridge when we get there.

Sleep was restless, and I'm nearly a zombie as I pull into an empty spot in the parking lot when my phone vibrates.

Aiden: What's your trial's NCT number?

I frown, keying it in and hit send before it hits me.

Kilian: Try to get in if you can!

Aiden: Yeah, maybe. I'll take a look.

Feeling a new sense of urgency with Aiden's interest in the trial, I take long strides from the car to the front doors. My eyes gravitate to the corner near the alley, looking for the familiar sight of Red's crocheted blanket.

Being in northwestern Pennsylvania, it gets cold. The amount of snowfall is arguably worse, but for individuals who are homeless like Red, the cold can be a killer.

Last winter I drove him to the local shelter seven times because I wasn't sure he'd make it through the night. Even now, the bitter air overnight would be enough to make me worry about him, and it's not truly the deepest part of winter yet.

We're still in the half-autumn, half winter phase of weather where it snows one day, and you're in a t-shirt the next.

Hauling the door open, a blast of warmth blows my hair from my face, and I make my way past the front reception desk to the flight of stairs to the second floor, making a mental note to check on Red later.

It's not long before I'm settling into my desk, keying in my password as it loads up. Staring at the circling icon in the middle of the screen, my mind wanders to Talon, and I swallow hard when the mental image of him tearing up the entire house comes to mind.

Nope. Stay positive. I'm sure it's all fine.

The computer finally loads, and I download the file of five thousand applicants from our main database with a yawn that sends a shiver through my body. The first three are automatic denials based on certain indicators of quality of health.

They were both within the age group of eighteen to sixty-five, and each had adenocarcinoma; the most common colon cancer that exists. They weren't smokers or drinkers, but for whatever reason, their recent lab results showed a drastic decline in enzyme markers that would make them ineligible.

For the next hour, I sort through volunteers and end up rejecting more than half of them, and I'm about to take a break when my gaze snags on the name of the next applicant.

Thomas Rempson.

Staring at the screen, I blink once, twice, three times.

Nope. It's still the same.

There's no way one of the Rempsons is applying to join this clinical trial.

This has to be a coincidence.

Opening a new browser, my fingers fly over the keyboard before I hit enter, and the first result has my eyes widen.

Thomas Rempson, father of William Rempson, and the CEO of Ethena Health, which is the largest healthcare company in the state. Thomas recently stepped down in the past year stating he wanted to retire and leave his legacy to his eldest son, but clearly, it was more than that.

Thomas checks all the boxes for an eligible applicant though, so I add his name to the list and continue on, doing my best not to wonder too much how many of these people need this treatment most, but won't get it.

It's hard to accept that oleander's anti-cancer properties weren't found earlier, given its known toxicity and cardiac effects… but positive human clinical trials could redefine this.

This could, quite literally, cure adenocarcinoma entirely.

I'm not disillusioned enough to think it won't be hard, though. We've already had setbacks because as much as people don't want to admit it, there's money to be made in people being sick.

If we didn't have our largest donor, Astra Inc. funding us, we probably would have had to pause testing even longer. When the rumor of our trials got out, we went from having eight companies backing us to three. I'd heard through the grapevine that two indirectly threatened us to stop our research because it could break the market.

The market.

As if dying people are a clientele.

Still, Astra Inc. remained steadfast and increased funding to us to cover costs now exposed with the others dropping. Thankfully, our preliminary research was more promising than expected, but throughout all of it, I couldn't help but feel like I was waiting for the shoe to drop. But there has been no evidence of a shoe plummeting to the earth, so for now, all I can do is stay positive.

Half the day goes by, and I'm finally nearing the end of denials with bittersweet relief. It's not my first rodeo to file through trial volunteers in such a sheer volume, but this one feels different. It feels like it's more significant than any I've been part of prior. Scrolling down to the last name, I freeze.

Chapter 8

Aiden Wilde.

My gaze scans over the eligibility criteria, pausing on the sexual orientation that absolutely does not match the man I know, and I cover my mouth with my hand.

Shit. I didn't think about that.

I could lose my job if anyone finds out that I marked him as eligible knowing he lied on his application.

Goddamn it.

Checking the eligible box, I swallow hard against the lump in my throat before saving the file and loading it into the final database. We're only in phase two, so there's still much to learn in how this treatment could affect the volunteers, the long-term safety of it and determine what side effects it has.

For all my confidence earlier telling Aiden to get into the trial, a large part of me worries that my best friend could end up more sick than he already is.

The chime rings out as the upload into the database completes, and I click the randomization button, watching as it loads once more, the bar on the bottom slowly turning green before a bright green checkmark appears.

Within seconds, the spreadsheet automatically opens, displaying which group will be the control group and which will receive the experimental treatment. The main page shows the total number of applicants and the number of attributes that make up each. We typically ensure an even distribution of numbers, preventing an overrepresentation of elderly participants in either the control or test group. There are countless ways the data could be spread, but this new software splits the volunteers according to the preferences we input before the list is uploaded.

Usually it takes the human error out of it as much as it takes the human bias out. Now, I just need to go through and make sure it all makes sense, and no errors happened during the upload.

Scrolling through, I notice Aiden's name on the right side with the rest of the control group, and my gut twists.

I don't know whether I'm upset or relieved.

Part of me knows that he could have seen a positive change from this, but the other part of me knows it could very well be the opposite.

My fingers twitch as if to scroll, but hesitate when I see Thomas' name in the group to receive treatment. Staring at the screen for a long moment, my gaze slides to the arrow next to Thomas' name that would allow me to shift him to the control group and Aiden to the test group.

It would be so easy.

Of all the trials I've done, not once has anyone questioned when changes were made to the groups. That being said, I had only made changes when it was necessary for balance.

My mouse wheel scrolls and scrolls as I scan for any excuse to swap Aiden to the treatment group, looking for any variance in the way the algorithm separated the volunteers that could validate or support the change.

But I find none.

Sitting there for what feels like an eternity, I stare at my best friend's name like it could give me the answers I need before releasing a long sigh and glancing at the clock.

Five forty-five?!

I didn't even go for lunch!

Grumbling to myself about how long I'd taken on one task, I rub my eyes with my palms before regarding the screen once more.

Aiden's name stares back at me, as if taunting my indecision with its existence.

My mouse slowly glides over the screen and hovers over the arrow to swap the names as a noxious mix of guilt and anxiety washes over me. A long moment passes, and I exhale, moving my mouse away from the arrow, gliding to the save button with a shake of my head.

I don't know if I can do this.

The file saves, and I push to my feet with my head feeling light, an odd contrast to the heaviness weighing on my mind as I slowly make my way to the car.

Outside of the fact that I told Aiden to get in, and the guilt of knowing he will be part of the control group, I nearly broke every rule in the book by switching him and Thomas Rempson.

Maybe I should step away from this trial while Aiden is here, especially because we're so close, and I've already broken the rules by ignoring his sexual orientation submitted.

Unlocking the car with a beep and my wheeze worsening in the cold, I spend the rest of the drive home in a daze, and it's not until I'm pulling into the driveway that my mind finally wanders away from the guilt.

I scan over the windows that don't appear trashed with a modicum of relief.

Actually, they don't look like they've moved at all.

The thought of Talon getting hurt or his condition worsening while I was gone makes my gut twist, and I find my feet carrying me faster out of the car to the door.

The door creaks open, and a rustle fills the air as I step inside, bracing myself to see chaos as more of the entryway comes into view. The coats to my right are still on their hangers, and my shoes have remained untouched. I spot Talon in the center of the hallway, his head cocked as he eyes me cautiously.

"Good to see you're okay." I murmur, my gaze trailing the front room that's fully intact, and as more of the kitchen comes into view, I relax more, seeing it in the same state as I left it.

"Are you okay?" Talon's deep voice emphasizes the 'you' more and my brows shoot up.

*Where did he learn **that** one?*

"Uh, yeah. Just glad to be home, I guess. Long day." I don't know why I'm talking like he can understand me, but it feels right considering the way he inflected his own words.

There's still so much to this raven that I don't know, and that includes his vocabulary. He had to have belonged to someone before or been from a rehabilitation center, because there's no way he'd have picked up on things this quick.

Talon's head cocks to the side, and that's when I notice his bandage is no longer wrapped around him.

"Come on, I should make sure your injury is okay."

Without a second thought, I take the two steps over to Talon and scoop him into my arms, carrying him into the kitchen.

His wing isn't sticking out anymore as I hold him, and though I know that means he's likely feeling better, part of me was enjoying having him around.

Chewing the inside of my lip, I glance down at him and settle into the chair. "Alright, let's take a look at that wound."

He steps aside and ruffles his feathers, puffing them up as I reach over to gently lift his wing. As if taking the queue, he outstretches it, and I frown when it's nearly impossible to see any injury.

Even using my other hand to shift some of the puffy feathers aside, I still can't seem to find the injury, so I lean back, blowing out a breath.

"Well, the good news is you seem to be better. Bad news is, I have no idea if you're **actually** better."

He cocks his head to the side, and a knock at the door makes us both jump.

"Kil, it's us! Open up!"

My pulse calms down at the sound of Aiden's voice and I set Talon on the counter. "Wait here one sec."

Hurrying to the door, I suppress a laugh at the clatter following me, and I know Talon has followed me to the front door as I swing it open.

"About time. I can't feel my toes." Aiden and Connor both grin before Connor's eyes drop to my right.

"Holy shit. Is that a raven?!" Connor's jaw goes slack as he steps inside and takes off his shoes.

"His name is Talon. He's..." My gaze turns to look at the bird that's eyeing both men warily. "He's a rescue."

The cold air hits my lungs, and I shut the door out of an abundance of caution. The last thing I want is to have a sudden attack in front of them.

Pacing back to the kitchen, a rustle of feathers sounds out just as Talon's claws dig into my shoulder. I flinch slightly and wince as his wings fold in.

"Babe, that's not a rescue and you know it. That's your pet now." Aiden laughs, and Talon bristles.

Clearly, he doesn't enjoy being called a pet.

"Well I don't think he'll be here much longer. He seems to be all healed up, and since he can fly just fine, I'll take him away from the neighborhood and release him back to the wild soon."

"Why take him out of the neighborhood?" Connor asks, opening the cupboard and grabbing a bag of popcorn.

Talon puffs out. "He shot me."

Connor drops the bag of popcorn as he and Aiden stare at Talon with wide eyes.

"Did he just–?"

"Holy shit."

I can't help the huff of laughter that escapes me. "Yeah. Talon picks up words really, *really* fast and most of the time, I don't know where he got them from."

"Why so surprised?" Talon's deep voice fills the room, and I see Aiden swallow.

"That's so cool." Connor breathes, and finally collects himself as he paces to the microwave.

"Do you wanna do movie night another time?" I offer, not wanting them to feel like they need to put up with having a creature interrupting at all, but they both shake their heads.

"No, I mean, as long as you're okay with it." Aiden shrugs, and I reach into the fridge to grab us each a drink.

"Right. Well, what are we watching today?" I ask, seeing excitement suddenly erupt in Connor's expression as Aiden sighs.

"Well, I wanted to watch something in particular, but Connor said he has a surprise for both of us."

My eyes widen, and he must notice as he nods his head with feigned exasperation.

"Yeah, I'm worried too. The last time he tried to surprise me, he made me watch this horror movie that I still have nightmares about to this day."

"It wasn't that bad," Connor groans, and Aiden gives him a deadpan look.

"I made you keep the night light on for a week, and I still won't go into the basement unaccompanied to this day."

I just laugh, grabbing a bag of chips from the cupboard and waltzing to the front room with Aiden following close behind.

"Is that why you made me go down there last week?" Connor calls out from the kitchen as the sound of popcorn fills the air.

"And three weeks ago when I needed that box of my dad's."

Sliding into the left side of the couch, Aiden takes his spot beside me just as Talon crawls down my chest. He clicks his beak in approval as he settles in my lap, and Aiden chuckles beside me.

"He really seems to like you." He whispers, and a lump forms in my throat.

"It's probably just a trauma bond from me saving him from Paul after he shot him."

Connor sinks into the seat beside Aiden. "Wait, Paul as in, *your neighbor*, Paul?"

Aiden shakes his head. "I thought he was all about preserving precious life?" He air-quotes his last two words and rolls his eyes as I let out a dry laugh.

Connor grabs the remote and turns on the television. "Yeah, apparently precious life stops at fertilized embryos, and doesn't include wildlife."

Aiden snags a piece of popcorn. "Has he ever shot at birds before? Why shoot at Talon?"

I just shrug. "No idea. He was making a lot of noise, so that probably set him off."

The movie opening credits play, and I mindlessly glide my hand along Talon's feathers. A few minutes pass before Aiden nudges me, and when I glance over, he nods his head toward Talon.

The raven's eyes are closed, with its head fully slackened as he rests against my body, making my throat tighten with emotion.

God, I'm really going to miss him.

Chapter 9

The ending credits roll across the screen, and Connor flips the channel to the local news station.

"So, what did you guys think?" He turns to us with a tentative excitement plastered across his face, and even though mine hurts from laughing the entire time, I force a scowl.

"Terrible. Zero stars."

Connor's eyes narrow on me as Aiden nods his head. "I'll give it one star because of that one scene that made me laugh."

When Connor shakes his head with exasperation, we both laugh. "Clearly we hated it."

"Loathed." Aiden agrees sarcastically, and Talon clicks his beak at us.

"Hilarious." Talon's deep voice fills the air again, and Connor's face lights up.

"At least **someone** here has good taste. Thank you, Talon."

Breaking news today on News Alliance, an exclusive look at the war overseas.

Aiden glances at the screen. "They're finally covering this shit?"

Connor scoffs. "Only because Channel Five covered this last week. Shits embarrassing."

"Covered what?" I ask quietly, but my question is answered by the video of an explosion in what looks to be a densely populated area in another country. Children scream and cry as people scatter, and the video cuts to a hospital in crisis with people being treated in the hall-ways.

"Fucking shameful." Aiden murmurs, and the video cuts out as the news anchor comes back on the screen.

Connor flips the television off. "It's not getting anywhere near enough coverage on the media. They've just been forced to cover it because it went viral online and Channel Five already covered it, but all the other stations are watering it down."

Aiden scoffs. "If that were our families under attack so blatantly, you know people would riot in the streets."

"War shouldn't even exist." I murmur and Talon cocks his head as he blinks at me.

"In a perfect world, it wouldn't." Aiden whispers as he pushes to his feet.

"And we do not live in a perfect world, I'm afraid." Connor agrees as he does the same, stretching over his head as Aiden yawns.

"I'll take care of the garbage and dishes. You guys should get home before Paul decides humans are next on the target practice list."

Connor chuckles as I set Talon on the couch, and both men lean in to hug me tight.

"Thanks for the movie night, babe." Aiden murmurs as Connor breaks his hug early and heads to the door.

"Thanks for coming over." I grin, turning my gaze to Connor. "And thank you for not picking a horror movie."

Aiden laughs as Connor salutes and they both call out a goodbye before leaving out the front door. Turning to Talon, I yawn deeply.

"Let's get some sleep. We have a big day tomorrow."

My heart squeezes as his head cocks to the side, and I don't know that I'll be able to let him go without a piece of me leaving with him.

This damn raven has already stolen a piece of my heart even after the short time that I've known him.

Scooping him into my arms, he blinks at me before leaning into my chest, and carry him into my room to sleep.

God, tomorrow is going to be so hard.

Placing Talon on the bed, I strip off my clothes and change into pajamas before crawling into bed with him. His feathers rustle as he walks over and settles himself beside me, and my eyes slide shut.

Chapter 10

Standing in the center of Ron's office, he slams a piece of paper onto the desk with a scowl. "What the hell is this, Kilian?"

My heart slams against my chest as I look at the blatant lie on Aiden's application, and guilt coats my veins. "I don't know what you're talking about."

"Why didn't you add me to the test group, Kil?"

I whirl around to see Aiden standing in the doorway, tears pouring down his cheeks as he sniffles. He looks haggard, and exhausted, with sunken in eyes. There's a fogginess that covers him, and I feel the lump in my throat grow.

"I'm so sorry, Aiden."

His eyes harden, and his gaze flicks behind me as an icy wind sends a shiver down my spine.

"Ms. Kilian." I whirl around to see a handful of my recent doctors walking into the doctor's office as I sit on the examination table, with Dr. Newlin at the head. "It's time to give up now, Ms. Sterling."

"No." I whisper, rolling off the table and scrambling to my feet. "No, stop. Get away."

"It'll be over soon." One of my doctors from years ago whispers, and I look into their dead eyes before turning to run away through another door.

I run as fast as I can, but they always seem right on my heel as I scream for help. Sprinting through empty hallways, I turn a corner and slam into something solid that knocks the wind out of me.

"Kilian? Are you alright?" Relief crashes over me as I look into two familiar, otherworldly eyes.

"Please, oh God, help me. They're after me." I gasp, my entire body shakes with adrenaline as I turn to look over my shoulder for the doctors, but the serene forest around me has replaced the vacant doctor's office and hospital I was sprinting through.

"I don't—" Gulping down a breath, I turn my attention to the familiar man standing before me once more. "It was a dream." I say quietly, more like a soft realization to myself than as a statement to him.

His large hands remain steadfast on my arms, and I can't be more thankful for it as my pulse rages in my ears. Somehow I know he's not a threat, and seems so incredibly familiar, so I cling to his safety like a net.

It felt so real. They all seemed so incredibly real.

"What was it?" The deep tenor of his voice is plagued with concern as he glances around us on high alert.

"I think it was nothing. Just my subconscious acting like the enemy."

His brow twitches upward. "And who is the enemy?"

It's too much to say out loud, and my memory of the events is already fading, so I just shake my head. "I'd rather not go into it. Thank you for... well... catching me?"

He chuckles. "I did nothing in particular. I heard you screaming for help, and then you ran into me."

I glance around at the forest. "Your name is—"

"Stolas."

"Ah!" I snap my finger. "Yes, that's it. I should have remembered."

If my lack of memory offends him, he doesn't show any indication as he shrugs. "Memories from this realm are hard to recall. Don't be too hard on yourself."

Realizing I'm still held tight to his chest, I ease back a step, and he releases my arms entirely. "I'd like to remember more when I wake up."

He searches my face for a moment before bringing his hand to rub his jawline. "I could help keep us more connected, which would make you more likely to remember things here."

My eyebrows shoot up. "Connected how?"

Considering my question for a breath, his intense gaze burns into me as he answers. "I believe it would thin the veil between our minds, allowing a greater connection, but it could have risks, Kilian."

I frown. "Risks as in death?"

Stolas' eyes widen and he huffs a laugh. "No. That's not something I'd ever offer or agree to. Risks as in, the veil could thin too much over time, resulting in a connection between our minds."

It takes a second to understand what he's suggesting, and my heart thunders. "Permanently?"

He shakes his head. "No. It would last a couple of months at most."

I swallow. "So we'd be able to read each other's minds?"

"It's possible." He nods, crossing his arms over his broad chest. "There's a chance it could just thin the veil enough for you to remember this place."

Taking a deep breath, I toss him a grin. "Well, what's the worst thing that can happen?" His mouth drops open to respond, and I hold my finger up. "Ah. That was rhetorical. Don't tell me."

Stolas chuckles and steps in close, unraveling his arms to place his palms on either side of my head. "Close your eyes." He's leaned in close as my heart thrums loudly in my chest, and when I don't do as he says, his brow raises. "Close."

As if I've snapped out of whatever trance his proximity had put me in, my eyes snap shut, and I feel his forehead press to mine. His hands cup my jaw, with his fingers curling around the back of my head.

This is so much more intimate than I'd expected, and I silently thank the universe that he can't hear my thoughts just yet because as his nose brushes mine, they take a turn they shouldn't.

"Breathe in and count to ten, then exhale as you count to five."

Already feeling intoxicated from our breaths mingling together, I nod ever so slightly, and slowly inhale, holding my breath at six for another four seconds. A burst of warmth washes over me from the top of my head, rushing along my skin as I release my breath slowly, counting to five.

"Good. Do it again."

I repeat the action, feeling another wave of warmth cover my body as I release my breath once more.

"Last one."

By the time I've exhaled fully a third time, my entire body is buzzing with energy. Stolas leans back slightly to put distance between our faces, but keeps his hands in place as I wait.

He lets out a low chuckle, and my cheeks burn. "Open your eyes, Kilian."

My heart thunders as I obey, and when my gaze finds his, everything seems to be a bit more clear. My focus has sharpened, and I don't know if that's a good or bad thing right now.

"How do you feel?" He searches my face, and I have to fight back a smile.

"I'll take that as we can't read each other's minds yet." I murmur and his lips twitch. "Good. All things considered. What did you do?"

His eyes seem to burn bright as he releases my head. "I thinned the veil. It might take time to remember but, you should be able to recall what we discuss here more over time."

"How did you... thin the veil...?"

Stolas tilts his head in a familiar way. "I'm surprised you're asking that now, after I've already done it."

I shrug. "I guess I trusted you enough to not ask then."

"Yet you're asking now."

I can't fight the smile that's forming as I give him another shrug. "A girl can be curious, can't she?"

He searches my face for another long moment before he concedes with a sigh. His expression turns guarded as he reaches over to grasp my hand, guiding my palm upwards between us.

"There are certain things in the known world that can help cognitive function." He whispers, and the wind blows the branches surrounding us. "To put it in the simplest terms, I gave you their benefits, using a sliver of my power to bind them to you, and focusing them where it would be most effective."

My eyes widen. "You have powers?"

He laughs, and the mirth reaches his eyes as nearby branches stretch further toward us. The leaves twist and turn as they inch closer.

"Holy shit." I breathe, watching with wide eyes as the branch glides along my arm, the leaves caressing as it travels down to my hand.

"The earth and God's many creations might just be as beautiful as the stars in the sky, dear Kilian."

I have so many questions to ask him. There's so much I want to know, but some part of me can feel my consciousness pulling out from this realm.

He must sense it too, as he tucks a lock of hair behind my ear. "It seems your time here is nearing its end."

I nod, feeling a tightness in my chest as I give him a soft smile. "Time to test that veil, Stolas."

His lips twitch, and his mouth opens to speak as everything goes dark.

Chapter 11

A clicking beak near my face has my eyes snapping open, and Talon's enormous form fills my vision.

Light filtering in from the window burns my eyes and I squint as they water. "Good morning to you too, Talon."

The realization that I'm going to be releasing him on my way to work hits me like a bag of bricks, and I stare at him for a long moment. He tilts his head to the side in a way that feels oddly familiar, but I brush it off as I scoop him into my arms.

"Well, you're officially going to be a free bird today, Talon."

He says nothing as I set him on the dresser to pull on some clothes. In fact, he goes eerily quiet until I'm ready for work, and scooping him into my arms once more.

Part of me wants to fill the silence as I walk to the car with him in tow, but for the life of me, I can't think of anything to fill it with. Not now. Not when everything in me is screaming to just keep him at home.

I think back to how well-behaved Talon has been since I'd brought him in with a bittersweet note.

No. There's someone somewhere out there waiting for him. Who am I to keep him from them?

The car ride is agonizingly silent and far too short for comfort. When I pull into the parking lot at the office, I turn to look at Talon with a lump in my throat so large that I'm not sure if I'll be able to say anything at all.

He blinks at me and tilts his head to the side. "Leaving?"

The tears that had slowly formed fall down my cheeks as I nod. "Yeah, it's time to go."

Swiping at my eyes, I scoop him into my arms once more. "You're welcome to visit, but I'm sure there's someone out there looking for you and missing you. I can't keep you cooped up in my house anymore. It's not fair to you."

He blinks as another tear falls, but I can't wait any longer. If I do, I'll never let him go.

Not when my heart feels like it's being torn in two.

How in the world I became this attached to a bird I'd rescued, I have no clue.

Maybe this is my sign to get a cat after all.

Climbing out of the car and into the brisk air, I close the door and turn in a full circle. My gaze scans the area and I frown.

Should I have chosen a more forested area?

Do I just set him down and walk away?

Chewing my lip, I adjust him in my palms. "Alright, here you go, Talon. Stop by and say hello, sometime... Just don't get shot again, please." I whisper before launching him into the air, and his wings spread wide to catch the wind.

I watch him ascend as he gets further and further away, making my chest tighten with each second. By the time he's disappeared into the treetops, it feels like I've lost something precious.

Sucking in a hitched breath, I lock the car and head toward the front door. I get to the sidewalk when I notice Red's blanket sticking out from a crevice in the building wall, blocking the wind from hitting him as a wave of relief washes over me.

At least I know Red's doing alright. I don't know that I could handle more than one loss today.

My chest squeezes at the thought of Talon, and I sigh.

This is going to be a long, long day.

"What's eating at you?" Trinity asks, easing herself into the chair across from mine.

I shake my head, knowing there's no way I can tell her even a fraction of what's happened without sounding insane. "Just a long day at work." I murmur, and she glances at the clock.

"It's lunchtime." She states flatly.

"And yet, it's been a long day." I grumble, and a knock at the doorway has both of us turning our heads only to see Jen peering inside.

"So this is where the cool kids are hanging out." She strides in and plops into the seat beside Trinity. "We need to go get dinner soon and do something fun. I'm drained."

Trinity laughs. "Yeah, well, tell that to the grouch." She jabs her thumb in my direction as Jen's eyes widen.

"What's wrong?"

Fighting the urge to sigh, I just shake my head. "Nothing, really, I'll be fine. I probably just need a day to recharge."

They both nod in agreement like it's the most sensible thing they've heard in weeks. "So true. Maybe we need a girl's night."

The two of them chatter about possible events to go to until Ron walks by, and the look he shoots them is enough to send them back to their own offices in a hurry.

By the time I've sorted through the rest of the applicants and added them to the file, it's five thirty, and I yawn deeply.

Something tells me that I'm going to sleep like a baby tonight.

Locking up my office, I turn into the hallway and head toward the parking lot.

"... something special."

My head turns to look down the hallway to my right, only for there to be no one in view. I scan around in all directions to see where it came from, but there's no one there.

Weird.

I'm half on alert until I'm in the car, and my mind wanders to Talon. The image of him flying into the horizon comes to mind again, and I can't help but wonder if he's living his best raven life now that he's free.

Honestly, there's no way it was comfortable to live in a cramped house as big as he was. Letting him go was the right thing to do, even if I hated every second of it.

A crow flies across the road before the light I'm at turns green, and my phone vibrates on the center console. Lifting it to my ear, a woman's voice fills the air.

"Hello, is this Ms. Sterling?"

"This is." I'm mere minutes from turning onto my driveway as I yawn.

"Ms. Sterling, my name is Maris Sylvara, and I'm an investigative reporter with News Alliance Network. I was hoping you had time to speak about a couple of doctors you've seen over the past few years."

Frowning, I turn off the main road and onto the driveway. "Uh, sure."

Papers sound like they're flipping, and I try to recall any of the multitude of doctors I've seen over the years. With how frequently I've had to switch providers, it's nearly impossible to recall all of them.

"First, I'd like to discuss Dr. Hanish. It's my understanding that he was your medical provider in 2027 for a total of six months. Is that correct?"

Pulling the car to a stop in front of the house, I turn off the ignition. "Yes, that's correct."

"Great. Thank you for confirming. What can you tell me about your relationship with Dr. Hanish?"

I huff a laugh. "You mean other than that, he just disappeared in the middle of my treatment?"

There's a pause from the other line. "What do you mean, he disappeared?"

Climbing out of the car, birds squawk from the treetops as I lock the door. The bitter air tightens my chest and I hurry inside. "I mean, all of a sudden, he was gone, and I was reassigned to another provider."

The line is silent for a long moment before Maris clears her throat. "And you were upset by this?"

I scoff. "Well, it's frustrating to have to restart all over again."

Maris' voice softens a touch. "Ms. Sterling, off the record, are you comfortable telling me what Dr. Hanish was testing you for?"

"Chronic asthma and other lung issues." As if on queue, my lung crackles as I exhale, and she hums in acknowledgement.

"I understand. Thank you for sharing. And what can you tell me about Dr. McIntosh?"

Coughing away from the microphone, I place the phone to my ear as I kick off my shoes in the hallway, and shut the door.

"Well, I saw him three times for a total of two months before I was reassigned, I think. From what I remember, he didn't have very good bedside manner, and he was talking about doing surgery on my lungs before I was reassigned."

A moment of silence fills the air before the sound of a pen thumping paper follows it. "And Dr. Gregory?"

The number of doctors she's listing off makes my pulse quicken. "Same deal there, no bedside manner, and I think he was ordering another round of some new medication for me when I was reassigned."

Why is all of this relevant?

"Great, and Dr. Thompson?"

My eyes widen. "Dr. Thompson had just gotten through all of my testing and said that he was close to a diagnosis outside of just my asthma when I was assigned to Dr. Newlin."

There's another long pause. "Thank you, Ms. Sterling. Can you tell me if any of these doctors or the others you've seen did they exhibit any signs of illness when you saw them? Coughing, neurological, cognitive decline?"

My jaw goes slack. "Uh, no. Not at all. They seemed fine. Can you tell me why you're asking?"

"I'll get to that. Can you tell me if you've been experiencing any of those symptoms in the time you've been visiting their office?"

Oh, God.

"Nothing outside of my asthma that can be severe at times, but usually when I'm at home. Why? Is there something I should know?"

Another long moment of silence from my phone makes me feel as if I could scream.

"Ms. Sterling, I hate to be the one to tell you this, but looking at each provider's patient history, every doctor you've seen from that facility has died in the past three years."

I feel the blood drain from my face, and my mind goes a mile per minute, running through every interaction I can remember. "All of them?"

Her voice is solemn as she confirms with a low hum. "They all died from cyanide poisoning, resulting in cardiac arrest after suffering severe seizures. The medical examiner stated that the concentration of cyanide was ten parts per million. The lethal dose in a grown adult male is three."

I swallow. "Holy shit."

"Ms. Sterling, do you have any reason to believe that someone might target the doctors for Ethena Health?"

Blowing out a breath, I shake my head even though she can't see me. "No. They were just doctors doing their jobs. Oh my god, this is horrible. I had no idea."

"I think that's all my questions for today, Ms. Sterling. Please call this number if anything comes up."

Murmuring a quiet thank you, the line disconnects and I walk mindlessly to the front room before collapsing onto the couch.

I can't believe they were all killed. All of them.

Chapter 12

Two weeks later

"Houston, we might have a problem."

I glance up at Trinity as she slides the door shut and flicks the lock in place.

"I hope you mean that in a 'I didn't get what I ordered for lunch' sense, and it doesn't have anything to do with the trial..." When she winces, I groan and put my head in my hands. "What is it?"

"I think there's something wrong with the trial..."

I frown, and I'm about to argue how that's impossible when I see the tense concern etched into her features. She slides into the chair and sucks in a breath before placing a stack of papers in front of me. "These are the recent lab results of the scans and bloodwork of all the volunteers."

There's a tremor in my hand as I lean forward to pull the pile closer and flip through the first few. One is a control volunteer, with minor fluctuations in various markers. The next is a test volunteer, who received blood work a week after receiving the drug.

My eyes stare at the paper as my entire body goes cold.

This can't be real.

Flipping through the next three, seeing all control volunteers with minimal changes to their symptoms. When I land on the fourth, yet another volunteer receiving the drug, the scan showing the volunteer's tumor increased size by half an inch, and I slam the papers down with force.

"I need to tell Ron." I choke out, and she throws her palms up.

"No!" I'm about to push to my feet, but the alarm on her face stops me as she blows out a breath. "Not yet. It's only been two weeks. We don't know for sure."

My eyes widen. "In another two weeks, the damage could be horrendous, Trinity."

She chews her lip for a moment. "Kilian, you can point the finger at me if it comes back to us, but I don't think we should raise the alarm yet."

A knot of dread forms in my stomach, and I shake my head, my voice hardly above a whisper. "People could die, Trin. We can't just do nothing."

The knowledge that Aiden could be seeing worsening symptoms cycles through my mind, and I have to shove the thought away with force.

"How about this," she says, pushing to her feet. "I'll start investigating the machines that took tests and samples, see if there's anything there. In a couple of weeks, if the tests still show negative progression for the test volunteers, we go to Ron, and we recommend pulling it."

The look on her face is pure desperation, and I sigh. "Fine. But I want updates if you find anything."

She nods and hurries to the door as I gather the stack of papers to put into my desk drawer. I'm bent down as it rolls back into place when a deep voice in the distance catches my attention.

"... have to start all over again..."

The familiar voice sounds like it's coming from down the hall, and I slowly make my way to the doorway.

"That's just how it'll have to be."

By the time I'm peering down the hall and no one is there, I frown. Waiting for a long minute, no one rounds the corner and with work piling up the longer I wait, I head back to my desk with a sigh.

Maybe the stress of all of this is getting to me.

Chapter 13

Two weeks later

"So, in conclusion, the trial results have yet to bring forth the expected outcomes we saw in the initial phase one study."

Ron stares at me with furrowed brows, the crease in his forehead deepening as he takes in everything I just said. When I came in this morning, Trinity was waiting for me with a nauseated look, and I knew. After spending the next four hours validating that the test results have somehow gone sideways, we had to tell Ron.

He blows out a breath and runs his hand through his short grey hair.

I'd been dreading this meeting for the past two weeks, even asking the other researcher named Giselle to redo all her results reporting for the control group, even though I already knew them.

For the past week Aiden had seemed worse for wear, but he hadn't said a word until he'd been over for dinner on Saturday, and he'd been in so much pain that he finally broke down.

That was one of the more painful conversations to have, knowing that he's in the control group when he has no clue he's not getting treatment.

Another painful conversation to have is this one.

Telling the manager of the trial that even though phase one showed promise, phase two displays none of the same consistencies will cause sheer chaos and more questions than answers.

The vein in Ron's forehead has become more pronounced than normal, and I mentally run through the responses I'd prepped with Trinity in my office earlier.

"Not only has the drug not shown a modicum of efficacy, but if what I'm hearing is accurate, it's creating a drug induced exacerbation of negative symptoms. Am I understanding that correctly?"

I swallow hard with a nod. "Yes sir." *This isn't looking good.* "Phase one showed the tumor markers drastically improved within one week, whereas for phase two, it's been over three weeks with signs of worsening symptoms..."

His eyebrow raises at the way I trail off, and I suck in a breath.

How the hell can I frame this in a way that doesn't shut our trial down immediately?

"The tumor markers are actually steadily increasing, which makes me concerned that there is even more inconsistency between phase one and two."

He flips through the seven-page summary once more and rubs his hand over his mouth thoughtfully. "You suspect something is off?"

With my heart thundering in my chest, I give him as close to an honest answer as I can. This is my only chance to salvage our research and not get the entire trial thrown out.

"I can't say for certain until we dig deeper. Right now, with the glaring differences, it's only fair that we investigate further to understand why there's been such drastic differences in the results."

He clicks his tongue and suddenly tosses the paper on the desk in front of him as he slumps back in his chair. "Get me answers, Kilian. If phase two of this trial concludes as anything worse than ineffective, we may lose funding completely."

It hasn't escaped me that Ethena Health is the main group responsible for sponsoring this trial, giving us the facilities, the equipment and other essentials, so if the treatment doesn't work for Thomas Rempson, I'm painfully aware that William Rempson will pull out from it.

"I'll do some more digging. Give me three to four weeks and I'll have a full report."

"You get two weeks."

My mouth drops open to protest, but the look on his face has me snapping it shut automatically as I nod. "Two weeks. Got it."

He glances at the clock, and I know it's because we're at the top of the hour, leaving him with less than an hour to spin this somehow to Ethena Health executives.

"Set a meeting for this time in two weeks. If you don't have answers by then, I'm ending this trial."

My feet automatically step to the door, pulling it open as I nod my head. "Loud and clear. Two weeks."

How the hell am I going to do this in two damn weeks?

The moment I close the door behind me, my chest tightens up with each step, and by the time I've breached the entrance to my office, I double over and cough until my throat feels like it very well might be on fire.

My fit calms down, though my lungs sound like crinkling paper, and I slump into my chair with my head tilted toward the ceiling.

If I'm going to do this investigation, I'm going to have to pull records of everything and start from the basics to prove whether someone performed each step in sync with phase one.

A deep-seated sigh crawls out of my throat that makes my lungs ache even more.

I have no idea how the hell I'm going to manage this while still working through my normal reports, but I'm going to have to make it work.

My gaze slides to the folder on my desktop labelled "Phase One" and I roll myself forward to the desk to double-click on it.

"Here goes nothing."

It takes the rest of my day to gather the details needed, and section out my plan of validation, but by the time five o'clock rolls around, I'm beyond ready to leave as I turn off my computer.

My mind is a chaotic mess of guilt and frustration after feeling like I got nothing accomplished to an overwhelming degree. Usually during the summer months, I'd take a walk through a park or go for coffee to unwind, but drastic times call for drastic measures.

And these are indeed drastic times.

The computer screen goes dark, and I sigh, pushing to my feet before walking out the door with my purse in hand. I can already feel the anxiety in my body from the pressure of needing answers as it's built up, and even though my lungs will protest, I already know what I need to clear my mind.

Each step to the car door has me contemplating my decision, but when I slide into the driver's seat, and my breathing remains even, my resolve solidifies.

Maybe this is just what I need.

It's a short drive to the state park, and as I turn off the main, well lit road, a mix of anticipation and something else I can't quite place washes over me in waves.

The once familiar treeline has changed with the seasons, and the full branches of leaves have become near barren. The few remaining having turned varying shades of yellow and brown. Each bump in the road rocks the car back and forth ever so slightly, with the jingle of my keys filling the air as I venture further into the park.

Lights along the road are few and far in between the further I go until I finally reach the giant boulder on the side of the road, marking the distance to my favorite path to clear my mind.

Chapter 14

The wind blows hard, and leaves sprawl over the street, tumbling over one another as I glimpse the break in the trees to my right.

The light feeling in my chest swells, and I turn off the road, pulling into the small parking area that's just wide enough for a couple of vehicles. Yet there's no one here. Even on the drive in, I hadn't seen any other car lights or signs of visitors to the park coming or going at all.

It's probably just too chilly or the wrong time of year.

Pulling the car to a stop, and I reach over to haul my jacket on, tucking my mitts into the pockets before pushing the door open. The brisk wind surges in, and I shiver, feeling the cold travel along the length of my body all the way to my toes.

It's not unbearable, but I'll need to walk to keep my body temperature up.

The vehicle beeps twice as I lock it, tucking the key into my pocket as my lungs fill with the early winter air. The bite to it nearly sends me into a coughing fit, but I swallow it down as my body adjusts.

I'm fully aware my inhaler is at home, and I could be walking into a mess by doing this, but my mind's needs feel greater than my body's right now.

My phone vibrates in my pocket, and I pull it out to see Aiden's name on the screen.

"Hello?"

"You will not guess what just happened to me."

"You won the lottery and you're moving to Italy?"

Aiden's voice is choked by laughter on the other end, and I bite back a smirk as the cold nips at my exposed fingers.

"Close, actually. Connor got a bonus from work, and he surprised me with a trip to Mexico!"

My chest tightens, but I don't know if it's because of the loving gesture Aiden so rightfully deserves or because of the cold.

"That's amazing. When are you going?"

There's a pause, and when his voice comes through the speaker once more, he sounds more solemn.

"Well, since the medications in this treatment aren't working, he found an oncologist surgeon who will remove the tumor, and has some treatment that has really good results. He booked our flight for the last week of the trial."

Each word reminds me of the painful fact that my best friend is in the control group, and I can't help but feel thankful that not only has he found treatment elsewhere, but that he's not in the test group.

Not with how their tests have shown accelerated tumor markers recently.

There's a large part of me that can't help but wonder what if he was cured of it, though.

A rustle of feathers fills the air as a bird flies past, quickly obscured by the shadows of trees as I continue to hike up the trail.

"Well, that's great. Are there any risks?" It's the nicest way I can ask if I should be worried, because I don't want to bury my best friend.

Although, arguably, there's a chance I may still bury him at some point in my lifetime.

A shiver runs through me at the thought.

"From what Connor said, it's relatively low risk. There were just no doctors that would do it here for the same cost, and my insurance wouldn't cover it. I'd be in hundreds of thousands of dollars of debt if I did it here."

I nod, because I understand entirely. The healthcare system here has always worked against us, and you have to fight and argue to advocate for yourself. For many people, they're too exhausted to fight for themselves, and good people are lost because of it.

I'm thankful Aiden has someone who is already in his corner.

"When will you be back, then?"

There's a long pause from his end of the line, and I turn right at the fork in the road absently as I wait.

"Three, maybe four weeks?"

My jaw goes slack, but I recover quickly. "That's, I mean that's great, right? You get to recover and spend time with Connor."

"Yeah. I think so. I just can't keep waiting, Kil. It feels like each day I wait, I'm digging the shovel deeper toward my grave, you know?"

My throat tightens up, and I nod. "I'm glad you're going," My voice wavers and I clear my throat. "When you come back, we need a full weekend though, yeah?"

Aiden laughs, and I can hear the smile in his voice. "Yeah, babe. We'll finally do that movie marathon you'd wanted to do months ago."

There's another long moment of silence, and the guilt of knowing he was in the control group continues to gnaw at me, regardless of the test groups results.

"I hate that you're going through this, Aiden. I feel terrible." Even to me, my voice sounds so small.

Aiden just scoffs as I make a left turn at another fork in the path.

"There's nothing you could have done, Kil. I'll be alright. Do you want to come with us?"

I chew the inside of my cheek at the thought, feeling the tips of my fingers becoming numb.

"No, I have to do too much for this trial over the next few weeks. There's no way I'd be able to."

"Well, if you change your mind, you know you're always welcome to join us."

I huff a laugh, nearly sending my asthma into a tizzy as my lungs sound crunchy. "And be a third wheel? Absolutely not. I said I like Connor, but I'm not into sharing *that* much."

He laughs harder, and I bite back a shit-eating grin as I turn the last bend to my favorite resting place.

"Alright babe, well, you know you're welcome to either way. Connor just pulled up though, so I'm gonna go let him in."

"Okay-love-you-bye." Aiden hurries his goodbye out, and I'm still laughing as I slide my phone into my pocket with a deep breath.

The path hugs a cliff that overlooks the rest of the forest below, with the lake in the distance reflecting the crescent moon that peers from behind a cloud.

Without the light pollution of the city, countless stars scatter across the sky like the most beautiful and ethereal kind of glitter. The sight is one I've seen more than a handful of times, but it never loses its luster.

Spotting the tree that hangs low on the far edge, I slip between the thick branches and follow the edge of the cliff, slowly getting further away from the worn path.

I'd only come here a handful of times after stumbling upon it by accident, but it's mere seconds before I spot the large oak tree with a long, low-hanging branch that runs parallel to the edge.

My lungs continue to sound like a wrinkled bag, but I climb over the branch, swinging my legs off the other side as the lone cloud in the sky finally moves out of my field of vision.

When I first saw this view, I'd tried to take a photo, but no matter how many I'd taken, it didn't do it any justice. The way the water reflects the myriad of stars, mirroring the patterns, and the light from the crescent moon brightens the treetops, highlighting the green of the pine trees as a stark contrast to the barren branches of the oncoming winter.

The unforgiving bark bites into my clothes, the cold seeping into my skin as I relax into the view with each passing minute. Even with how chilled the air is, I'd still easily be able to spend hours here.

My breathing evens out, and the horrid sound lessens with each lungful.

Maybe I should go see a doctor out of the country, too. Even if I do, though, there's no guarantee that the outcome will be any different. Sure, Aiden found a surgeon who can help, but for asthma? That isn't something you can remove with surgery as much as doctors have suggested it now and again. Originally I'd been excited, but when I had really looked into it, it didn't make sense.

Still doesn't.

No, I'll just hope that Dr. Newlin can figure out what is wrong where my other million doctors seemed to be stumped or stuck on testing.

I mean, I work in the medical field technically... I should be able to trust the system to work.

Some part of me wants to believe that, but there's the other part of me that has spent the past years undergoing endless testing and treatment to come up empty-handed and still sick as ever.

Words will never express how I desperately want to believe the system works.

"Beautiful view."

The familiar baritone voice jolts me from my reverie, and I twist toward the sound to see *him*.

Chapter 15

Yet again I'm struck by the most intense feeling of déjà vu, but this time, it doesn't last long, and his name forms on my lips.

"Stolas?"

My gaze flicks to his arms, and the foggy memory of him wearing the same polo comes to mind as my pulse hikes.

There's no way this is a figment of my imagination, right?

I didn't meditate.

My attention slides to the steep cliff-side below, and I swallow hard.

God, I hope I didn't meditate.

A flicker of humor crosses his features as he steps closer, his tall form still towering over where I sit on the branch, even though it's a few feet off the ground.

He leans forward to rest his forearms, and the tree just barely dips, as if he's not leaning much weight on it at all, but resting his arms comfortably.

"You remember?" The way his brow tugs upward as he eyes me, he seems genuinely surprised.

"Just barely. I only recalled bits and pieces... like echoes of memories..." My attention flicks to either side of him. "How is this possible? Am I..."

When I trail off, he shakes his head, and his rich voice is like silk to my ears. "No. You're fully awake, Kilian." He tilts his head in a wholly familiar way, and his dark hair shifts with the movement.

"So then how are you..." I gesture to him with my hand. "Appearing so real here?"

His lips twitch, and he levels me with a stare. "I'm not simply *appearing real* here. I live in this world as much as you do."

Stolas must see the confusion on my face as he laughs, and the genuine grin on his face only brings heat to my cheeks as he continues. "Is it so odd to know that I exist in both places?"

I swallow hard. It's not like I know much–if anything–about the meditating I'd done. Hell. I watched one video and then tried it.

"I just thought that spirits were only in, uh, the spirit realm."

Part of me cringes internally at how awkward the words sound coming from my mouth, which is only further emphasized by the way Stolas' eyebrows pinch together.

"That might be true if I were a spirit."

My jaw goes slack as I hold his gaze.

He can't be telling the truth, right? Because that was meditation to meet my spirit guide I'd originally followed. If he's not a spirit, then...

"What are you?"

He turns his focus to the sky, and I track the curves of his cheekbones, the stubble along his strong jawline if only to remind myself. I vaguely remember thinking he was something **more**, but even those thoughts are foggy.

"I've been called many, many things over the years. I think my favorite was—"

The memory returns with a vengeance, and he abruptly stops as I whisper. "Just Stolas."

His lips twitch upward, and his piercing blue and green eyes slide to me. "That's the one."

I blow out a breath, turning my attention to the sky once more, watching as the moon ever so slowly rises in the sky.

"So what's troubling you so much that you've ventured into the middle of the woods at night?"

A ball of knots forms in my stomach, and my gaze drags down to the reflection of the moon in the lake.

"I had the chance to really help someone that I care about, but would have broken just about every rule in the book to help him, so I didn't. I don't know if I made the right choice, but there's this feeling of guilt that's eating me alive. What if it could have been the thing to cure him, even though there's no evidence that it would have worked? I am mortified that I was considering breaking more rules than I already had, and yet, I equally feel like the shittiest friend for not breaking more rules."

A long moment passes between us, and I glance over at him, only to find his attention already on me. "There's not a single person in this world that doesn't have a price or a threshold where they'd give up their morality for something that benefits them or someone they care for."

I'm about to argue, but the look on his face has my mouth snapping shut. "A mother would give her life for her child. A lover would kill for their beloved. A poor man would steal for food. A rich man would deny basic quality of life to the many to maintain his wealth. A country would bury masses to maintain their secrets. Everyone has a price, dear Kilian."

As much as I want to disagree, I know in my heart of hearts that I can't. My molars grind, and I look out at the serene lake once more. "I don't know if that makes me feel better or worse."

He just chuckles, and the sound feels like it's vibrating within my very bones. "That you are this concerned should tell you more than enough about your character, Kilian."

I blow out a breath. "Maybe you're right. I just wanted to help. I wanted him to be okay, but I'm afraid that I'm a coward and could be the reason he gets more and more sick."

Stolas shifts in my peripheral, and the tips of his fingers brush my temple. The contact suspends the air in my lungs as he tucks a lock of hair behind my ear, and a shiver wracks down my spine as a cool breeze glides along my cheek.

"Do you know for certain that whatever you were going to do to break rules would have yielded a positive outcome for your friend?"

I shake my head, and my gaze slides to Stolas. "I don't."

"Then you made the right decision."

Frowning, I open my mouth to argue only for him to shush me with a challenge in his eyes and a raised brow.

"Careful, Kilian. You're dangerously close to making me wonder how much you trust me."

A hint of boldness rushes through me as my tongue traces the sharp edge of my canine. "That's assuming that I can even trust you to begin with."

A flash of amusement paints his features as he considers me for a moment. "I'm concerned that you're this comfortable in the middle of the forest, at night, with someone you don't trust, then."

"Well, just remember that I'm not stuck out here with you right now. You're stuck out here with me." My huff of laughter catches in awkwardly, and I cough, feeling the crinkling sound in my lungs as I double over.

I'm vaguely aware of Stolas' hand on my back, but it's a long moment before I can recover, still feeling like my chest suddenly has a five-pound weight on it.

"You need to get that checked, Kilian."

I'm about to toss back some sarcastic retort, but the words die on my lips when I see the genuine concern in his expression.

"I have been. My doctor is running tests, and I've been taking an antibiotic to clear the infection. I just can't seem to get rid of the cough."

His jaw tenses, but when his eyes slide to the lake, he says nothing more about it, and for a long moment, we're suspended in silence.

"What do you see when you look at the stars, Kilian?"

I survey the brighter stars in the sky, comparing them to the others. "They're beautiful. Like nature and the universe's very own form of art."

His sight remains glued to the sky as he seems to consider my answer. "I've watched the present until it becomes the past, but never have I peered into the future like my brothers. The stars we see are mere glimpses in time long ago, like recalling your oldest memory. Beautiful in their own right, but far out of reach and though faded into nothing in time, it existed nonetheless. Stars are reminders that time is a fickle thing that waits for no one. No man, woman, creature or god can slow it, never mind stop it. Death himself has no power over such a thing, yet we always assume there's more of it than we have."

I don't have the heart to ask him if he's trying to say that I don't have much time left with my condition, but thankfully I don't need to.

"Stars are a reminder that this life is fleeting for us all. We are all mere glimpses in time in the grand scheme of things, though sometimes you need that reminder to appreciate the present and just how temporary it may be. Dwelling on decisions of the past may be just as futile as wishing to change the past itself. You cannot change it, nor alter it."

The realization sinks in that this entire conversation hasn't been about the time I have left, but how I focus my energy, and a mix of relief and embarrassment washes over me.

"So you think I should just forget it?"

His gaze holds mine, and for a long moment, I'm pinned in place. "Never forget anything, Kilian. Memories are the blood of our existence, the water in our souls. But you should acknowledge the feeling and allow yourself to be free from it, knowing that you made the decision that was right at that moment."

My throat constricts with emotion as I consider the dilemma I faced when I could have swapped Aiden's name with Rempson's.

I swallow against the lump that's formed. "What if it had helped him?"

Stolas leans in within a couple of inches from my ear, and the breath catches in my lungs as his voice fills the space between us. "What if it hadn't?"

I shiver involuntarily, and he reaches over my shoulder to pull my hood over my head.

"Are you certain you're not a spirit guide?"

He straightens, and I tilt my head up to look at him as he grins. "Perhaps this is me turning a new leaf. We'll have to see." His eyes travel along the forest to the lake before turning to me once more. "You should get going before you freeze to death out here."

Noting the numbness in my legs, I can't help but agree as I nod. "Thank you for everything, Stolas, my not-really-but-might-still-be-spirit guide."

He laughs. "Maybe Hell has finally frozen over."

Chapter 16

I spend the entire drive home mulling over what Stolas said with the heat on full blast.

There's no doubt that I feel more at ease with what happened, even though I still feel bad that Aiden is having to get surgery because of how the trial has played out.

But that isn't something I can control.

I just had to look past my guilt to see it.

Plus, Stolas was right. Even if Aiden had been in the test group, there's a good chance he never would have gotten any results... That's not to mention that those who are in the test group are seeing acceleration of symptoms and markers.

That's most definitely **not** what I want for him.

Perhaps this really was for the best.

I'm minutes from the house still, and chunky flakes of snow fall from the sky as I chew the inside of my cheek.

Every few seconds, the memory of Stolas leaning in close to lift my hood overhead comes into the forefront of my mind, and my cheeks burn.

It's normal to feel flustered about that, right? Like he's clearly some ethereal being. It would be normal for a human to feel like this.

It's not like I have feelings for him.

He's just very helpful, and smart... and attractive.

That's it.

That's all it is.

I pull into the driveway and put the car into park before shutting off the engine. The rhythmic ticking sound as it cools fills the air, and I chew the inside of my cheek.

Clearly, the reason I can't get him out of my mind is because this entire situation is bizarre. To meditate and meet spirit guides is one thing, but he's clearly so much more. It's not like I'm practiced in how to meditate or what to expect from it, but I sure as hell don't think that this is a typical experience for someone just starting out.

I still have so many questions for Stolas, and the time we got in the state park was nice, but I didn't have the time to really get to know him.

Climbing out of the car, cold air hits my lungs, and they instantly tighten in my chest, with each exhale coming out in a wheeze.

I really should move somewhere warmer to give my asthma a break. There's no way it's good to always have this heaviness in my lungs or to cough this much.

Once upon a time, I was actually in decent shape because cardio wasn't a fight for my life. Now, I'm what people would call a curvy girl.

Thick thighs save lives, right?

With the door clicking shut behind me, I flip the bolt and slide my shoes off. The house feels too quiet for comfort, and even though it was only a short time that he was with me, Talon definitely kept things interesting.

Maybe this really is my sign to get a cat.

Although I didn't know there was a raven distribution system, I'm thankful for it regardless... Too bad they're illegal to keep as pets without a permit.

Though, it seems like Talon was someone's pet, anyway.

My lungs still labor through each breath, and the thirty-second trek to my room feels like an eternity as I press my lips to the inhaler and suck in a cold spritz of medication.

It takes a couple deep lungfuls for me to feel relief, but I stagger to the bed and flop onto it, feeling oddly more tired than expected for not doing much physical labor today.

Staring at the ceiling, I recount the past twenty-four hours and breathe deep, relaxing into the bed more and more until my eyelids grow heavy.

"Should I be concerned with how often you're choosing to visit me here?"

My eyes snap open to the familiar view of the ethereal garden, and I whirl around, tilting my head to where Stolas stands grinning at me. The sight makes something in my chest flutter, and I run my tongue along the edge of my teeth.

"Who is to say you're not the one pulling me here?"

His brow raises, and he releases a deep chuckle that has my stomach doing flips. "You've got me there. Guilty as charged." He puts his hands up in surrender, and I cross my arms triumphantly.

"I knew it. Now how can I report an ethereal stalker, I wonder?" An icy breeze glides across my skin, and I shiver.

Stolas winces. "There's no ethereal stalker hotline, I'm afraid. You could call a priest, perhaps? Though I doubt that would do any good."

The multitude of questions I have for him come to the forefront of my mind, and I chew the inside of my cheek. He must notice as his head tilts to the side and searches my face.

I don't give him the chance to ask as the words tumble from my lips. "What are you, Stolas...?"

My hand twitches to cover my mouth at the blunt nature of my question, but I hold firm as his lips tilt upward.

"I'm what many would call a demon, Kilian."

A nervous huff of laughter escapes me, but when he holds my gaze expectantly, the humor dies on my lips.

"You're serious?"

He glances away and amusement graces his features before his piercing eyes burn into me again. "Well, yes. Does that bother you?"

Blinking at him, my mouth drops open before it snaps shut, and I really consider his question. I suppose somewhere deep down I knew if he wasn't a spirit guide, that it was possible he was another entity.

Weighing the importance of it, I chew the inside of my cheek some more. "Are you going to hurt me?"

His brows knit together, and he shakes his head. "I wouldn't dream of it."

"Are you going to hurt anyone I care about?"

I watch the muscle in his jaw feather, but he shakes his head again. "No. I might be a demon, but I'm not a monster."

"So, what do you do then—as a demon?"

The question comes out more awkward than intended, and I fight the urge to backtrack, since I'm viciously curious about what the answer could be.

"I do the same things as you on most days... maybe less wandering in forests, though." He adds with a grin.

My cheeks burn, and I suck my tooth in feigned exasperation. "Yet that seems to be where I just saw you. I should have known the forests were a dangerous place for a girl like me."

He laughs, and the depth of it seems to reverberate in my chest, but I can't bring myself to look away from his smirk. "Forests, meditation to astral plains.... Nowhere is safe, really." Stolas eyes me thoughtfully. "Speaking of meditation, you're not in a bathtub this time, are you?"

My eyes widen, and I laugh, shaking my head. "No. Goodness, no. I'm never doing that again. Even without my asthma, I nearly died."

"I could help you get better, you know."

My brows shoot up, and my gaze snaps to his. "That sounded dangerously close to the start of a proposition or deal with a demon."

Stolas' lips twitch with barely restrained humor. "Perhaps it is."

"Right, and next you'll tell me to meet you at a crossroads and only ask for my insignificant soul in exchange."

"Your soul is far from tiny, and if anyone tries to convince you of its insignificance, they do not deserve to live."

I'm about to laugh, but seeing the seriousness etched into his expression, my mouth snaps shut. Even if he wasn't joking about being able to help with my asthma, I don't know that I want some magical cure.

If my doctors could just figure it out with their testing, I'd be in a better place. Getting him to help me would be like I'm cheating the system.

"Who says I just don't need to lose weight and eat healthier? Do I really need demonic intervention for asthma?"

His brows pull together, and there's a long moment of silence between us as another cool breeze of air graces past me.

"Why the hell would you lose weight or eat differently? You're perfect the way you are."

I scoff. "Half of my doctors recommended losing weight as the first point of treatment."

"They're all lazy idiots." Stolas murmurs, before gently grasping my hand, tugging me along behind him as he guides us through the garden.

"Where are we going?"

He glances over his shoulder at me, and the look on his face sends butterflies through my body. "Are you afraid, Kilian?"

"My self-preservation instincts must be malfunctioning, because I am not." I give his hand a slight squeeze. "I'll try almost anything at least once, so hit me with your best shot."

He pauses, eyeing me thoughtfully. "Gemini?"

It takes a second for me to understand what he's asking, and I nod. "How'd you guess?"

"You mean other than that brilliant display of impulsiveness disguised as open-mindedness?"

I gape at him, and he just laughs knowingly. "The stars never lie, dear Kilian."

We come to a stop near a small section of the garden where a handful of blooming flowers display their bright orange and white petals. The potent smell of pollen in the air has me thankful I'm meditating so that I don't have an asthma attack as he turns to me.

"Let me help you."

I frown, and my mind wanders to Aiden as guilt tremors through me. "Why help me when there are so many other people in the world sick?"

He releases a dry huff. "It's impossible. That would be the equivalent of extinguishing the heat in a volcano when the magma itself seems hell-bent on erupting." Letting go of my hand, he picks a flower from an extended bush beside us and turns to me, twirling it between his fingers. "There's a balance in this world, Kilian, and it's been disrupted. Normally, this would not be a problem, however, I have found recently that it is becoming increasingly bothersome."

My brows pinch together, and I watch as he offers the flower between us. "That doesn't explain why you want to help me."

"Is it not enough to say that I care?" He asks, his expression guarded yet oddly hopeful for a supposed demon.

I nod. "Yes. That is not nearly enough. You hardly know me, Stolas. How could you care at all when you don't know my life, my struggles, my joys, or my accomplishments?"

His mouth drops open to speak, but I shake my head, not giving him a chance before continuing. "You might think you know me, but you have no idea what I go through every day. Until you can show me proof that you see all of me, and that you actually care, I don't want your help."

The muscle in his jaw feathers, and he goes to speak as everything suddenly goes dark. I surge upright with a gasp, sending a sharp jolt through my chest as I lean forward, coughing until my throat feels raw.

There's an odd feeling in my body as I collect myself, sending butterflies soaring through me, and I exhale a ragged breath. I still don't know that I fully believe him about being a demon. I suppose I have no reason not to, but the notion that I might have just made him angry sends a nervous thrill through my body.

Maybe he's right about my impulsiveness...

Sighing lightly to not trigger another coughing fit, some part of me feels so incredibly stubborn for denying his help, but I can't accept it when Aiden's struggling with something that could kill him.

Frustrated, I tear off my clothes, tossing them to the floor before rolling onto my side.

Sorting through all of this is tomorrow's problem.

Chapter 17

"Hey Kilian, a bunch of us wanna go to Thornton's tomorrow for dinner and drinks. Do you want to come?"

My head twists to the door, seeing Trinity's bright smile plastered across her face.

The last time they invited me out to Thornton's, Mark and I had gotten way out of hand doing karaoke, even going so far as climbing onto the tables and dancing on them while singing Cher.

Somehow they didn't ban us from the bar, but that hasn't stopped everyone from trying to go back since.

"Maybe. I have a lot to do before the end of next week——"

"Kilian, please. You've been working yourself to the bone. Just come out and unwind with us. Blow off some steam and recharge."

Chris pops his head out into view and glances between us. "Yeah, it's not the same when you're not there. You gotta come, if only for our sakes."

I roll my eyes. "Alright, alright. I'll go, but only for a bit."

Trinity's smile widens, and she shares a look with Chris. "Great, I'll message the others. We'll aim for seven-thirty for dinner! That should give us enough time to get changed here after work and head right there."

They both disappear from view, and I chuckle to myself as I sort through the logs from the first phase of the trial.

Everything outwardly appears normal. The drugs administered were all the same dosage, same frequency, and the pool of volunteers was much smaller, but the results were all consistent.

Within a week, the tumor markers drastically decreased, and after two weeks they'd basically disintegrated, and there was no cancer left in the volunteer's body. There were elevated levels of certain enzymes that lasted a couple of weeks before all levels returned to normal, but nothing that could have been dangerous by any stretch.

Why those results are the opposite of what we're seeing now, I don't know.

Rubbing my face, I run my fingers through my hair and stare at my screen, trying to think of what the hell I might be missing.

I've covered drug type, administered method, duration, and who was receiving the drug.

What else is there?

A long moment passes before it hits me, and I snap my fingers, leaning forward excitedly.

"Preparation. That has to be it." I murmur to myself, clicking over to the shared folder where the records are kept, typing in the password to it before getting an error message.

Password failed. Please try again.

Frowning, I type it in once more, only to see the message reappear.

Weird.

I glance at the time. I have about twenty minutes before Jen is gone for the day, so if I want to get the records, I'll have to get them soon.

Pushing to my feet, I walk down the hall, hearing ambient chatter carrying through the space until I reach Jen's office.

"Jen, I need the password for—"

I stop abruptly, seeing Ron sitting in the chair across from Jen, her face pulled into tense concern as she glances at the doorway where I stand.

"Oh, Kilian. Glad you're here. I was just telling Jen about your short timeline to investigate the disparities between our phases."

Jen nods. "Yes, and if there's anything I can do to help—"

"Well, I'm glad you're offering, because there is something you can do." Her brows shoot up, and I lean against the door frame. "I need to get into the folder for phase one's drug and trial preparation."

"You still have the password, right?"

I shake my head. "It isn't working."

Ron glances between us before pulling out his phone and texting, but I watch as Jen turns to her computer, her fingers flying across the keyboard as she clicks around.

It's not long before her brows furrow, and she shakes her head in disbelief. "I don't understand."

Ron's head snaps in her direction. "Understand what?"

"I–" She types something again and hits enter, staring at the screen with wide eyes before glancing between us. "The password I set isn't working."

Ron's face turns a tinge of red, and he gestures to the computer. "Get that data, or I'll expect your resignation on my desk by the end of the week. I'll put it next to mine."

I step aside, swallowing as Ron breezes past me before hurrying to Jen's desk and sits down. "Are you sure you don't have caps lock on or a sticky key?"

She just shakes her head. "I'm positive, and I've never changed the password. It'll take me some time, but I'll be able to get in." Her gaze locks with mine and her voice quiets down. "Are you really thinking there was something changed or altered?"

"I don't know for sure, but everything else I've looked at suggests there should be no difference between the phase results, nor anything that supports what we're seeing happening to these volunteers."

There's a long moment of silence before she speaks, and it's almost as though she's more talking to herself than to me.

"Alright, well, we'll get this password shit figured out first. We'll worry about the rest of it later."

"The rest of it?"

She looks at me before returning her gaze to the computer and typing. "Yeah, Ron said one of the donors, some company called Astra Inc, just made a large contribution for phase two. He's worried about press if it gets out that the first and second phases were wildly inconsistent. People might accuse us of manipulating results to get funding."

"Shit..." I breathe, and she just nods as her fingers continue to fly over the keyboard.

"Yeah, so needless to say, we need to find out what's going on."

I fall silent beside her as she spends the next twenty minutes working on the password. I nearly jump out of my skin when she finally stands up, slamming her hands against the table.

"It's no use!" She groans, yanking her phone up off the table and scrolling through her contacts.

"What is it? What are you doing?"

Pausing, she looks at me with a sigh. "It won't let me change the password, and any attempts I make to recover it aren't working either. I'm going to see if Chris can come look."

Chris is the tech guy out of all of us, so I nod. "Okay. I'm going to head out then since there's nothing left for me today to do, but call me if you get in."

"You got it."

Chapter 18

Walking in the door, I set my phone down, and it immediately starts vibrating as I release a deep sigh.

I swear to god if this is another debt collector.

Tilting the screen, I see Aiden's name and quickly swipe to answer.

"This better be a call to tell me you've made it there safely."

Aiden laughs as I finish the sentence in a sing-song voice, and I grin, putting him on speaker as I venture further into the house.

"We just got to the hotel. I wish you would have come with us, Kil. You could use a vacation."

"Vacation? I thought you were there for treatment?" I tease, tossing my car keys on the counter and heading to the kitchen.

"Both things can be true, you know? I might be here for treatment, but I refuse to be miserable."

"Good, because Connor probably spent a lot of money and if you're miserable, he could have just brought me instead."

Aiden laughs harder, and I set the phone on the table before opening the fridge to grab a pre-made meal.

"Ugh. I know I'm excited to be here, but I hate that you're so far away, Kil. Be safe over there, okay?"

"Safe? We live in one of the safest places. Nothing ever happens here."

"Your neighbor held target practice in your backyard."

"Yeah, you know, that was a one-time thing. He hasn't done something like that before, and he's kept to himself since."

"He better. Otherwise, he will have me–" Connor echoes the words 'and me,' in the background. "–to answer to for his crimes."

I can't help but laugh as I peel the plastic from the container and throw it in the microwave with a beep.

"So far, no crimes need to be answered for. What are you both planning for the rest of your night?"

"We're actually about to run out to grab food, so I'll let you go. We just wanted to check in."

My chest squeezes almost to the point of pain. "Well, thank you. Go enjoy your dinner and let me know when your treatment starts."

"Sounds good babe. Love you."

I hear Connor yelling goodbyes in the background before the line disconnects, and I pull my food from the microwave, teetering the plastic on my fingertips, rotating the distribution of weight to keep from burning myself as I set it on the counter.

By the time I've settled into my seat at the kitchen table, I'm absently looking through my notifications on my phone when I notice the voicemail from yesterday still there.

Putting a forkful of chicken in my mouth, I chew slowly as I hit play.

"This is Kristina with Gentry Debt Collections. I'm looking to speak with a Kilian Sterling..."

My heart sinks, and even though I haven't received a call today, I swallow my mouthful before dialing the number.

I know I have several bills outstanding from the past two years that have gone to various collections companies, but I don't have much to pay right now until I get paid... Perhaps they'll do installments or settle for a lesser amount.

The phone rings a few times before Kristina's voice fills the air.

"This is Kristina with Gentry Debt Collections. Who am I speaking with today?"

"Uh, hi. This is Kilian Sterling." Typing fills the air as I take a small bite of food.

"Hello Kilian. May I ask for your social security number, your phone number and the reason for your call today?"

I provide Kristina with the requested information, feeling like there's a ten-pound boulder in my stomach as I put another forkful of food in my mouth.

Kristina types away for an agonizing length of time, leaving us in pure silence.

"Ms. Sterling, I don't show any open debts on file for you."

I frown. *Is this some kind of prank?*

"That's impossible? I've been receiving calls every day." For weeks. But I won't tell her that, even though I'm certain she knows.

"It looks like as of today, your balance is showing paid in full."

Rearing back, my body feels like it's in a weird state of numb excitement. "How is this... How could this be possible?"

Kristina's voice is softer than before as she murmurs. "I'm not sure... It looks like someone called in this morning, and he paid them."

My brows shoot up. *Stolas?!* "Okay. Thank you, Kristina."

"You're welcome. Is there anything else I could help you with, Ms. Sterling?"

Disbelief coats my senses as I shake my head. "No, that's it. Thank you."

The line clicks, and within seconds, I'm scrolling through my other missed calls. When I reach the next debt collector whose payment I know is overdue, a wave of nausea overwhelms me.

This can't be happening.

I click the number, and rings. By the time I've given my information to the agent on the other line, and he's silent for a full minute, I already know what he's going to say.

"Ms. Sterling—"

"Someone already paid it, didn't they?"

The man hesitates for a moment. "Uh. Yes. This morning."

"Thank you—" I whisper and hang up before he's able to say anymore.

I don't bother calling the handful of other debt collectors that have bogged up my voicemail inbox for years as I finish the last of my microwaved dinner.

He thinks I can be purchased? Is that it?

He thinks that my willingness to be helped is directly tied to me owing him? Or maybe he is trying to prove he is good for it?

Either way, this doesn't show me in any way that he knows a damn thing about me.

If anything, it shows me the opposite.

Tossing the plastic container in the garbage and the fork into the sink, I storm toward the bedroom with one person in mind.

Stolas.

Chapter 19

"Do you think this is some kind of game?" Stolas turns to face me with concern etched across his features, and I stomp toward him, jabbing my finger into his chest. "You think you can just flaunt your wealth around, and I wouldn't notice?"

His brows furrow, and his fingers glide up my wrist before curling around my hand. "I didn't know it would bother you, Kilian. I've made donations before, but I suppose you just didn't know it was me."

Donation? Is that what he's calling it? Like I'm some charity case?

"You can call it whatever you want, Stolas. You had no right to do that."

I move to retract my hand, but he holds it firm in his grip. "It's my company. I can support whatever I want with it. It just so happens that supporting trials I know will be successful helps to keep them running."

I blink at him.

"Your company–" The realization hits me, and I search his face. "Astra Inc. is your company?"

His lips twitch, and he cocks his head to the side. "What did you think I was talking about?"

"I–" My mouth snaps shut, and I go to pull away, but he's still gripping my wrist in his hand. When my body twists away, his other hand catches the back of my free arm, turning me to face him again.

"Kilian." The rich tone of his voice has my heart raging in my ears, though I'm not sure if it's because of his voice, his proximity, or both.

"I learned today that someone paid my medical debt, and I just thought..." I shake my head, feeling heat rise to my cheeks from embarrassment. "I assumed you'd done it because I told you that you didn't know me. I shouldn't have assumed."

Stolas remains silent, and my gaze drags over to see the restraint in his expression that looks reminiscent of a wince.

"It was you, wasn't it?"

He grimaces with a nod, and I turn to walk away, but he just tightens his grip slightly, keeping me from moving. "Was that truly so wrong of me?"

"I cannot be purchased, Stolas."

He rears back slightly. "My intention was to ease your mind, Kilian, not purchase it."

"How is that any different?" He looks genuinely confused, so I continue. "Your gesture only made me owe you. I am not debtless. My debt has just been purchased by another without my permission."

The shift from confusion to regret in his eyes is clear as he shakes his head. "I didn't know—"

"You could have asked me." I have to stop myself, because part of me knows it was a kind gesture, but the other part of me doesn't want to owe anyone anything.

It was bad enough to owe collections, but to owe thousands to Stolas instead?

That's somehow even worse.

"How can I pay you back?"

His brows pinch together even more. "Kilian you don't have to–"

"How?"

Stolas' jaw feathers, but his expression turns contemplative for a long moment. "There's an art exhibition coming up, and I need to attend. If you attend with me, I will consider your debt paid."

That's it?

His head tilts down, bringing his face mere inches from mine as he searches my face expectantly, and I feel as if my heart's in my throat.

"Done." I whisper, but he just grins.

"So, we have a deal?"

I nod, but the way his grin widens has me wondering what the hell I'm getting myself into.

"Wonderful. I'll pick you up at six on Saturday."

"Wait." Suddenly overly aware of how close he is as each breath I take brushes my chest against his, my pulse only heightens. "Six in the morning? What do I wear? Where is it?"

"This year it's being hosted in Los Angeles, and we'll have about six hours of flight ahead of us, so preferably something comfortable."

I can't help but gape at him.

"But... Los Angeles?! I can't just fly to LA! I need to work–"

"Nah, ah, ah." He wiggles his finger from side to side. "You don't have any trials next week."

"How do you–" I shake my head. "You know what? Never mind. I don't want to know how you know."

The way his eyes search my face makes butterflies soar through my body chaotically. "Six AM Saturday, then?"

I nod. "Six AM on Saturday."

He releases my arms, and I take the smallest half-step back, if only to give myself enough space to think.

"Stolas," I whisper, feeling his eyes on me as I absently look at the forest before returning to where he stands. "You said you had donated to the trial before?"

"I've donated to it since its registration."

Surprise rifles through me, and it takes all my effort to not sound accusatory. "Why?"

"I've been watching it closely. This treatment is one of the few which holds the most promise to curing cancer in humans."

My eyes widen, but I shake my head. "Sorry to be the bearer of bad news, but it isn't."

The realization that I could have just tanked our funding sets in as he frowns. "What do you mean?"

Shit. Too late now.

"Phase two was a dud. I'm investigating why phase one was different, but phase two only sped up the volunteers prognosis and increased their tumor markers."

Stolas crosses his thick arms over his chest and rubs his hand along the stubble on his jawline. "And your investigation?"

My gaze drops to the ground. "Has yielded nothing yet to explain the difference."

"But you're still investigating?"

"I am," I whisper with a nod, and when my attention drags back to him, he looks suddenly more serious than before.

"Good. Don't let it get swept under the rug."

"I don't understand. If you know it will cure cancer, why wait for humans to prove it? Do you know how many people will die? How many people have already died?"

His jaw feathers. "It's complicated, Kilian."

"What's complicated about saving people?"

When he tilts his head to the sky, he releases a long breath. "I don't expect you to understand. There are things we are bound to, things that are forbidden. There's a–"

"A balance."

He nods slightly, but the look on his face is apologetic as I sigh deeply. "Of course there is."

There's a long moment of silence before Stolas' hand brushes the back of my arm, dragging my attention to him and away from the garden.

"You should go rest, Kilian." The garden around us grows dark, and his hand glides up my arm to tuck a lock of hair behind my ear. "I'll see you Saturday."

Chapter 20

Jen: It was too late to call. Left the new password on your desk.

My heart pounds as I stare at the text with wide eyes. Turning the key to the engine, it rumbles one last time before silence fills the space around me.

This is it. This has to be it.

Grasping the straps of my purse, my palms stick to the leather as I tug it over the console and climb out of the driver's seat. The bitter wind bites at my lungs with each breath as my feet carry me the short distance to the doors.

Each second feels like a lifetime.

My conversation with Stolas last night has had my mind in a mess of thoughts, and I'd spent the entire morning so focused on that, that I'd forgotten that I was going out tonight with the others.

It was only after I'd taken my second last round of antibiotics that I'd remembered we're getting drinks tonight, and then with five minutes left I'd realized that I needed to pick an outfit to change into.

So, I'd grabbed one of the cute dresses I hadn't worn in a while from my closet and hurried out the door without a second thought. But now, with each step into the building, feeling the chill wrack through my body, I can't help but wonder if I should have grabbed one of my thicker cardigans to go with it.

I'm only half paying attention as my feet carry me absently to my office, and I slide into my chair, staring at the sticky note on my desk with a pit in my stomach.

"Here goes nothing."

The computer fan breaks the tense silence as I wait for the monitor to come to life, and every moment feels like an eternity before I'm finally able to log in.

By the time I've opened the folder for phase one, there's a slight tremor in my hands that makes me second guess each letter I've typed of the password Jen scribbled onto the sticky note.

The folder opens as my heart beats like a war drum, and I scan through one report, then another, and another. I drop the files from phase two in to compare, and I'm about to lose hope when I get to the logs of drug preparation.

My gaze snags on the drug identification numbers, and for a moment I freeze.

The last digit of the drug used for treatment for the initial phase was an eight, but the last digit used for phase two is a three.

How are there two drug identifications with the same name?

Usually the name auto populates once you type in, so it still doesn't make sense how this could happen.

I quickly tab over to the code directory, plugging in the identification number for the drug used in phase two, but as soon as I hit enter, a bold red message appears under the search bar.

Drug code not found.

Swallowing hard, I print out the comparison of the two files and the resulting message for the phase two drug code search.

I'm going to have to tell Ron about this.

"About what?"

Halfway to the door, I freeze at the rich voice that sounds like it's in the room with me. By the time I've turned in a full circle, I'm certain he's not here.

... Stolas?

His answering chuckle reverberates in my ears, and my hair stands on end. I turn to look around in the room, halfway relieved to see it's empty, and he didn't magically appear.

What the hell are you doing here?

"I'm not actually there. I warned you about the side effects of thinning the veil. Suppose it is quite thin now, since we can hear each other from this distance."

I swallow. *What's the risk of it being this thin?*

"You mean other than our minds melding into one and losing our independence? Oh, not that much."

My heart slides into my stomach. *What?!*

Stolas laughs, and I roll my eyes. *You asshole.*

"There's no risk, Kilian. I already told you. If there was a risk, I wouldn't have done it."

If you say so...

A moment of silence follows, and I sigh before pacing to the door, feeling reality sink in about what I need to do now.

"I take it you're having to tell this Ron individual about what your investigation uncovered?"

The drug administered in phase two isn't real and is not the drug that was given in phase one.

"Interesting."

Leaving him with that knowledge, I let the door to my office close behind me. On one hand, I'm thankful the trial wasn't a complete failure, but on the other hand, I'm concerned about which drug the test volunteers actually received.

The latter has me especially thankful that Aiden wasn't part of the test group.

Step by step, I finally approach Ron's open door and knock, seeing him gazing down at papers strewn over his desk before his head snaps toward me.

"Come in."

My hearts thrashing in my chest as I close the distance to his desk, sliding the papers on top of it in silence.

My head swims, and my blood rages in my ears. *I'm going to pass out.*

"Would it help to know I'm trained in CPR?"

My cheeks burn, and for a breath of a moment, I forget the anxiety running rampant through me.

Perhaps a little.

"What is this?" He asks, scanning over the reports before flipping to the next page, and his brows furrow, creating a deep line in his forehead.

"It's the reason phase two failed."

His eyes flash as he scans the first page again, and I know the moment he realizes because he stares at it for a long moment and flips to the second page once more.

"Shit." He rubs his hand over his mouth. "This is going to put us in PR hell. What drug did they administer?"

I shake my head. "No. It doesn't exist."

Ron mutters a curse before leaning back in his chair. "Phase two ends now. I'll talk to legal while we recess for the week. Next Monday, I want you triple checking what is being administered."

"Yes, sir."

I'm turning to leave when Ron's voice halts me in place. "Oh, and Kilian, I think it goes without saying that if our second iteration of phase two goes awry, we're both going to be without jobs."

He didn't have to say it for me to know if the pit in my stomach was any indication, but hearing it out loud like this only makes the pit feel more like a bag of boulders.

I give him a single nod before leaving his office behind and wipe my palms against my thighs as my pulse finally calms.

That was moderately less painful than expected.

"No CPR needed, I take it?"

Heat engulfs my entire being. *Not yet.*

"Shame."

Inhaling deeply, a twinge pulls in my chest, and I cough as I turn the last corner into my office, doubling over as each lungful feels more and more labored.

I don't know whether Stolas, this asthma or this trial are more likely to be the death of me.

Chapter 21

After writing a final summary for phase two, I save it to my hard drive in a password encrypted file before shutting my computer down with a sigh.

My phone vibrates and I glance at the screen, seeing Aiden's name as I hurry to unlock it.

Aiden: About to go into surgery... In case I don't make it... delete my browsing history on my computer please.

Kilian: Delete it yourself when you're back. You're not going anywhere.

Aiden: Your confidence in my survival is inspiring.

Kilian: One of us has to be positive.

Aiden: My blood type is B positive. I think that's enough for me.

I huff a laugh, typing out another text to distract him from his procedure.

Kilian: We're going out for dinner tonight. You're going to miss my shenanigans.

Aiden: Do a blow job for me. I won't be satisfied unless you do.

Aiden: But make sure you get a video of it, so I can enjoy my recovery to the fullest by playing it over and over.

I roll my eyes, and Jen's voice sounds out from the hallway.

"Leaving in ten minutes. Are we okay to carpool?" She peers her head in the door. "Chris, Mark, and Trinity are already waiting."

"Shit." I mutter, pushing to my feet and hurrying to grab my dress from the drawer. "Okay, I'll be right there."

She disappears, and I hurry to shut the door behind her before stripping off my jeans and t-shirt. I've got the dress half up my body when the material fits more tight than usual, and a warm wave of self-consciousness washes over me.

I should have tried this on before I left.

"Tried what on?"

My eyes widen, and I curse myself for forgetting I'm not alone in my thoughts now.

Just a dress for dinner with coworkers tonight.

He hums in acknowledgement, the deep sound vibrating in my head as I smooth the material out along my body, tugging the hem down lower. The material that used to barely brush against my skin when I moved now hugs my hips tight, and my chest feels constricted as I tug the side zipper up.

I snag the pair of heeled boots from the closet and glance in the mirror hesitantly, my eyes quickly spotting all of my imperfections in the red and black floral dress. My stomach sticks out more than I want it to, and because my body doesn't fit it like it used to, the dress no longer hovers just above my knee, but rather sits around my mid-thigh now.

I can't say it looks terrible, but it's much less flattering now than it ever has been in my eyes. My attention snags to where my love handles look more pronounced, and I shut the closet door with a sigh.

Whatever.

Let's just get through tonight.

Maybe after a couple of drinks, I'll just forget about how uncomfortable I feel.

I slide on my boots, take my last dose of antibiotics with a swish of water before pulling out my phone to text Aiden.

Kilian: I'll get you a video, but only if Connor gets a post-anesthesia video of you. We will trade embarrassment for entertainment purposes only.

Aiden: Ugh. Fine. They're wheeling me back to pre-op. Love you.

My chest feels tight as I grab my purse, texting as I head out the door of my office.

Kilian: Love you too.

"About time!" Mark exclaims as Jen and I step out of the building into the brisk afternoon air, and I feel my lungs constrict as my breath forms a cloud of fog in front of me.

"It's not like we have reservations." Trinity grumbles before climbing into the back seat, with Mark and Jen following close behind, leaving shotgun to me.

Can't say I'm not thankful for it. There's no way I'd be able to crawl into the back seat without flashing someone.

Chris puts the car into drive as I buckle my seatbelt, and the car lurches forward as I lean over to turn the music on. When the car turns the opposite direction of Thornton's, I'm about to ask where we're going when Jen beats me to it.

"The bar is the other way, Chris."

He glances at her in the rearview mirror and grins. "I might have a new spot for us."

My eyebrows shoot up, but Trinity's voice fills the air. "We're heading downtown?"

"It's been a while since I've been down there!" Jen chimes out, and Mark chuckles as we chatter about the construction that had been going on for so long.

Another fifteen minutes later, we're passing apartment buildings surrounded by businesses, and Chris takes a couple of turns before pulling over in front of a restaurant.

Through the dark tinted window, a handful of people sit at the entry bar together, and Jen gasps in excitement behind me.

"Oh, my, gosh, is that the new nightclub, Luminous?!"

Mark leans forward in my peripherals and claps his hand onto the back of Chris' seat. "Who's down to check it out after dinner?"

"Yes! Let's do it!" Trinity chimes in, and Chris turns the car off before turning to me.

"You down?"

I just grin. "They'll have to drag me out."

Trinity and Jen let out a collective 'whoop' before we all climb out of the car and file into the restaurant. The moment we step inside, as excited as I am, I'm immediately self-conscious of my choice in clothing.

Most of the others in the restaurant have long sleeves, jeans or something of the like appropriate for winter. Compared to the others in the restaurant, Jen and Trinity wear the most form-fitting, appropriately sized clothing that still makes me feel somewhat scandalous.

I'm spiraling in my thoughts as we each scoot into a circular booth and the server brings over a pitcher of water.

"What can I get you all started with?"

I glance around the table before the server makes eye contact with me first.

"I'll get a vodka cranberry."

The server moves down the table before disappearing down the hall and I check my phone briefly, seeing nothing from Aiden as the others quietly chatter amongst themselves.

"What are the chances this trial gets cancelled completely?"

My gaze snaps to Trinity as Mark shrugs. "Phase two was a complete and utter failure, so I'd say chances are high."

I shake my head. "We restart a new phase next Monday with fresh volunteers."

Everyone's attention at the table turns to me, and Jen's eyes are wide as she leans in. "Not that I'm upset about it, but what do you mean? How can we start fresh if the drug doesn't work?"

I'm not sure if any of them could have had a part to play in why phase two was a failure, and a small part of me screams that it very well could have been on purpose, so I tread the fine line between fact and fiction.

"We're still investigating why phase two was such a failure, but we're going to redo the testing with a fresh wave to rule out inconsistencies."

Mark nods and Jen's brows shoot up. "So the week after next is just rinse and repeat?"

I know I need to shut their questions down, so I just smile and nod. "Yep. Ron's orders." Thankfully, the server steps up to the table with a platter of our drinks, so I go quiet, letting the distraction take their minds from the topic entirely.

By the time we've each ordered our food, the news seems to have died down, with the entire table focused on chatter about various topics. It's not long before we get and finish dinner, and I'm already feeling like the dress that was tight has gotten impossibly tighter. Thankfully, as expected, the vodka cranberries I'd had with dinner have taken the edge off of my self consciousness.

"Off to Luminous, we go!"

We all scoot from the booth, and the moment I stand up fully, my head swims. I sway a bit before grasping the back of a nearby chair.

Following close behind the others, it takes a conscious effort to focus on walking straight with how my head is spinning. Thankfully, the walk to Luminous is short, and we're hardly waiting in line more than five minutes as the music from the club reverberates into my very bones.

The line moves up, and the bouncer glances over at our group.

"The ladies get in free." He gestures to allow us to walk past him before addressing Mark and Chris. "Ten dollar cover charge each."

They each hand over a bill as Trinity giggles, leaning in to whisper to Jen before we all head inside.

The entryway has pulsing lights strung over the top, illuminating the dark hall before we breach the main entrance where groups of people crowd together.

The rest of the club lives up to its name, with ambient lighting built into the pillars around the room, some lights hanging from the ceiling like vines that flash in time to the music.

The sight somehow reminds me of the garden, and an odd feeling tightens my chest.

Can you see any of this?

A moment of silence has embarrassment coating my veins until he finally answers. *"Seeing what?"*

The club.

"You're at a bar?"

I roll my eyes at his tone. *I'll take that as a no, then.*

"The veil doesn't share sight. Imagine walking into your boss's office and seeing what I see where I am. I don't think you'd be able to handle that and reality."

My brow raises. *You'd be surprised what I can **handle**, Stolas.*

"Perhaps." I can hear him smiling in his response, and my cheeks burn.

Strobe lights and lasers from the DJ table stretch all the way to the opposite side of the room where we stand, and I see Trinity turn in a full circle with her jaw slack.

"Wow." Trinity sighs wistfully.

"This is so cool!" Jen shouts over the music, and Chris leans over to us.

"I'll get our jackets put up." He offers his hands as the others shimmy out of their winter jackets, and I can't help but feel silly that I hadn't bothered to wear one.

At least I don't need to worry about it being stolen or losing it.

My phone vibrates, and I unlock it to check the message, only to see a video of Aiden lying in a hospital bed, clearly under the effects of anesthesia, though I can't hear a word he's saying to the camera.

Aiden's bargain for a video comes to the forefront of my mind and I resign myself to my fate as I tap Jen on the arm.

She turns to me as I flip my phone to the camera video setting, offering my phone between us. "I was dared to do a blow job. Can you record it for me as evidence?"

Trinity gasps. "I'll do one with you!"

I just grin at her, silently thanking God that I won't be doing it alone, and Jen cackles, taking my phone dutifully as we cross the room to the bar.

The bartender's gaze scans each of us before he leans forward. "What can I get you?"

My mouth drops open, but Trinity's voice chimes out. "Two blow jobs please!"

To his credit, the bartender just nods before turning his attention to the others, and they order three lemon drops.

I see Jen grinning as she points the camera at the bartender who's lining up five shot glasses methodically, and I watch with fascination as he fills the three lemon drops first before pouring darker liquid into the last two and topping them with whip cream.

We each slide over some cash before Jen's voice chimes out. "Blow jobs first!"

My cheeks burn, and Trinity grins as she puts her hands behind her back.

"What are you doing?" I ask, and she blinks at me.

"You can't use your hands." She wiggles her arms, showing her fingers interlaced together to emphasize her point. "That's the point of the shot!"

Oh. That's why they're called blow jobs.

"Should I even ask where your line of thought is going?"

I can't help the chuckle that escapes me as I lock my arms and interlace my fingers together.

I'm about to do my first blow job. Wish me luck.

A choking sound filled my mind, and I bite back a grin.

"You got this, guys!" Jen cheers, pointing the camera at us as a warm wave of nervousness washes over me.

Better get this over with... Aiden better love me.

Positioning myself next to Trinity, Jen focuses the camera on us. "Three... Two... One... Go!"

Leaning down, the whipped cream fills my mouth first, and my lips wrap around the rim of the glass as I squeeze ever so slightly and straighten, tilting my head back as the liquid runs down my throat.

It's a challenge to swallow it gracefully, and I feel liquid still run down my chin as I take the glass from my mouth and cough awkwardly.

When I look at Trinity, she's got whipped cream on the tip of her nose and I laugh, coughing even harder as Jen hands my phone over.

"You got a message while I was recording." She shouts over the music, and I swipe the whipped cream from Trinity's nose as she cackles.

Jen walks over to Chris and Mark, tossing the lemon drop back with ease before I go to check my messages, seeing another video from Aiden in his hospital bed.

I open the video of me taking the shot but send it without watching to save myself the embarrassment, and shove my phone back into my purse as my stomach turns uncomfortably.

Stubbornly, I brush it off as the shot not mixing well with dinner, and I'm hardly paying attention when the bartender slides another row of shots over to us.

"What–?"

My question dies on my lips as Chris slides over a couple of bills with the realization sets in that he purchased us another round. Staring at the glass, my stomach turns and flips.

Maybe washing it down with a lemon drop will help settle it?

Part of me knows it's unlikely, but the other part of me, the one with inhibitions and concerns, watered down by liquid courage, doesn't seem to care.

"Bottoms up!" Jen cheers out, and I grab the glass, tossing it back quickly, tasting the sour and sweet on my tongue just as my stomach flips one final time.

Oh, god. That was a terrible decision.

I look around frantically for the washroom, and my mouth waters as the wave of nausea worsens. Each LED light along the wall brings my hopes up, and I turn, scanning the room until I spot an illuminated sign for the restrooms.

"What are you looking at?" Jen asks, but I don't give a second longer to respond as I hurry over to it.

Each second feels like it's my last, like I could lose the grip I have on the way I've squeezed my mouth shut, and the moment I push past the door into the restroom, I feel the first heave in my abdomen.

Seconds.

My palm slams against the door to the stall as it bursts open, clattering against the side as I drop to my knees, hurling the contents of my stomach into the bowl.

The remnants of dinner, all the alcohol and everything else flushes down the toilet as I groan, leaning back on my heels.

"Kilian?" Jen's voice sounds awfully close, and I turn my head to see the stall still wide open, with Jen's concerned expression in my line of sight between me and the sink. "Are you okay?"

"Yeah, I think something just didn't agree with me." My stomach feels like it's shaking, and a shiver runs through my body as I slowly push to my feet with a dizziness I can't seem to shake.

"Do you want us to take you home?" Trinity chimes in, and my heart drops. "I can see if Chris can–"

"No, you guys should enjoy your night. I'll just catch a cab home."

I look at both women who have concern etched into their features, with their brows pulled together tightly, and Jen's mouth drops open, but I interject before she can argue.

"It'll be okay. I probably just need to sleep it off."

Come to think of it, it's more than likely a side effect from the antibiotics and alcohol that I stupidly took together.

"Okay." I walk past Jen to the sink as she tracks my movements, her voice still filled with concern. "Do you want us to wait with you outside for your cab?"

Guilt tremors through me at the thought of dragging both girls outside, and I shake my head as I wipe my mouth off with water, feeling my stomach churn uncomfortably again.

"No. Just go enjoy the club. I'll be fine."

Trinity leans over the sink slightly to look at me. "Are you sure? We don't mind."

Nodding, I turn to look at them, mustering more confidence than I feel. "Yeah, I'm sure. Go enjoy the club and dance enough for the three of us. I'll text you once I'm home."

Jen walks over to Trinity and hooks their arms together. "Okay, just be careful, Kilian."

Giving them a weak smile before they leave the restroom, the moment they're out the doors, I hurry back into the stall and heave bile into the toilet.

God.

There's nothing more that I want than to curl up in bed right now.

By the time I've cleaned up, it's half an hour later, and I slip out of the restroom, spotting the others dancing in the middle of the floor, surrounded by crowds of people as I make my way out the front entrance of the club.

Chapter 22

When I brush past the final set of doors, cold air hits me like a bag of ice, and I shiver uncontrollably as I pull my phone out, dialing the number for a cab.

I get halfway through the set of numbers when my stomach cramps and panic washes over me.

Oh, god.

There's no washroom out here.

Spotting an alley nearby, I hurry over to it, my lungs burning with each frigid breath that sends a cloud of mist outward. I hardly turn the corner before doubling over and dry heaving repeatedly. My eyes water, and I spit the acrid saliva out, bracing myself on the brick wall of the building with a trembling hand.

"You look like you're having a rough night."

The familiar rich voice that's no longer in my mind sends a nervous note down my spine, and I glance toward the street, seeing Stolas' silhouette against the bright streetlights mere feet away.

"I am." I croak. My stomach cramps again, and I double over more, clutching my stomach as my body tries to force something out that's not there. Out of breath, I lean more on the wall as I wipe my mouth and turn to face him.

"Would you like a ride home?"

Those six words seem so insignificant at face value, but beneath the surface, my heart soars as much as I feel like I'm standing on the precipice of something monumental.

Stolas, and everything he represents, is a terrifying type of beauty.

My abdomen growls, and I know it's merely a warning for something to come as I nod.

"Please. The sooner I can get out of here, the better."

He offers his hand between us, and I swallow hard, stepping closer unsteadily as my palm slides into his, and he gently encircles it.

"Is your sudden acute nausea due to drinking or your illness?"

Stolas guides me to the street where a black SUV's parked on the side of the road. The dark tinted windows make it impossible to see inside, but I don't have to guess as he steps forward to open the passenger side door.

"I'm fine—" My words cut off abruptly as I feel the familiar clench in my stomach, and I cover my mouth like that will stop me from heaving a whole lot of nothing from my body.

"Right, and I suppose next you'll say you don't have to take medications to breathe."

My attention flicks to where he stands with a raised brow, as if challenging me to disagree with him.

"The alcohol just didn't agree with my medications." I stubbornly slide into the passenger seat as his brows furrow.

"You drank while taking medications?" He asks incredulously and I groan.

"I–" The look he's giving me has my mouth snapping shut before I try again. "Not my best moment, okay?"

Stolas shakes his head and slowly closes the door with a hint of amusement on his features. It shuts with a click and I swallow against the nausea roiling in my stomach as he slides into the driver's side.

He glances at me thoughtfully before putting the car into drive. "Just... try to give me a warning if I need to pull over."

My mouth waters, and I swallow hard again, not trusting opening my mouth as I nod.

There's a good chance if I try to say anything back, it'll be game over for Stolas' interior.

"At least you can talk this way without vomiting everywhere."

Please don't say that word.

I see his lips twitch in the corner of my eye. *"Which one? Vomiting?"*

I squeeze my eyes shut and groan. *Damn you, demon.*

His laughter grows, and he navigates the vehicle out of downtown. *"Already damned, twice over."*

The vehicle rocks back and forth as it takes everything in me not to hurl.

If I throw up in your car, it's your own damn fault, then.

Chapter 23

We're pulling into the long driveway, and I'm seconds from losing the battle to keep myself from hurling.

My body's like a leaf in the wind with how it's trembling, and I've broken out in a full body sweat. Beads drip down my collar to my chest as Stolas brings the vehicle to a stop, and within seconds I've surged out the door, only to hurl bile onto the snow covered driveway.

Leaning against the side of the SUV, my head spins as I hear Stolas' footsteps grow closer. The gentle brush of his fingertips rubs soothing circles on my back, and I desperately cling to the feeling, focusing on it. The cold air bites at my lungs, and I suck in a breath before coughing, feeling the crackling in my chest with each.

"Come on. Let's get you inside."

I straighten and turn toward the house with a nod, feeling the world spin before he grips my arm. It takes a second for my half-lidded gaze to find his, but the alarm in his expression is enough to send a note of worry down my spine.

"Alright, here we go."

He guides me gently to the front door, and I'm fumbling with my keys when he pulls them from my hands to unlock the bolt in one swift motion. Two, three steps in, he's leaned down to help remove my shoes, crowding my space as I brace one hand on his arm for support.

Stolas is a pillar beside me, and no matter how I lean, he remains steadfast, supporting my weight as I try not to fall to either side.

Lifting one foot, even though I've braced myself, I teeter off balance, feeling like the world around me is spinning as Stolas catches me by my biceps. He pulls me into his chest, wrapping an arm around my waist to support me as he curses under his breath.

"Is this what you typically do with your spare time?" He's moving now, keeping my waist held tight in his grasp as he does, with my legs dangling over his other arm.

"Not typically, no," I murmur between breaths as I fight to reconcile how we're moving.

How the hell is this possible?

My head swims and I chance a quick look at my feet as he somehow navigates to the washroom, only to see them completely suspended half a foot from the floor.

"Have you never been carried before?"

My cheeks burn, and I feel another wave of nausea twist my stomach. *I don't think anyone gets carried much after they grow up.*

He turns the final corner to the washroom and everything spins more, forcing my forehead to lean into his collarbone for support as my body trembles.

*God. This is the **worst**.*

"What kind of medication did you take?" His deep voice feels like it's reverberating in my bones with how close he is as he eases me onto the lid of the toilet seat, and I shiver at the chill against my bare legs.

He must notice, because his eyes trail along the length of my body before his jaw tenses, and he moves to the tub, twisting the knobs as water rushes out.

"Ant-t-t-t" My teeth chatter as another shiver wracks through my body. The chattering makes it near impossible to respond to him, so my gaze rises to his. *Antibiotics.*

He curses under his breath and steps out of the room for a moment, returning with a thick towel in his hand that he places beside the tub before sliding his jacket off.

"Stay put for a moment." He murmurs and wraps the jacket around my shoulders.

Wait, where are you—

"You'll find out in a second."

Within a heartbeat, he's disappeared out the door, and I reach over to grip the sides of the jacket, pulling them tighter around me as the light scent of a woodsy cologne invades my senses.

It's comforting, and even with the trembling and nausea that has my stomach turning uncomfortably, I inhale a lungful before his footsteps in the hallway grow closer.

When he comes around the corner with a duffle bag, I have a hard time reigning in my reaction as my brows pinch together, watching as he dumps something into the bathwater. He grabs what looks like various colored crystals and places them around the edge of the bath, placing a couple into the water before reaching back into the bag.

My focus sweeps from the amethyst crystal to the turquoise one before landing on what I assume is topaz, and I point to the one he places near the head of the bathtub.

What kind of crystal is that?

He glances at my trembling hand before following my index finger to the dark crystal that almost looks red in the light.

"Garnet." He says in a low tone before walking over to the toilet, and another wave of nausea washes over me as he leans in, wrapping his arm around my waist and easing me to my feet.

I sway and suck in a breath, squeezing my eyes shut against the way the world spins. Thankfully, he helps me to the edge of the tub, keeping his arm wrapped around me as the water shuts off.

"Kilian." My eyes snap open at the sound of my name, and I lock eyes with Stolas, looking more apprehensive than ever. "I can step out for you to undress, but if I do..."

I glance between him and the bath, and whether due to not wanting him to feel awkward, mixed with not wanting him to leave, I gesture to him in a circular motion.

Ironic that I'm asking him to do what my brain is already so inclined to do.

Can you just turn? I'll let you know once I'm in...

Without missing a beat, he turns to the side, keeping his arm out for support. For a few seconds, I watch his head tilted to face the opposite wall, but I quickly focus on the task at hand.

If he was going to watch, he wouldn't have offered to turn away.

Not like there's much for him to see anyway, other than a girl who likes to eat snacks a little more than she should.

I reach over with one shaky hand, tugging down my zipper that gets stuck halfway, and I squirm as I try to manipulate the stuck mechanism. After a long moment, I huff angrily before my eyes flick to where he remains still with his eyes shut, dutifully facing the wall opposite of the tub.

"Stolas..." I whisper, and his head turns to me slightly, with his eyes shut. *"My zipper is stuck... Can you—?"*

My voice stops abruptly as his lips twitch, but his eyes stay closed as his hand glides across my body, finding the zipper with surprising ease. We're chest to chest, with his arms on either side of me as he eases the zipper down.

"If you wanted me to undress you, Kilian, all you had to do was ask."

The sound of the zipper fills the air, and embarrassment coats my veins as I tug the material down my body. It collapses to the ground with a soft thump, and I step one foot into the tub.

The hot water feels like a balm to my core, and I lean heavily on Stolas' support as I climb the rest of the way into the bathtub. Within seconds, I've eased into the scaling heat, feeling it seep into my bones as I lean back with a contented sigh. The smell of lavender, hints of cinnamon and vanilla invades my senses as my attention returns to where Stolas stands with his eyes closed.

Heat rises to my cheeks. "You can open your eyes..."

I don't know if it's the heat of the water covering me, Stolas being in the room while I'm nearly nude, or the noxious mix of alcohol and meds, but when his eyes open, my entire body feels exposed and oddly light as my knees press together almost subconsciously.

He kneels down alongside the tub, yet somehow still towers over it. "How are you feeling?"

I glance over at myself, assessing how I feel from head to toe. The shivering has finally relented, and though I still feel nauseous, it's much more manageable than it was moments ago.

Whatever magic he put in the water must have been fast acting, because within seconds I've relaxed more into the back of the tub as he gently places the back of his hand against my forehead, before feeling the back of my neck.

A shiver finally makes an appearance down my spine, but I doubt it's because of the hot water.

"I'm feeling a bit better, surprisingly." Water laps against the bare skin exposed above my bra, and I lean my head further onto the edge of the tub.

My eyes slide shut, and I exhale a breath, feeling the nausea finally subside as Stolas moves beside me. When the rustling stops, I feel hands along my neck, and my eyes fly open to see him sitting on the edge of the tub.

He must see the alarm in my face, because he huffs a small laugh. "Close your eyes, Kilian."

My brow raises slightly. "You think I'd simply let your hands around my neck without awkward eye contact? I think not."

He holds my gaze for a long moment, and my cheeks burn as his lips twitch upward. "Eyes. Shut."

My eyes linger on him a moment longer before sliding closed, and his hand glides over my skin. His touch is gentle as his fingers find their way to the tense muscles in my shoulders, and the moment he massages them, my jaw slackens.

Within seconds, they nearly roll back, and I hear a quiet huff of laughter as my lips purse, if only to stop myself from smiling.

Are you a massage therapist in your off time?

He adjusts his grip from my shoulders to my neck, and I'm effectively quieted as he expertly massages his way slowly to my scalp.

"Not quite." He answers out loud, and I can almost hear the smile on his face. "Though I am **very** good with my hands."

My entire body flushes, and it takes a conscious effort to suppress my reaction. "I'll be the judge of that."

I hardly get the words out in a coherent string from his ministrations, and after what feels like ten minutes of silence, the sound of water going whirling down the tub drain pulls me from my half-asleep daze.

Did I fall asleep?

Squinting against the light, I feel like a relaxed blob as he moves to grab the towel from the counter. When he turns to me, he unravels it, and drapes it over my shoulders as a chill threatens to settle over my exposed skin.

I notice the way the moon peers in from the window with an odd note of panic.

"How long have I been in here?" My voice doesn't echo my concern, coming out as more of a tired murmur, and Stolas grins.

"A couple of hours... Long enough for me to refill it with hot water." My brows shoot up and his grin widens. "I'll wait for you to agree with me about how I used my hands."

Heat engulfs me once more, negating the bitter chill in the air as I shake my head. "Don't hold your breath."

Stolas' arm hooks around my waist, and he helps me to my feet, supporting most of my weight as I clutch his other arm. Surprisingly, there's no hint of nausea left, and my body feels more relaxed than it has in years.

Did I really hold that much tension in my neck?

He stands to his full height with his head still tilted to look at my face. My entire body warms, coils of heat burning through me when his chest brushes against mine. He pauses, and the way he's looking at me only brings the flush to my cheeks.

Stolas' hand glides up the length of my arm to my shoulder and even with the blazing heat engulfing my body, a shiver finds its way down my spine.

He's so close that our breath mingles between us, and I inhale the light woodsy cologne in a lungful.

The tips of his long, dark hair tickle my cheek, and it's like the world has faded to black. Like nothing else exists. His lips part before moving, and in my admiration of him, I only tune into the fact that he was saying words when he's done talking.

"Say that again?" I breathe, and the way he smiles with barely restrained laughter has my heart rattling in my chest.

"Can I help you to bed?"

Oh, God, that's even better than what I thought he could have said.

I nod, and he's biting back a grin as he encircles my hand with his. Leading the way out of the bathroom, I shiver, thankful that he'd had the forethought to wrap the towel around my shoulders.

I hadn't even noticed.

We turn the corner to my room, and I glance around at my unmade bed, the clutter of clothes, shoes and makeup scattered around the dresser and floor with particular embarrassment.

Stolas isn't human, though, right? So maybe he doesn't care about that kind of thing...

For whatever reason, though, he's here for me.

Something dangerously close to butterflies soar through my body, and when he turns to me, his eyes searching my face, I know I'm in trouble.

Not because he's here with me in my bedroom while I'm half naked, but because I don't want him to leave.

His intense gaze lingers on me for a moment before his fingers curl around the towel, lifting it to soak up the water from my hair as he squeezes it methodically. With his attention shifting to the dry part of the towel he uses to get the remnants of water from my hair, I have no hesitation to study his face that's hovering mere inches from mine.

From here, I can see each short hair in the stubble of his beard, his defined jawline beneath it and the slight hint of color in his cheek, contrasting against the rest of his warm, sun-kissed skin.

Where most people would expect horns on a demon, there is none. Not a forked tongue or slits for pupils. He's beautiful in a way that makes him stand out from humans, but he would blend in with them otherwise.

He moves to dry another section of my hair, leaning slightly closer, and when he blinks, my attention slides to the dark lashes framing his otherworldly eyes, accented by his dark eyebrows, strong cheekbones and a nose that is perfectly proportioned to the rest of his face.

It's only when his attention turns to me that I avert my eyes, clearing my throat quietly, and the towel returns to my shoulders, feeling more damp than it was before.

"Here."

Another shiver runs through me as movement catches my eye, and my heart feels like it's going to beat from my chest when he offers one of my large pajama tops between us.

I'm torn about what to do just as he turns to walk away, and my pulse hikes at the thought of him leaving.

"Wait—"

Chapter 24

He pauses and turns to me, holding the pajama top in my hand. His brows pull together, and my heart beats like a war drum in my ears.

"You're not..." *Oh, god, what am I doing?* "Are you..."

Stolas lips twitch, and my entire body flushes as I struggle with words for what seems like the first time in my life.

"You're going to the hallway for me to change?" My voice sounds so quiet in the space surrounding us, yet at the same time, it sounds all too loud.

When Stolas bites back a smile, I swallow. "Would you prefer I remain here to watch?"

The air catches in my lungs, and I stare at him before blinking, as if that could help my mind comprehend his sarcasm. Warmth reaches my cheeks, and I know without a doubt when his gaze drops to them, they're likely burning red, and something flickers across his expression that I can't quite place.

"What an odd idea to want to watch someone get dressed. I'd imagine it would be the opposite."

Not like he didn't just undress me hours ago.

His brow quirks up, and he glances away with heat in his expression that only serves to heighten the pulse raging in my ears.

What am I doing?

Am I really flirting with him?

When his attention returns to me, there's no doubt in my mind that the tension between us isn't imaginary and his gaze drops slightly, as if to remind me I'm standing before him in only my underwear.

He leans toward me until we share breath once more. "It would, and you are."

Shit.

I feel as though we're tiptoeing the edge of a cliff with either side a rocky, steep oblivion and the only certainty with falling is the promise of our ruination.

Stolas moves agonizingly slow as he raises his hand, and his fingers glide along my jawline to my chin. He glides his thumb along my bottom lip, and it feels as if the air's been sucked from the room as he brushes his lips across mine.

"I'll be back to pick you up in the morning. Try to get some sleep, Kilian." He whispers, the movement brushing his lips against mine with each word.

Reality crashes down like a sack of bricks as he pulls away, and I nod, feeling a dreaded note of rejection settle into my heart.

He disappears around the corner, and I listen to his footsteps receding down the hallway, my fractured confidence wavering more with each.

The thought that he might be toying with me crosses my mind, and I exhale a ragged breath.

What the hell am I thinking?

Part of me feels utterly idiotic because of course there'd be no way he'd feel the same, but if he doesn't, why would he act like this?

Glancing down at myself, a harsh wave of self-consciousness hits me, and I stare at each imperfection with a simmering disgust that roils anger within me.

The dimples in my hips from the extra weight on them, the puffiness around the V line along each hip that accompanies it. My love handles that always make tight-fitting pants a chore, and of course, the way my stomach sticks out slightly, rather than being flat.

Unhooking my bra and tossing it aside, I shimmy out from my underwear and toss the oversized shirt over my head with a frustrated and defeated sigh.

Perhaps it's nothing more than delusional and wishful thinking that he'd be interested in a girl like me in more ways than just a friend.

Chapter 25

By the time I'm rolling my carry-on to the front door, I hear a vehicle pull into the driveway, and my heart jumps into my throat.

I hardly slept.

Tossing and turning for hours, I kept thinking of everything that happened last night with a critical mind—picking apart every interaction until embarrassment coated my veins like hot oil.

So needless to say, I over criticized every outfit to bring with me, trying one on after another, getting more frustrated each time until finally I threw in a handful of baggy clothes and one decently nice dress that I can wear to the art exhibition.

Feeling defeated, I peer between the blinds to see Stolas' black SUV next to my car, and release a long, drawn-out sigh.

It took over an hour this morning to resign myself to the fact that I'd be going to Los Angeles with Stolas because I'd committed to it, but that doesn't mean I hadn't contemplated cancelling my own commitment.

In the end, it was the desire to get out of this indebted feeling toward him that made me get ready.

Okay, maybe it wasn't entirely that... but I don't think I'm really ready to accept or acknowledge the other reason yet. The extra time I'd spent getting ready this morning is enough of a confession and I refuse to speak why into existence.

Not when there was already so much yet so frustratingly little that happened last night.

I'm locking the front door when footsteps crunch in the snow behind me.

God, it's **him**.

I'm not ready to face him again.

Fuck.

I know I have to, though.

Time seems to slow as I turn and Stolas comes into view, his hand already grasping the handle of my carry-on as he sets it down in front of the stairs.

"Morning." I murmur, my voice wavers from exhaustion and Stolas raises a brow.

"I'd ask how you slept, but by the sounds of it—"

He pauses as I shake my head. "I slept terrible."

His concerned expression bleeds into a hint of amusement, and he offers his hand as I'm about to walk down the stairs. I contemplate against taking it for a breath of a moment, but with how tired I am, the last thing I want is to face-plant out of stubbornness.

My palm slides into his, and the moment his fingers encircle my hand, I'm thrown back into the memory of last night. The ghost of his lips against mine, even with how feather light it was still left me breathless.

Even after I've reached the bottom, he keeps our hands firmly clasped and leads the way to the SUV, opening the passenger side door for me before heading to the back. By the time I've climbed into the passenger seat, he's already loaded my carry-on in and butterflies soar chaotically through me.

When he slides into the front seat and backs out of the driveway, I spot Paul near the middle of his driveway on the border of our properties, and he glares at the SUV as we continue past him.

Something about how Paul has behaved recently strikes me as odd, considering how he randomly shot a raven and now, his attitude toward strangers near his house has left much to be desired.

He's old enough that I suppose illness is a possibility, and I tuck that away to reach out to see if he has family some other time. My phone vibrates and I glance down, seeing Aiden's name on my lock screen.

Aiden: You're officially doing a blowjob with me when I get back. You threw it back like a champion. I've taught you well.

I huff a quiet laugh and my fingers fly over the screen as I respond.

Kilian: Actually, I regret to inform you that I got sick, and I will never be doing them again, let alone drinking.

Stolas turns onto a main road, and keys something into the large display before taking his hands off the wheel entirely, and my eyes widen.

"What are you–?" The moment I'm about to ask, it clicks, and my mouth forms an 'O'. "Electric vehicle?"

He nods, angling his body toward me a bit. "Electric is the future. At least, for now, it is."

I glance between him and the display with my brows furrowed slightly. "So you have an electric vehicle, you go to art exhibitions, you are very much not human, and you know more about cures in medicine than we do. Is there anything else I should know about you?"

He grins. "Not human is putting it lightly, and there's much more you should know, however, that information is not freely available to give."

My eyes narrow on him. "What information **can** you give then?"

Stolas contemplates in silence for a long moment before his lips twitch. "Why don't you ask what you wish to know, and we'll go from there? If I can answer, I will." His expression turns more serious, and my heart pounds in my chest. "I will warn you though, Kilian. You may not like the answers I have to give."

I huff a quiet laugh that tickles my lungs, and I cough to clear it. "Right. Because telling me you're a demon wasn't the worst of it."

He says nothing, and I swallow. "Have you killed someone before?"

The look he's giving me is like I should know the answer, and my heart thrums steadily.

"I told you I was a demon."

I swallow hard. "Right."

"Did you think I was lying?"

My mouth drops open and snaps shut as I really give it an honest thought. "I suppose I didn't consider everything that being a demon would entail."

He just shrugs, as if this is the most nonchalant conversation he's had in...

"How old are you?" I blurt the question out without a second thought, and amusement paints his features as my hand shoots to cover my mouth.

To his credit, he just laughs harder as the car slows down with traffic. "Whatever number you have in mind, you can likely multiply it by any three-digit number."

My eyebrows shoot up, and I blink at him.

"Right, well, I'd say give me the secret to eternal youth, but I think that's more of a demon thing, huh?"

He laughs again and nods. "There are other ways to achieve it, but it's not pleasant."

"I'm intrigued, do go on. But first, and completely unrelated, do you have paper and a pen in here by chance?"

Shooting me a sidelong glance, he shakes his head. "Death is too short to need a notepad and pen. Besides, it comes for all humans."

"Death is the secret to eternal youth?" My question comes out more incredulous than curious, and I wince internally.

He just shrugs. "Most don't understand what death is, but it is not the end for any humans."

I blow out a breath. "Well, that's not a heavy revelation."

"What did you think death was?"

"Truth be told, I simply thought it was the end. An oblivion of nothing to welcome us after a life of everything."

Stolas' piercing gaze lingers on me for a long moment, and I feel like an ant under a microscope until his rich voice fills the air once more. "Do you want it to be an oblivion of nothing?"

"I–"

"You don't need to answer if you don't want to."

I shake my head slightly. "I don't want it to be an oblivion if there's something better awaiting us..." My pulse spikes, and I make the split decision to ask what's been burning in the back of my mind. "So, does this mean heaven is real?"

A long moment passes, and he looks like he's thinking through his answer, or choosing his words carefully when it hits me that this may be one of those times when he cannot give me a definitive answer.

Interesting.

"Ancient stories in religions everywhere came from somewhere. While some might be fables, you'd be surprised how many actually have inspirations that are mostly correct."

The researcher in me is screaming in excitement even though I know little to nothing of the religions across various cultures.

I mean, sure, I knew one to two Catholics and Christians in the family, but that's as close as I'd gotten to any organized religion.

"I won't lie, Stolas. This makes me want to pick up a bible."

He just laughs, but it doesn't reach his eyes as the car takes a wide turn into the main entrance into the airport.

"Just remember that regardless of the text, everyone has a side to their story, and only those who remain in power can lend words to paper. No struggling man would read a poor man's doctrine on how to be the richest man in the world."

The car comes to a stop in front of the main doors, and I'm lost in my thoughts as he climbs out of the seat and starts unloading our carry-ons.

He's given me so much to consider, and there's nothing more that I love than a conversation that makes you second guess everything you know, or research everything you don't.

Climbing out of the SUV, Stolas is handing the keys to a man near the front when I go to take my carry-on from him, and he slides it out of reach with a grin.

"Not a chance. I've got these." His rich voice fills the air, and I glance around at the bustle of people who don't even notice his presence.

"And they say chivalry is dead." I murmur, making him grin even wider as he wheels our carry-ons with one hand and passes me my boarding pass with his other.

I suppose it makes sense that no one would consider him out of place. The only outwardly shocking aspect of Stolas is how attractive he is, which includes his eyes, but it's not like he's got horns or bat wings or something.

Glancing at him, I somehow can picture him with both, and a whip-like tail that moves with each step he takes.

He notices my stare and casts a sidelong glance at me. "Something particularly amusing to you?"

My cheeks burn, and I step in closer, angling my body slightly toward him. *I was just picturing you with a tail, wings and horns.*

Stolas' brows shoot up, and for the first time I see genuine shock on his face before he bursts into laughter, catching the attention of a handful of people before they continue past to their destinations.

"Any reason for the sudden mental image?"

We slowly approach airport security, and when we come to a stop at the back of the short line, I glance at the people nearby and shake my head.

I don't even want to know what kind of list I'd get put on if I started talking about demons in an airport. *None that I want to get into in a place where they'd ban me from flying if I said it out loud.*

Chapter 26

By the time we're at our gate, we're just in time for boarding to begin for the first zone. Stolas takes a few steps to the line, pausing when he notices I haven't moved.

"Have you come all this way to stay at the airport?"

I frown, pulling my ticket up. "It's not our turn yet, they're boarding first–" I'm abruptly cut off as I notice the "1" next to the zone on my ticket.

My wide eyes slide to meet his, and he just chuckles. "Let's go Kilian. Time waits for no one."

I follow close behind as the gate attendant scans our tickets with a melodic beep, feeling my nerves slowly disappear with each step until we reach our seats.

Stolas stores our carry-ons in the overhead bins, and we settle in as the rest of the plane's passengers slowly make their way to their own.

Crossing my legs, I relax more into my seat, leaning my head back and closing my eyes.

These seats are spacious, no question about that.

Exhaustion from lack of sleep weighs heavy on me, and when the plane taxis to the runway, my eyes snap open, and a click sounds out from my lap as a full head of dark hair comes into view.

Stolas' head tilts up, and once again I'm sucked in as he searches my face. His arm moves in my peripheral just as the seatbelt tightens, and my heart thrums heavily in my chest.

"Safety first, of course."

His gaze drops slightly, and I already feel breathless. "Of course."

It's all I can do to echo him as he leans back into his chair, leaving me half dazed, and half wishing he hadn't leaned back.

What is wrong with me?

I'm on this trip solely because he needed a way for me to pay off this debt, not because of the relationship we don't have.

The plane hurdles forward on the runway, and the front lifts into the air with the back wheels following shortly after. Every second we gain distance from the ground, my ears clog until I swallow hard, and they finally pop, letting the loud rumble of the jets fill my mind.

I spend the next few minutes reminding myself that there's no way someone like him would be interested. He'll live forever; so it's only fitting that he'll look for someone who will exist as long as he will.

That's definitely not a human girl like me.

The constant hum drowns out all other sounds as my eyes slide shut, and sleep blissfully takes me.

Chapter 27

The sound of water seems entirely out of place on a plane, and my eyes snap open as I glance around at what looks like my bathroom at home.

Submerged in the full tub, I get an odd sense of déjà vu to when Stolas was at the house. Part of me wonders for a moment if the plane ride was even real, but when the corners of my vision blur in and out of sight, that's when I know for sure.

I'm dreaming.

The water's bitter cold, and I lazily crawl forward to pull the plug, feeling my movements lagged as I push to my feet. The air nips at my skin, and I shiver, stepping onto the chilled tile floor.

It's like there's a haze surrounding me, and I squint against it, searching for a towel as my arms cross over my chest. It seems to get even colder with each second, and my teeth chatter as I step quietly to the doorway. I'm about to turn the corner to the closet when I collide with a broad chest and gasp.

My heart thunders as I glance up to see Stolas, wide-eyed, as his hands support the backside of my arms.

"Sorry, I—" His attention drops to my arms, and even through the chill in the air, my entire body warms. "I didn't know you were there."

He quirks a thick brow, tucking a wet lock of hair behind my ear as goosebumps break out over my skin. "Do you want me to leave?"

His thumb glides along my arm, and I shake my head, feeling his hard chest against mine with each breath.

"No. Of course not." My voice comes out quiet, and Stolas leans closer, so imperceptibly that I almost miss it.

"Then why did you come here if not to be alone?" His breath skates over my cheek, and my heart's beating in my throat as I hold his gaze.

"You say that as if I chose to be here."

He looks at me as if that's the most ridiculous thing I've ever said to him.

"Oh, you definitely chose to be here, Kilian." His hand near my shoulder moves to my neck, and he tilts my head toward him. "Not only did you choose it, but I heard you repeating my name in this realm over, and over, and over again until I joined you here, and then you went silent."

I stare at him as my brows pull together. "You're lying."

The smile that graces his features could very well make my heart stop beating as it stutters in my chest. I've never been one to be left speechless, or at a loss for words, but when he leans his head down and I feel his lips against my neck, my mind empties itself of all rational thought.

Or it tries to.

"You think I would lie to you?" He murmurs against my skin, and presses another kiss against my pulse point as a shiver makes its way down my spine. "Do you?"

This has to be a dream. There's no way this is happening right now.

He trails his nose along my jawline, and my breath gets caught in my lungs when his lips reach mine. I'm afraid to answer for a fear of this ending, of him pulling away; but when I've finally mustered the courage, my mouth drops open, and he closes the distance.

His lips press to mine, and a mixture of disbelief and denial coats my veins. Everything I'd imagined this moment to be in the depths of my unspoken fantasies could have never prepared me for this.

"Answer me, Kilian." His fingers flex into my hips, and the desire I'd suppressed for so long comes full circle as I lean into his touch. He nips at my lower lip as if to reinforce his demand, and I gasp audibly.

I don't know.

A frustrated sound escapes his throat, and he hooks his arm around my waist, tugging me in close. *"That's not an answer. That's a safety net. Answer the damn question."*

When I don't say anything, he leans back to search my face.

Truth be told, I don't think you'd lie to me, but I don't think you'd tell me the whole truth.

His hands cup my jaw as he holds my gaze. *"Ask me what you want to know, Kilian."*

I swallow, my lower lip throbbing from where he nipped it. *What are we doing, Stolas?*

He glances at the counter for a second before bending slightly. His hands hook under my thighs before he hauls me into his arms and a shrill sound escapes me with the sudden movement.

"Presently? You're asleep in first class on this plane, and I'm about to cover you with a blanket." He sets me on the cold counter-top, and I jolt at the contact. The realization sets in that I was completely nude this entire time, and my tummy tumbles over itself.

My eyes widen. *You're still awake?!*

The heat in his face darkens as he grins. *"I **did** tell you I exist in both places."*

I appreciate the knowledge that he can be fully awake in both realms, but... *You know that wasn't what I was referring to.*

His lips twitch, and his hands glide up my thighs to my hips. One trails my skin along my breast to my neck, while the other stops at my nipple. *"I still plan on answering that question, Kilian."*

My mouth opens as I go to respond just as he squeezes my nipple, and I suck in a breath. *Then answer it.*

"What we're doing is spending this entire flight doing what I have craved since we first met."

His piercing gaze is all-consuming as he searches my face, cupping my cheek with his palm, pressing the length of his hard body into me. Every place our skin meets engulfs in unyielding heat, and my heart thunders, threatening to erupt from my chest as his lips crash into mine.

What have you craved, Stolas?

Unwilling to keep any semblance of distance from him, my arms winding around his neck. He pins his hips to mine, swallowing the moan that crawls out of my throat.

I want to hear it. I need to know why he's everywhere to me. Why I'm so drawn to him.

Part of me knows hearing it won't be enough, though, and I dread the moment I wake up from this.

"This." He devours my mouth in long, drawn out movements for a moment before squeezing my nipple in between his index finger and thumb as I gasp. *"That, too."*

Fingers trail lower down my breast, leaving a blazing trail in their wake until he cups my ass, and tugs me in close, the heat from his body seeping into my skin. I slip forward an inch on the counter until the bulge straining his pants presses hard against me. When I squeeze my legs around him and tighten my arms around his neck, he groans.

Why did you wait?

I almost don't want to ask for fear of him stopping, but I need to know why. It's a torturous **why** question that will eat at me until there's nothing left, and he's the only person who can answer.

Without skipping a beat, Stolas' lips slowly trail fervent kisses down my neck and chest as he continues lower. *"Because I had to be sure it's what you wanted, even if waiting felt like waiting for death to find me."*

He leaves a long line of kisses down my stomach to my thighs, and that's when I realize what he intends to do. My heart skips a beat as he looks at me from between my legs, with a look on his face that sends desire pooling in my core.

What happens if I—

My question trails off, but I know he understands what I'm asking as heat darkens his gaze.

"We're about to find out."

Setting my thighs on his shoulders, he reaches over and hooks his hand around the back of my ass.

Then his mouth is on me.

My hands grip the edge of the counter, and I lean into the mirror. The back of my head collides into it with a soft thud, but I hardly notice, honing in on every place we connect. His tongue rolls over my clit, and my eyes roll with it as he sucks and laves.

"You're fucking perfection, Kilian." He growls and my ragged breathing picks up. *"Every time you dream of me, every single thought, I feel it. I sense it like a siren's call radiating from each star in the night sky. Do you have any idea what that's done to me?"*

I don't know what it means, but I know he's telling the truth. In some odd way, I can feel the honesty in his words, and he grips me tighter against him, coaxing a heady moan from me.

Electric bolts of pleasure build in my core, and my hips move of their own accord, chasing the feeling as he grips my ass. The euphoria gets to be too much, and I buck against him.

Stolas, it's—

All at once, he uses both hands to support my weight, and he lifts me up as I scramble to hold on to his head. He doesn't stop circling my clit with his tongue, and when my back meets the wall, he grips my thighs tight.

I'm mentally mumbling jumbled pleas as he chuckles against me, the vibrations making my head swim.

"I'm a demon, Kilian. You didn't expect me to go easy on you, did you?"

His dark laugh echoes into my mind, accented by the vibration of his chuckle between my legs, and I shudder as he devours me in earnest. His fingers bite into my skin, and it's all I can do to grip his hair as my orgasm crests.

You're relentless.

As if to prove his patience, he drags his tongue along my pussy, and he groans. "And you're delicious." Before I can catch my breath, he's circling my clit, and my legs twitch so hard my toes curl.

"Do you feel it yet?" Pleasure builds more as I struggle against his vice-like grip. *"Do you feel how deep this goes for me? Does this make it clear that I want and will never get enough of you?"*

The truth is, it goes just as deep for me, but I can't form a coherent string of sentences to tell him that as he squeezes my ass.

He's inescapable as pleasure radiates from my core in waves, and I moan loudly with my hands tangled into his hair, my fingers fisting his locks so hard that the muscles in them cramp. His name tumbles from my lips in broken, staggered pieces, pleading as he pushes me further through each ripple of pleasure.

God, yes.

"That's it, Kilian. Give it to me. Give me every broken sound of you coming undone." His voice in my mind drops to a low, reverent whisper. *"Let me show you what it means to be wanted by a demon who's already burning for you."*

Slowly coming down from my orgasm, he lowers both my thighs off his shoulder, and slides me down the wall, kissing up the length of my body until we're face to face again.

Our breath mingles between us for a moment as he searches my face, and my pulse finally calms. "Good news is, you only gasped once in your sleep."

My eyes widen, feeling like a bucket of ice has doused my body. "And the bad news?"

His lips twitch, and he leans in, pressing his lips to mine. Tasting myself between us, it's hard to imagine this entire thing hasn't been real, but the desire pulsing between my thighs tells me it's real enough.

"Bad news is that I've gotten a taste, Kilian. A sample." The hunger in his rich voice sends a shudder through me. "You have no idea the lengths I was willing to go for you before this, I fear there are no boundaries now."

He pulls back to look at me, and I know once again that every word he's uttered is the truth.

But somehow, none of that scares me.

Only the reflection of his declaration should. The vast ocean of gravity that is **him**, pulling me into his orbit and holding me hostage.

Yet, it doesn't. That's perhaps the most terrifying part of it all.

Chapter 28

Stolas pulls the rental car in front of a modest-looking house with orange trees and tall bushes lining the sides, and my heart pumps steadily in my chest.

My gaze lingers on his hands on the wheel, and flashes of what they looked like wrapped around my thighs make my pulse quicken.

I obviously haven't calmed down from the flight, and the tension between us from the moment I woke up has been clear as day, especially now that we're alone.

My mind's been circling the memory of his face between my thighs, with me moaning his name like a scattered prayer since it happened. It was bad enough that I woke up soaked with my heart racing as if he'd devoured his way to my soul on the plane, but with so many people around, it was all I could do to cross my legs and ignore the ache between them.

The engine shuts off, and my heart's in my throat as he climbs out of the vehicle, leaning down to peer at me from the open door with a hint of amusement on his face.

I'm near certain that amusement is due to how red I've been the entire drive, if the heat in my cheeks is any indication.

"Are you coming inside, or should I assume you've decided to sleep in the car?" My mouth drops open to answer him, but he continues. "That is, of course, until you meditate and demand to see me again."

My entire body burns, and I scoff before getting out of the car and joining him near the front walkway. "I told you it wasn't on purpose."

His lips twitch as we approach the front door, and his gaze slides to mine. "Maybe not consciously."

He unlocks the door and steps inside, holding it open for me as I take two steps in. I'm glancing around as he moves to close it, and I'm attempting poorly to focus on anything but him as I look at the decor.

"Are you insinuating that my mind and body aren't aligned in their desires?"

The way my heart thrums in my chest tells me they're painfully aware of my desires. A click sounds out as I turn to look at Stolas, seeing him already eyeing me slowly from head to toe with a look that sends heat to my core.

"I'm insinuating that regardless of your busy mind, the moment it calms, it calls for me." Our eyes meet, and I don't miss the way his expression darkens. "I dare you to disagree."

A huff of dry laughter escapes. "I disagree."

He tuts in disapproval and steps in close as my breathing picks up. "Say it again."

At this point we're chest to chest and I have to retreat a step to put space between us, but he continues his advance. It's not until my back hits a wall when I stop, and he places his hands on the wall on either side of my head.

My chest heaves as he tilts his head, searching my face with his blue and green eyes. His voice drops low, and my attention flicks to his lips. "Say it, again, Kilian."

Everything in me screams to say it. My body sings as he leans further onto his forearms, and his chest presses into mine. I'm not sure who's leaning into who as my shoulders flatten against the wall, and my hair blows aside as he huffs a dark laugh under his breath.

"I–"

A flash of excitement graces his features, and I feel his gentle touch against my skin as his thumb glides down the column of my neck, making me swallow hard.

"Disagree."

With a mere inch between our lips, he nearly closes the distance entirely. They brush with his words whispered in the silent space between us, almost as loud as my pulse raging in my ears.

"Stubborn. I'm going to enjoy that. It'll make it more satisfying when your body gives in before your pride does."

His finger glides along the inside of my thigh, and my breath suspends in my lungs when he pauses halfway.

The dark chuckle that escapes him sends a wave of heat through me that I stubbornly decide is anger.

As if testing me, he leans in and crowds my space just as his finger glides along the material over my clit. I can feel the desire pooling in my core, and I grind my teeth.

Something about wanting to prove him wrong strikes a chord in me, and I glare at him to sell my stubbornness.

"We should get ready." I breathe, and he just laughs.

"Today, we do things on our time." His features turn considerate for a moment. "Well, on my time."

Within seconds, he's hooked his arms under me, and I let out a shrill noise as he hoists me into his chest, carrying me down the hall. We pass abstract paintings hanging on the walls, intricately shaped by talented artists and carved into various patterns.

"Does *your time* include a tour of the house?"

His eyes slide to mine as he uses his foot to bump a door open with a chuckle. "After we've fixed your stubbornness, you can have whatever you'd like."

Heat washes over me, reaching my cheeks, but I can't ignore the thrill running through me. "Am I stubborn or are you just uncompromising?"

Stolas takes long strides before he tosses me into the air, and I shriek the moment I'm airborne, landing with a soft thud into a plush blanket. The clank of a belt buckle fills the air as his hand grips my ankle and he yanks me toward the edge of the bed.

My wide eyes find his, and the thrill in my spine melts into my core. "You would like a tour of the house?"

Chewing the inside of my cheek, I nod. "I would like one, yes."

His lips twitch as his fingers work the button of my pants. "Then I'll start with giving a tour of your body first."

The sound of my zipper fills the air, and he holds my gaze, as if waiting for me to protest.

But I don't.

"You can't give me a tour of something I know everything about, demon."

His answering smile makes me reconsider my statement for a moment before he tugs my pants down and off my ankle. "Are you certain?"

*Not when you ask like **that**.*

He laughs, leaning in closer to unbutton my top, and even though he's seen me completely naked, there's something so much more intimate about him undressing me like this and it not being a product of my mind.

"I heard all the thoughts you had about yourself the other night when you went to dinner and the club, Kilian."

I freeze, feeling like a bucket of ice water was just poured over my head. "You heard..."

"Everything."

Swallowing, my eyes slide to his, and he leans in to tug my shirt down the length of my arms, tossing the material aside. "So it appears you *do* need a tour."

"You're biased." I retort, and he just laughs under his breath, gliding his hands to the center of my back.

"As are you, arguably more than I could ever be." He unclips my bra and slides the straps down my arms. By the time he's hooked his fingers under the waistband of my underwear, I feel more exposed, more vulnerable than ever.

"Tell me, Kilian." He murmurs, trailing his fingers down the length of my body, leaving a blazing path in its wake. "How much would it take to prove to you that the pieces of you that you loathe are worth the reverence I plan to treat them with?"

When he pops the buttons of his own shirt, he untucks it and tosses it aside as my gaze lingers on his face. Something about appraising every newly exposed inch of his muscular body while criticizing my own feels overly hypocritical.

His hands jerk slightly before another thud fills the air, and I know the sound was his pants hitting the floor as a wave of desire flips in my stomach.

"Answer me, Kilian."

I swallow, shaking my head. "I don't know."

Tilting his head in a manner that seems oddly familiar, his lips twitch. "We'll know soon enough." Crawling on top of where I lie on the mattress, he pins me with his hips, and I feel him throb hard against me.

"Is that how you plan to get rid of my stubbornness?" I ask sarcastically, and he grins as I squirm beneath him.

Stolas leans in, his hair brushing my skin as it falls loose around him, and I feel his lips brush my ear as he tugs my arms overhead.

"I plan to explore every inch of this incredible, strong, resilient, and stubborn body." His words resonate in my mind, each word pointed by his lips pressing further down my skin. *"And remind you that you're more than the terrible things you think of yourself as."*

His touch in the recesses of my mind was as soft as they were demanding, even though he gave more than he took. But now, with his weight on top of me, reality has started to sink in that Stolas truly means what he's saying. There's nowhere to escape to as he places reverent kisses down to my chest.

I just don't get it. Since we've met, he's been here at every turn. Every meditation, on purpose or accident, then the bar...

But why?

Stolas doesn't miss a beat as he presses his lips just above my nipple, and I suck in a breath.

"I've been here because you called." Releasing my hands, I'm about to bring them down from over my head when his voice becomes a low growl in my mind. *"Keep them there and do not move them, or the only menu item for dinner tonight for either of us is you."*

Part of me wants to argue that his proposition sounds like a good time, but he takes my nipple into his mouth and rational thought leaves my mind as quick as it came.

My back arches into him, and he presses his delicious weight into me more, his hips squeezing mine into the bed. My heart beats like a war drum in my ears as he releases my nipple to press another kiss to the inside of my breast.

Finally in a second of clarity, I try and fail to ignore the desire pulsating in my core. *I didn't **do** anything to call for you.*

His eyes lock with mine, and I feel his featherlight touch glide down my stomach. With his fingers grazing my skin along my hips. His palm slides between my thighs, and I shudder.

"You might not have done it consciously, Kilian, but you called to me, nonetheless. Your soul transcends the space where your body dwells, shining brighter than any star in the night sky." His fingers find my clit, circling it as my eyes nearly roll back. *"Imagine my surprise when the beacon calling my name belonged to one who doesn't even know how worthy she is."*

His touch is light, teasing, and equally addicting as I squirm to find more pressure with his movements.

"Even with everything you'd been through these past few years, the malpractice wasn't enough to dim your light."

My mind can't comprehend a word he's saying when he's teasing me to the edge of an orgasm faster than I can find my voice to beg him for more.

"So each time you called, I answered. In some way, I was there, whether or not you knew. But now? Now I need you more than you need a protector, Kilian."

He presses harder as he circles my clit, and presses his lips to my other breast, taking my nipple between his teeth as air suspends in my lungs.

"You searched in another realm, looking for a guide, and god help me, a guide you will get. But with my help, you'll let go of this stubborn need for control once and for all."

My legs twitch as desire crests to the surface of my core. The ache between my thighs screams for release as my hips gyrate, my clit throbs, and I'm a panting mess as he withdraws his hand entirely. I mourn the absence of his touch as my eyes snap open to the look of approval on his face.

This was all about me being stubborn?!

"I did say that I planned to address that." His lips twitch, and I try to choke down the anger building in my chest. "Besides, it's not like it'll take much effort."

Squirming beneath him, he releases a deep chuckle that only serves to make the butterflies in my body even more chaotic. My arms itch to drop to my sides, but I keep them in place.

I chew the inside of my cheek. "Smug ass demon."

His eyes flash, and my heart leaps into my throat as he presses his lips down my chest to my stomach. Memories of the plane ride flit through my mind, and by the time he's spread my thighs, my heart is racing.

"Try to make it a challenge, Kilian." Without a moment to lose, his mouth is on me.

Chapter 29

Inhaling a sharp lungful, the twinge from my asthma is hardly noticeable as my hands wring the sheets overhead. Stolas devours me like nothing else exists in the world, and I writhe in his grip, my thighs trembling as pleasure builds in my core.

His tongue circles my clit, and my gasp forms his name as he smiles against me. *"That's it Kilian. Give it all to me."* My hips gyrate away from the bolts of euphoria building in my core, but he's relentless as his husky voice echoes in my mind. *"Every sound. Every tremble. Every breath. Give me everything, Kilian."*

A soft moan escapes me before my breathing picks up, my orgasm on the verge of taking over my body when he pulls back.

No, no, no—

His deep voice mixes with my quick breaths as he moves to hover over me. "If you want to come, Kilian, you need to agree that your soul and mine are tied, and that you are worthy of the love you do not give yourself." The fierce look on his face tells me there's no way he'll let me argue or negotiate. "However, I suspect you won't be able to form a full sentence soon, so any form of pleading will be an acceptable substitute."

My eyes narrow on him as the ache between my thighs grows. "You're evil."

A flash of humor crosses his expression. *"I'm a prince of hell, Kilian. This is me being merciful."*

Without another spoken word, Stolas' fingers brush my clit before circling it, and my eyes roll back.

God.

I've been so close to coming twice. If he stops a third time, there's no guarantee that I won't lose my mind.

My heart skips a beat when he slips a finger in me, and my hips lift to meet his hand. It's nowhere near enough, and I think he knows that because he slides another in to join it, drawing a long, husky moan from my throat.

His thumb circles my clit, and it aches to the point of pain. The sensitivity of being denied an orgasm twice brings tears to my eyes as he works my body, coaxing pleasure from me once again.

The moment I'm close to coming, and my breaths come in near strangled as I choke down air, he pulls back again, and I nearly sob.

"This could all be over now, Kilian."

I hate you.

A dark chuckle escapes him, and he reaches down to circle my throbbing clit. His touch doesn't reach it, just circling around it as I whimper, fisting the bedding over my head with frustration.

His finger gets closer to my oversensitive clit, and my eyes squeeze shut as he presses his forehead to mine. *"Say it, Kilian. Say it out loud."*

His touch is too far, yet just close enough that desperation coats my veins like hot oil, and I only last another half minute before I can't take it anymore.

Fuck. "Please, Stolas."

He freezes, and I instantly mourn the movement.

"What was that?" His voice drops another octave, and I shiver. "Did you say *please*?"

Writhing as my clit throbs, my body trembles, aching for release. "I swear to God, Stolas. I need you."

"There it is." He whispers, his expression as dangerous as it is reverent. "My beautiful ruin."

"Surrender to me again. Give me everything you are, Kilian."

I know this is more than he originally bargained for, but I don't care. He eases between my legs and within seconds his mouth is slowly coaxing pleasure from my body.

"I'm—" His tongue flicks my clit and I gasp. "Oh, God. I'm yours."

The moment the words leave my lips, it's as if something inside him snaps. A growl escapes from his chest, and he spreads my thighs further, holding them open with a vice-like grip as he buries his head between them.

But this time, he doesn't stop.

Stolas is ruthless, persistent, and attentive as he devours me. If I didn't know better, I'd have thought that he really was trying to eat his way into my soul.

His grip on my thighs tightens as they struggle against him involuntarily, desperate to escape the pleasure he brings as much as I chase it.

Stolas drinks me in as if he's been starved for me his entire life. Like he's determined to memorize every inch of me, etching himself into every ounce of pleasure he gives.

When I'm on the blissful edge, panic and desperation coats my veins at the thought of him pulling back.

"That's it, Kilian. Come apart just like that."

Oh, God.

A string of words I don't recognize tumbles from my lips, my vision goes white, and my entire body shudders as I ride out each wave of euphoria washing over me. Stolas stifles a groan as he spreads my legs wider, dragging me through the aftershocks and only stopping when I squirm from over stimulation.

It takes a long moment to come down, but I finally manage to, with my eyes cracking open to where Stolas crawls up alongside me.

"Giving up your stubbornness isn't so bad now? Is it?" His lips twitch, and my cheeks burn at how they glisten with my arousal.

"It sucked..." I whisper as he leans in, gathering me into his arms. "Until it didn't."

My shoulders are tender from holding them overhead for so long, but all thought leaves my mind when his lips brush against mine. Our eyes meet, and something in his expression sends a shiver down my spine.

"You're mine, Kilian. Now and always."

Searching his face, there's a seriousness to him that sobers me. "I still don't understand why."

He rolls onto his back, tugging me further into his chest as I rest my head against him. The steady beat of his heart fills the silence until I hear his voice echo in my mind once more.

*"Is it not enough for me to say that I've seen **you**?"* I swallow hard, and my eyes slide shut. "I've been around for far longer than you could imagine, Kilian. I do not take this lightly."

His hand on my jaw has my eyes snapping open to his other-worldly irises gazing back at me. "You're one of a kind, Kilian. Your soul burns with the light of a thousand suns, and I would gaze upon it until it blinds me if only it were the last sight I'd ever see."

It takes a moment for me to notice the tear that's fallen down my cheek, and he tracks the movement, placing a tender kiss on my forehead. "Now... Let's get ready for dinner."

Chapter 30

After a full day of sightseeing and a late dinner at a local restaurant, we're walking back to the car, passing a handful of stores with purses and perfumes lining the brightly lit shelves in the floor to ceiling windows.

My line of vision snags on one display and my steps slow to a stop as I stare at the red dress tightly wrapped around the mannequin.

The way the material hugs the mannequin's hips, the low dipped V-cut chest and off-the-shoulder sleeves have me picturing it on myself, as if staring at a mirror.

Although the mannequin has curves, I can still picture how the dress would fit tighter around my own, and chew my lip.

Stolas approaches from behind, his arm encircling my waist as his lips brush the shell of my ear.

"Sorry, it just caught my eye." I murmur, turning to leave as he gestures to it, halting me in place.

"Why not get it?"

It takes a long second for me to turn my attention back to it, almost as if I'm reluctant to get caught up in admiration, but it doesn't take long as the deep crimson fills my line of vision.

"I suppose I could wear it to the exhibition." I suggest, but Stolas shakes his head, shifting my hair between us.

"You already have what you need for tomorrow."

My brows shoot up. "The dress I brought is nowhere near appropriate for a global art exhibition."

I can already see it now. Stolas and I, walking into a grandiose building beside countless others dressed to the nines or artistically dressed, and then there will be me, the only person in a twenty-nine dollar dress from a local retail store.

"You won't be wearing the dress you brought at the exhibition, so don't worry about tomorrow." He gestures to the dress in the window again. "But I'm certain there are other occasions you could wear this, no?"

"There are, but—"

He walks us into the store, and I huff as he guides me forward, hearing his voice nonchalantly fill the air. "Then it's settled. We will get the dress."

We hardly get two steps in when an attendant appears from nowhere. "Can I help either of you find anything?"

Keeping one arm loosely wrapped around my waist, Stolas gestures to the window behind us. "She'll take the dress on display."

The young woman smiles kindly as her attention turns to me. "Wonderful. Come with me and we'll get you sized."

When I look at Stolas, he's still watching me with such intent that heat rises to my cheeks before following the attendant to the back.

God, I hope this dress actually fits me well.

My palms grow slick as I step into the dressing room, turning to look at the attendant as she gives me a warm smile.

"Do you know your measurements by chance?"

Feeling way out of my element, I shake my head. "Not measurements, no. I wear triple D cup thirty-eight bust bras, large shirts and pants vary depending on the brand."

She nods, and the warmth in her expression doesn't falter as she unties the curtain on the side. "That should do, then. I'll bring over a couple, but I think I know which one will fit best for you. Keep this closed and undress. I'll be right back with it."

She slides the curtain shut, and I release a tense breath.

It's been so long since I went shopping at all.

My asthma made it impossible to do cardio, so I've avoided buying new clothes if it wasn't online shopping where I can buy multiple sizes and return the ones I don't wear, all from the security of my home.

Tugging my shirt overhead, I hang it on the hook beside the full-length mirror and scan over my body.

Funnily enough, Stolas' insistence on my over critical perception seems to have made a difference, because I find myself not as fixated on the areas that would normally frustrate me.

I still notice them, and they're still pronounced as usual, but I'm not as upset by their existence as I was.

"Here you go, Ms. Sterling!" The attendant chimes, and I turn to see the deep crimson dress suspended from her grasp through the curtain.

Taking it from her, I blow out a breath. "Thank you."

It doesn't take long for me to pull the soft material up my body, zipping the side as the material cinches along the stomach. The way the fabric's constructed creates a complimentary curve from my waistline to my hips, where it tightens and drapes to my mid-thigh. The top of the dress hugs my breasts tight, with a deep-set V-line that exposes enough cleavage that I worry it might be too much.

Thick crimson straps keep them held firmly in place while not digging into my skin, and when I turn around with my gaze locked on the mirror, it's hard to believe my own eyes.

I think I might be in love.

"Should I take you shopping more often?"

My lips twitch. *I was talking about the dress.*

His deep chuckle makes my cheeks burn for reasons I'd rather not consider, and I slowly extricate myself from the delicate material and put on the clothes I came with.

It feels odd to change out of something so extravagant into my normal every-day clothes, and I have to remind myself that the dress would only be for special occasions.

Fancy dinners and celebrations would be the only time it's appropriate.

Tugging the curtain open, the attendant glances at the dress and grins. "I bet it looked amazing, didn't it?"

I can't help the smile that tugs at my lips as I return her smile. "It did. I'll take it."

The rumble of the engine coming to life shakes the box in my lap slightly, and I place my hands on top to steady it.

Stolas reverses out of the parking spot before keying in the destination and my phone vibrates.

Seeing the unknown ID on the screen, I unlock my phone and bring it to my ear. "Hello?"

"Hi, Ms. Sterling. This is Maris Sylvara from News Alliance again."

"Oh, right. How are you?"

She chuckles. "I'm doing just fine, thanks. I wanted to know if you'd had anything come up since we last talked?"

I frown. "No, sorry. Nothing."

There's a long moment of silence from the receiver. "And Dr. Newlin seems to be okay?"

"Yeah, he was fine at my last appointment."

Keyboard typing fills the air. "Okay. If anything comes up, could you please—?"

"I'll let you know the moment I find out."

"Great. Thank you for your time."

The link clicks as the call ends, and I slide my phone into my purse.

"What was that about?"

My gaze turns to Stolas' guarded expression, and I sigh. "Just some reporter. She's investigating the deaths of a bunch of doctors here."

His eyebrows twitch upward. "Why is she calling you about it?"

I just shrug. "They were all doctors I'd seen in the past three years. I'm sure it's just an environmental thing since they all worked in the same office, though. It's probably nothing."

"Probably." Stolas murmurs in agreement before falling silent.

For the rest of the drive, I'm lost in thought about everything Maris had said during our previous call.

Whatever happened to those doctors, I doubt it had anything to do with me. Correlation doesn't mean causation.

By the time we've pulled up to the house, I've shoved it from my mind and resolved to leaving it in the past as we climb out of the SUV.

Unless something comes up that actually ties me to them, best to ignore it entirely.

I'm following Stolas to the door when he turns to look at me, glancing at the garment box in my hand. "When we get inside, I want you to put that on."

My eyebrows shoot up. "What? Why?"

Turning the knob and throwing the door open, the heated look on his face sends a thrill down my spine.

"Because I'm going to enjoy tearing it off of you."

Chapter 31

We turn onto a busy road bordering a long, modern looking building, with countless vehicles pulling up in front. I subconsciously smooth my black dress against my thighs as I see a woman in a pencil skirt and a blouse climb out of a white SUV with dark tinted windows.

The way her hair and makeup look professionally done has me already feeling insecure, even after seeing another person much less dressed up follow her into the line near the entrance to the building.

Stolas turns down a side road before pulling into the back parking lot, and he shuts the engine off.

We're going in the back entrance?

He gets out of the car without a word, and I follow suit with my heart in my throat.

Part of me is excited to see what these creative minds have done, but another part of me is really wishing I'd worn the red dress, even though Stolas firmly reminded me I didn't need it.

As we approach the door, it opens, and a man with a shaved head holds it open. Tattoos cover his arms and neck that disappear under the suit he's wearing. He glances at the tablet in his hand and scrolls as we come to a stop in front of him.

He taps the screen a few times before looking at us once more.

"Stolas?"

It takes a conscious effort to keep myself from looking surprised as Stolas nods once, and the man gestures inside.

"Room seven please."

Stolas leads through the doorway and I follow in close, taking every opportunity to survey what I'm near certain is a sort of back-stage prep of the exhibition.

What I can't figure out is why Stolas is here, or why an exhibition would have a backstage.

We walk for what feels like minutes down a long hallway before turning down another corridor lined with doors labelled one through nine.

Perhaps he's a special guest and needs to get ready here?

Stolas reaches for the knob of door seven first, turning the knob and pushing the door open before holding it for me.

"What are we doing here?" I whisper, and Stolas lips twitch.

"Attending the exhibition. Are you going to renege on our deal?"

My brows shoot up as the door slides shut behind him. "Never."

Something flashes across his face, but it's gone so fast that I nearly think I've imagined it as he steps in close, placing either palm against my skin, cupping my cheeks gently.

"Are you certain? This is your last chance to change your mind, Kilian."

I nod, feeling more confident than I have any right to. "I'm more than sure. Whatever happens, I can handle it."

Another flash of emotion I can't quite place is gone faster than I can grasp it, and he tilts his head up to press his lips to my forehead before stepping back.

"Well, if that's settled, then," he gestures to me with his hand. "Remove your clothing, Kilian."

Heat rises to my cheeks at his command, and I hold his gaze as I slowly reach up with one hand to slide one strap off. His eyes follow the movement until it dangles loose along my arm, and I move to do the same with the other.

My heart hammers in my chest as I slowly slide the material down my body, having to tug slightly harder to get it over my hips. Stolas' expression darkens, and the look he's giving me makes me wonder if actually came here for an art exhibition or something else entirely.

"Underwear, too."

If I thought my cheeks were burning before, my entire body's become an inferno as I unclip my bra, sliding the straps down my arms before it falls to the ground.

My fingers hook around the elastic at my hips, and I ease both sides down.

"Stop."

I freeze, and Stolas' gaze drops to my feet before slowly trailing up the length of my body, and when our eyes meet, I'm feeling more like a slab of meat by the second.

"Take it off." His voice has dropped an octave, with a rasp that sends a thrill down my spine as I tug the material over my ass, letting it fall to the floor.

The cool air against my newly exposed skin, sends a shiver down my spine as he visibly tears his eyes from me to walk a few feet to the dresser.

When he turns to face me with a couple of items in his hands, I frown, eyeing the two small paint cans and paint brushes

"How long do we have before the exhibition?"

His lips twitch, and he tugs the lid off the can. "An hour and a half. Two, if we want to be fashionably late."

He dips the bristles into the can of golden paint, and my brows shoot up. The bitter chill in the air sends another shiver through my body as I try and fail to connect the dots between me standing nude in the middle of this room and Stolas holding paint in his hands.

"What are you painting?"

He glides the brush against the inner edge of the can before pausing and holds my gaze as each second feels like an eternity.

"You."

I blink.

"Me?" My eyes drop to the gold liquid in the can, and he uses the wooden end of the brush to tilt my chin up to face him.

"Is that so surprising?"

If my heart was hammering in my chest, before it's a war drum that surely would be heard for miles as I struggle to find words.

"I–" He tilts his head and I swallow. "I don't understand. Why are you painting *me*?"

The humor in his expression melts into seriousness as he searches my face. "Because covering you with any material is a sin."

He doesn't mean to—? "But what about my dress?"

I watch as he glances down at my dress before trailing the length of my body on the way back up to my face.

"As I said, it would be a sin to cover your body. Even using paint is as close as I dare get." He tilts his head to the side. "Is this making you uncomfortable?"

My pulse rages in my ears. I'm torn between wanting to stay true to my promise and thinking this is wildly inappropriate. If I knew this was how I'd pay off this debt, I never would have agreed.

"You can't be serious about painting me." When he says nothing, I exhale a ragged breath. "I'm not wearing **anything** to the exhibition?"

The smooth wooden tip of the brush glides down the center column of my neck to my collar bone before stopping between my breasts.

"You will wear nothing. You are both the masterpiece and canvas. You are both life and love given form and flesh. Why would anyone cover such beauty?"

I can't breathe. This can't be real.

Stolas twirls the brush before focusing, and I feel the bristles glide across my skin as another shiver wracks through me.

It's only when I realize what we're attending that an icy wave of dread sets into my stomach like a stone. "Don't people **buy** art at an exhibition?"

His eyes flash, and for the first time, it really sets in that I'm standing nude in front of a demon after making a deal with him.

I swallow hard.

"You're not for sale." The authority in his voice has butterflies stirring in my body as he glides the brush against my skin again. "I've always brought forth the most beautiful pieces of art to exhibitions, because art is meant to be observed and experienced. You are, quite simply put, the most valuable and timeless work of art that this universe has ever created."

He studies me for a moment before his eyes narrow. "You don't agree?"

He can't be serious.

"Wouldn't it be not only narcissistic but also delusional to think I'm a work of art?"

"Everyone has a string of narcissism in them." He muses before his expression turns serious once more. "Tell me why you doubt me so much, Kilian. You think I will lead you into a display where they will jeer and jest at you?"

I swallow at the accuracy of his words, to the unspoken insecurity I've felt, fighting the urge to cover my body in silent protest.

"Beauty is objective. Just because you think I appear attractive doesn't mean that I am."

"What is it?" My gaze snaps to his, and my mouth drops open, but he shakes his head. "What is it that has you insecure?"

Each heartbeat hammers against my chest, and my voice comes out breathless, as if I've been running for miles.

"My stomach, my thighs, my hips..." I whisper, hearing the words shatter the surrounding silence, only contesting my pulse in my ears, threatening to deafen me. "I easily saw twenty women on the drive here who would be better suited to be painted and on display than me."

His lips twitch slightly, and he shakes his head. "That is where you're wrong, my dear Kilian." He sets the paint cans and brushes aside before cupping my cheeks with his palms, and tears spring to my eyes. "I will spend every day of my life proving to you how wrong you are about that."

A rogue tear trails down my cheek to his hand, and when his lips gently press against mine, it's not filled with hunger, desire and need that I've been so used to.

No, this is different.

Stolas kisses a trail down my jaw to my neck, to my collarbone, my breast, and he settles onto his knees. I watch as his otherworldly gaze flicks to my stomach, and his eyes slide shut as he leans his forehead against my belly button, inhaling a deep breath before placing a kiss so tender against it that tears fall in earnest.

"This body you scrutinize so harshly deserves so much more appreciation than you give to it." He glances up at me before placing another kiss against my hip, and another lower, and lower, until he's at my mid-thigh. "And since you're so stubborn about starving yourself of the adoration you deserve, I will gladly make up for it."

Chapter 32

He kisses his way near my inner thigh before his gaze flicks up, and the air gets caught in my lungs as his hand glides up my leg, pausing behind my knee only to hook it over his shoulder.

I don't get more than a second to consider how exposed I am when he glides his tongue up my inner thigh. My mind blanks as he presses his mouth to my clit, and I gasp as his tongue flattens against me.

My eyes roll back as he holds me upright with one arm braced under my ass. Gripping the hair at the top of his head, desire builds in my core with every passing second until I'm panting and writhing against him. I'm getting so sensitive that I edge away, but his grip just tightens on me as he puts more pressure on my clit.

I'm trembling, leaning most of my weight on his shoulder as he pauses, and his breath skates over me. "The next time you think negatively about yourself, my dear Kilian, just remember that I would spend the rest of my eternal life between these thighs, for I know without a doubt in my mind that your body is my temple, and the sounds you make could bring even the holiest angel to his knees."

I don't have time to respond before his mouth is on me again with more intensity than before. My legs twitch, and my hips gyrate of their own volition as he grips me tighter against his face.

If he hits that spot again, I might—

He must have heard my thoughts, because his tongue rolls over my clit again and my hands tighten in his hair as my eyes flutter back. The intensity has me wanting to pull back, but Stolas just squeezes me into him harder, and I wonder how the hell he's breathing when he repeats the action and my mind goes blank.

I've got nowhere to retreat to, to escape the overwhelming pleasure building in my core, and Stolas is buried between my legs as if he plans to eat his way to my soul. His tongue, like his own personal brand, works me until I'm a trembling mess. I'm hardly keeping myself upright as my orgasm crests.

I shudder and cry out, but he doesn't let up until I'm mumbling a pleading prayer between breaths, and he drags his tongue along the length of my pussy one last time.

He eases me back to my feet, helping brace my arms to steady myself as the muscles in my legs tremor in aftershocks.

My hands move of their own accord, quickly tugging at his belt to unclip it. "I need you." I murmur, and he groans as I toss his belt aside, sending it clattering to the ground.

"Who am I to deny you?" He muses, walking me backward to the wall, with his hands moving to cup either side of my neck. "To do such a thing would be sin."

I want to argue that a demon shouldn't care about sinning, but he doesn't give me a chance to respond before his lips crash to mine, and the taste of him on my tongue mixed with my arousal sends my mind into a haze.

He's all consuming as he kisses me senseless, and I just barely unzip his pants, with both of us haphazardly tugging them down his legs. I'm hardly aware that he's done the same with his underwear when he hoists me into the air, pinning me to the wall as my legs wrap around his hips.

In the time it took to get us to the wall, he's positioned the length of himself between my legs, squeezing his dick between us as it throbs.

I moan into his mouth and he shudders. *"I would kill to hear you make that sound for the rest of eternity."*

The admission makes something in my chest flutter. *As long as you fuck me after, I'll make the sound all you want.*

Whatever self-control he had must snap, because he quickly lifts me higher, only to position the tip of his dick against my pussy. Pushing in, he takes my lip between his teeth, and I wince at the pain as he pauses to let me breathe.

Our eyes meet, and I dig my heels into him slightly. "Did I say I couldn't handle the pain?"

Heat flashes across his face, and he pushes in harder, sending jolts of pain through me. "Tell me if it's too much, Kilian."

I nearly let my overconfidence win and tell him I won't need to, but when he's halfway in, I wonder if I've bitten off more than I can chew.

He pushes in more and I suck in a breath as he freezes. "Kilian—"
I'm fine.

Withdrawing slightly, it gives me the reprieve I desperately need, and I dig my heels in harder as he eases back in agonizingly slow.

Stolas... His teeth pinch my lip before kissing me again. *Please—*
The word hardly leaves my mind when a growl escapes him. He withdraws and snaps his hips as I cry out; the sound swallowed by his mouth as he repeats the action.

Something about the angle, the pressure of our position, and the desperation that I feel in my body for him makes each movement feel like I'm on the edge. I'm caught between the need to feel him and the urge to grind into his thrusts as I fight for breaths.

I've never in my life been fucked like this.

Desire with an edge of animalistic need, with an overarching desperation that makes my head spin.

It's all nearly too much.

The sound of our bodies slamming together mixes with my pulse raging in my ears, and my mind blanks as I hold on for dear life.

Each thrust squeezes my clit, and it's not long before I'm on the edge of another orgasm.

Stolas must know it as his pace picks up, laced with the same urgency that I feel as my hips grind to meet his. He slams up into me one, two, three more times before burying himself deep.

His dick stiffens, pulsating as he comes, and I moan into his mouth, feeling blissfully full. My pulse is still raging like a war drum as he eases me back to my feet, with my legs trembling.

My legs threaten to give out as he kisses me lazily, dragging out the aftershocks as I cling to him for support.

"Now..." He whispers, grasping the brushes and paint from the floor before returning to stand before me. "Where were we?"

Chapter 33

I'm still trembling as I stand near the door to the hallway, and Stolas folds my dress before setting it gently on top of the table beside him.

Glancing down at my breasts, where a golden hue completely obscures the pink of my nipples, with lines in the paint almost appearing like fibers.

I have no idea what he's painted onto me, but he seems entirely satisfied as he moves to the door, his eyes trailing over me one final time.

He slowly licks his lips, and some part of me wonders if it's because he's thinking about earlier, but he snaps from his reverie and twists the knob of the door, tugging it open.

I stare at the now empty space, the precipice of safety and security into the unknown, the dangers of ridicule and shame. The chill from the hallway glides over my skin and I shiver as Stolas waits patiently, holding the door open.

The pride and reassurance in his expression is nearly contagious, and I take a deep breath before taking the first step.

With each step, I remind myself that I wear this paint as if it were my armor, covering the areas that Stolas was determined for others not to see.

He's a towering presence beside me as we walk down a long corridor, and when we turn the corner to an elevator, a man with a clipboard in hand suddenly rises to his feet.

His eyes automatically move to Stolas first, but when they turn to me, he blinks, and I can visibly see how hard he's trying not to look below my chest line as he returns his line of vision to Stolas.

"I-, uh, name?"

In my peripherals, I see Stolas cross his arms over his chest as he gives his name, and the man scans over his board before checking something off.

"Third floor. Good luck."

He averts his gaze entirely, pressing the button on the elevator, and it beeps as he gestures for us to go inside, keeping his sights on the floor.

The nagging doubt that lingers in my mind rears its ugly head once more as we step inside, and I swallow against the acrid taste of self-consciousness.

Who cares why he wouldn't look at me. It's probably better that he didn't anyway, right?

It's not like I want that attention.

The quiet voice in the back of my mind can't help but whisper that it's because I'm too gross to be looked at, but I shrug it off as the doors slide shut.

"Kilian."

My attention flicks to Stolas, and the knowing look on his face sends a wave of guilt over me.

"Do you remember what I said earlier?" I nod, but he just raises a brow. "Then why do you appear so small?"

A small huff of air escapes me. "Because you're more than a foot taller than I am, maybe."

He gives me a deadpan look, and I know I'm going to have to confess, even if a large part of me wants to crawl into a hole.

Why did I ever agree to do this, again?

"Because you don't want to owe a demon a debt. Now answer my question."

It takes a moment for me to find the right words, despite that, it's not enough. "He wouldn't look at me."

Stolas' eyebrows furrow, but before he can ask what I mean, I decide to just get it all out.

"How do I know whether he was avoiding looking at me because I look horrendous or out of respect?"

Stolas slams his fist against the red emergency stop button, and I jolt at the sudden movement.

"He was avoiding looking at you because he would have had one hell of a time getting rid of the evidence of his appreciation if he had looked."

I blink, and Stolas steps in close, crowding my space as my heart hammers in my throat.

"Kilian," he whispers, "you understand what I am, yes?"

I nod, backing up to the side of the elevator as he braces his arms on either side of me, searching my face as if searching for the honesty in it.

"Then believe what I'm telling you. He didn't look because he still has to work, and what's more, he knows I would kill him for it. He might not know what I am, but human instinct is sharp, even if he doesn't fully understand." His thumb glides along the column of my neck. "When we leave this elevator, Kilian, I will want to gouge out the eyes of every person in this exhibit who dares to gaze upon you, but I cannot blame them for wanting to witness the most exquisite creature ever born of this world."

I look at him for a long moment before nodding once more, and he backs up to release the emergency stop. The elevator lurches into motion, and all too soon the doors slide open, with voices filling the air as my heart leaps into my throat.

Stolas walks to the doors, keeping them open with his arm as I gather myself.

Regardless of what happens out there, does it really matter?

My heart thrums steadily, and I blow out a breath before squaring my shoulders.

I take the first step toward him, and though it feels unsteady, I throw more confidence into the next until I'm passing him in the doorway with a raised chin.

He leads us down the hallway with countless meandering people, but when we breach past the entrance into the main room, the chatter quiets, and he leads me to an area with two enormous white marble pillars that are nearly twice my height.

The pillars swirl as they extend up to the ceiling, and between them stands a thick golden object that looks oddly like an enormous tree trunk, with the metallic surface shimmering all the way from the floor to the ceiling.

I glance at Stolas, and his lips twitch. *"You can touch it."*

My heart beats hard, and I step toward the golden tree. As I grow closer, the busy room around me melts away until I'm standing before it, and I've never been more sure that it's far more than just art. The way the light glitters on the surface makes it seem alive, and my palms reach out to it. My movements are measured, as if I were approaching a wild animal, reassuring it that I'm safe.

Hovering an inch from the surface, the air itself vibrates against my palm. I almost think I've imagined it, but warmth radiates from the golden bark and, without a second thought, I close the distance.

I gasp as vibrations hum into my palm, growing more intense with each passing second. The sensation travels up my forearm and into my chest as I stare wide-eyed at the shining bark.

With my palms going numb, I feel no fear at the sensation. A breeze flows through the room, but I hardly notice it beyond my hair, shifting against my skin.

Warmth baths over my entire body as the golden bark brightens beneath my touch, swirling as if alive. My being feels like it's turned into sunlight, and my eyes fixate on the golden hue that's swirling up my arms.

Clicks fill the air around the room, mixed with quiet chatter, but I can't bring myself to tear my gaze from the tree. I'm in awe as tears spring to my eyes, and I follow the length of the golden bark to the ceiling, where a branch disappears into the next floor along with the rest of it.

There's no way this was man made.

The utter beauty of it, and the sensation coursing through me, is anything but synthetic.

"No, this tree was not created nor planted by any man..."

A flash to my left reflects off the bark, nearly blinding me, and I flinch, retracting my hands from the tree to cover my eyes as Stolas barks at someone. Beyond the sound of his voice, I can hardly hear anything else as the humming vibrates from my chest into my head.

My body might be physically grounded, but something about my contact with the tree has made my soul float among the clouds.

I can't say that I dislike the feeling, but part of me wonders what the tree did to make me feel so... peaceful and airy.

My attention sweeps through the room full of people, many of which are staring at the tree or me, and I turn to look at it once more in all its glory.

A million questions circle my mind, all vying for priority.

Who planted it?

Feeling Stolas approach to my left, I turn to look at him, but the serenity that washed over what could very well have been my soul seems so small compared to the soft expression on his face.

"It wasn't planted, but it was grown here as a gift."

A gift to whom?

"Humans, servilians, everyone who lives here."

I'd heard of them before... another species of beings who can wield magic. When I was in high school, one of my teachers taught us about a more controversial topic, which I later learned was banned from schools.

The school district claimed she purposefully disrupted her pupils' and the district's educational interests before firing her for misguiding students.

By the time I looked everything up, people seemed so divided on the topic that it just seemed like it was all conspiracies. That is, until I saw viral videos on social media of a fireball in the air overseas that took down a fighter jet. It seemed so real.

But it's so different experiencing something like this in person. Social media can be denied or challenged.

This is tangible.

Who gifted it?

My gaze slides to Stolas, and his lips twitch. *"A goddess who reinstated magic to this world years and years ago."*

I have to physically keep myself from gaping at him, and my attention drags back to the tree that seems more fascinating by the second.

What is it made of?

"Gold."

Is it supposed to feel electric and serene at the same time?

Stolas doesn't answer, and when I glance at him, I have to do a double take because of the way his jaw tenses.

What is it?

Our eyes lock, but he shakes his head as movement to our left catches our attention.

"Stolas, Mr. Bernard wishes to speak with you." For the first time, I see Stolas scowl at the petite woman standing before us with her hands clasped in front of her. Another flash of light half blinds me as she glances between us.

"Bernard can come here."

She just shakes her head, seemingly unfazed by Stolas' resistance to her conveyed request. "He said you might say that and to let you know it is rather important, and you will want to hear what proposal he has for you."

My gaze slides to Stolas, seeing the muscle in his jaw work as he stares at her. The reluctance that's on display in his demeanor sends a note of unease down my spine.

"Fine. I'll be there in a minute."

She inclines her head and steps back into the crowd before disappearing into the sea of people before Stolas turns to me. He places his back to the crowd, effectively blocking me from view from most onlookers with a pained expression.

"What is it?"

A long moment passes, and when he finally speaks, the deep tenor of his voice has grown even deeper as he keeps his tone as quiet as possible. "Remain here, Kilian. Don't speak to anyone while I'm gone. Do you understand?"

I swallow hard at his sudden caution and nod. "Right. I'll just stand by the golden tree and look pretty."

His eyes drop for a breath of a moment and a flash of heat crosses his expression. "Pretty is not the word I was thinking."

"And what word is that?"

I'm fully aware I'm flirting with Stolas while naked in a room full of people, but at this moment, I couldn't care less about them.

He leans in, and his lips brush the shell of my ear as a shiver works through me, doing nothing to combat the heat that's risen to my cheeks.

"Enchanting. Ravishing. Delectable. All of the above and everything in between. Every word that could describe the way you've caught the attention of every person in this room with your beauty, but ensnared me with a mere glance of your soul."

He nips my ear, and I jolt as my heart leaps into my throat, but he pulls back, glancing around for a moment. "I'll be back shortly. Remember–"

"Yeah, yeah. I know."

He tosses me an apologetic look before stalking in the direction the lady disappeared into the crowd, and when he's out of sight, an odd feeling of emptiness washes over me.

It's like the familiarity, the comfort or safety in the room has drained from every corner the moment he left my line of vision, and I survey the crowd with a note of unease.

Another flash fills my vision and I squeeze my eyes shut, retreating a tentative step as I blink the white spots away. When my teary-eyed gaze scans the crowd again, I don't see anyone with a camera, to my relief, and exhale a breath.

I understand wanting to take a photo, but do they need to use flash so much? Shit is blinding.

More people file into the room, with a handful at a time stopping to look at the tree, and I suppose me, as I do my best to focus on the marble pillars or the tree itself.

Though as much as I itch to touch it, I keep my hands to myself.

A clatter sounds out, and I drag my eyes from the pillar to the source, only for another flash to fill my vision as it goes entirely white.

Squeezing my eyes shut once more, and I shake my head uncomfortably as tears pool in the corners, feeling as if they've been burned. Hesitantly, I peel one open before the other, blinking furiously.

"Sorry about that." A voice fills the air, and my head snaps toward the sound. I'm still almost fully blinded with most of my vision a mess of white, but I'm certain that wasn't Stolas' voice.

I nod awkwardly, hearing Stolas' warning in the back of my mind as I continue to blink to clear my vision.

"Does she not speak?"

Chapter 34

I scoff. "She speaks when she wishes to." I retort as my vision returns, and I see the outline of the figure in front of me come into view.

A rich laugh fills the air in front of me as I squint and I make out more of the man. First the brunette hair with specs of white and grey that peppers it, then the deep brown eyes and deep set lines in his forehead, the crinkled lines at the corners of his eyes and then the dark blue suit finally becomes clearer, but it's the grin that creeps across his face that sends another nervous wave over me.

I turn my head to look in the direction Stolas went when the man's voice fills the air once more.

"I suppose that means you wished to speak to me then, since you answered." My attention snaps back to him, and I'm nearly certain he stepped closer when I wasn't looking, because I have to tilt my head to look at him.

Not wanting to drag this out any longer than I need to, I hold on to that uneasy feeling in my gut.

"What do you want?" My hands gesture in front of me as I talk, and he suddenly snatches my wrist.

Everything suddenly feels owrong, and I move to pull away, but I'm frozen as he holds my arm in his grip, gently patting the inside of my forearm with his other hand as he grins.

Is this feeling because of the tree or is it because Stolas put it in my head not to speak to anyone?

"I simply wish to get to know who this wonderful work of art is?"

My heart thrums hard against a hollow feeling in my chest, and it's as if I'm underwater as the man's hand suddenly releases mine.

"She's not of any interest to you." Stolas' deep voice is clipped, and I don't need to ask to know he's pissed about something.

"Ah, Stolas. I was wondering where you'd gone." The man grins at him with a glint in his eye that I can't quite place.

The empty pit in my chest drops to my stomach and I clasp my hands behind my back as if that could force the same confidence I came in with.

"Cut the shit Bernard. What do you want?"

Bernard? This was who you went to see?

Why would he call you to his office but not be there?

Bernard smiles broadly and gestures toward me and the tree. "I wanted to make you an offer."

He doesn't mean...

I glance over to see him looking directly at me, and the world feels as if it's suspended.

If my blood could stop pumping, I'm nearly certain it would have already as the air catches in my lungs, but Stolas doesn't seem as phased by the request.

"No offers are being taken."

Bernard laughs under his breath, pushing up his glasses as if the rejection was nothing more than a joke to him.

"Nonsense. This is our most esteemed exhibition with the most rare pieces of art. Everything has a price, Stolas, you know that."

Stolas stares at him for a long moment, and I'm about to argue that I'm a fucking person when he finally speaks.

"How much is your highest offer?"

My attention snaps to him, but he's not looking at me. No, his gaze is laser-focused on Bernard, who seems only gleefully impressed at the turn of conversation.

"Seventy-five and a relic from death himself."

Stolas eyes narrow, but he just shakes his head. "Unfortunately, that's still nowhere near enough–"

"Two-hundred and fifty, and the relic."

My hands unclasp, and I'm about to grab Stolas arm to protest when he shakes his head again, and his deep voice fills the air.

"I said no, Bernard."

The man's jaw ticks, but he quickly recovers with a disarming grin. "Ah, well, I suppose you can't win them all on the first go." He steps over, and before I can retract my hand, he shakes it, and I want nothing more than to recoil into myself.

Something about him feels as if the very air's been sucked from my lungs and everything turns into a varying shade of wrong until he finally releases me.

"Until we meet again, Stolas." He says with a look of content in his expression. "Perhaps you'll be more willing to discuss a price next time."

"Unlikely." Stolas growls, and Bernard walks back into the crowd as I rub my hands together soothingly.

The crowd hasn't seemed to pay any mind to the interaction, and I'm starting to wonder if I'm over-exaggerating the entirety of it when Stolas reaches over to inspect my hands.

"What are you doing?" I murmur, eyeing the crowd as he continues to inspect my arms before turning me away from the crowd. It takes a moment to realize he's inspecting my back and probably my ass when I turn around and glare at him.

"What the hell—?"

"Careful, Kilian." Stolas warns, and I feel a jolt of nervousness through my core.

"What the hell was all of that?" I lean in and whisper the words as his jaw ticks.

"An asshole with too much money who thinks he owns the world."

"You were actually considering taking it for a moment."

He frowns and shakes his head. "Even two hundred and fifty trillion wouldn't be enough."

I feel the blood drain from my face, and Stolas' expression turns into pure concern as he steps in close, bracing either of my arms as if I'm about to faint.

"Are you unwell?"

I blink at him, fighting the urge to uno-reverse the question on him.

It's a losing battle.

"Why the hell would you turn down two hundred and fifty **trillion** dollars?"

He rears back as if struck before glancing around. "We should go."

I frown at his sudden shift in demeanor, but I came here at his behest as part of a deal, so I'm not about to complain. "Lead the way."

Following in close, we get to the elevator, and he presses the down button as it chimes to open, sending my heart rate through the roof before I step inside. The doors close, and I look at him hesitantly, noticing the way his jaw still tenses as he grinds his teeth.

"Did you consider it?"

Emotion flashes across his face, and his gaze softens as he shakes his head, but before he can say anything, the doors open. For whatever reason, I'm eager to get to the room and change. Eager to get one step closer to getting out of here, so I brush past him and head straight to the dressing room.

Not waiting for him to open the door, I stride to the dresser, grabbing my underwear off the top of the pile, and I'm about to bend over to pull them on when I feel Stolas at my back.

His arm wraps around my chest as his hand finds its way around my throat before he tugs me flush to him.

I'm fully aware that this is a vulnerable position, especially considering that he's a demon, but for whatever reason, my body relaxes, melting into him as he tightens his grip.

My head tilts back to lean against his shoulder as he gazes down at me.

"If you think there is any price tag worthy of you, you have not been listening to me." His free hand snakes around my waist to hold me tight to his body, and his thumb tilts my jaw even further. "He could have offered me every piece of gold, every diamond, every precious jewel on this planet, and I still would have turned it down, because no price they could offer me would be enough. Do you hear me?"

I swallow, and he tracks the movement as my throat bobs against his hand before I nod. "I hear you..."

His eyes flash as he flexes his fingers against my pulse point, and mine flutter closed as he groans. "As much as I want to bend you over and fuck you until your legs give out, we need to leave. I don't want Bernard to get an itch to come chat again."

Warmth explodes all over my body as my cheeks burn. He releases my neck, but his hands move to mine to grab my underwear, and he eases it up over my ass. His forehead leans against my shoulder as he sighs.

"God help me." He murmurs under his breath, before trailing kissing along the side of my neck. "But you'll have to dress, otherwise it will be hours before we leave."

Part of me wants to ask what's so wrong with staying a while, but the concern in his face earlier has me biting my tongue, and I grab my bra from the dresser.

I'll get answers at some point.

Tugging on my clothes, my mind is in a haze as we navigate down the hallways to the exit.

"Why was he going to pay so much?" I whisper, passing by the doorman and heading into the parking lot.

Stolas' SUV beeps twice as it unlocks, and his eyes meet mine over the hood before I climb into the passenger seat. His voice is like a deep caress in my mind as he climbs into his.

"Because you're special, Kilian. More special than you know."

I frown, and he backs out of his parking spot. "That doesn't answer my question."

His jaw tenses. "I wish I could say more."

"You can tell me anything, Stolas." I whisper, wondering if he's not telling me for fear of my reaction, even if he knows I can be impulsive.

"Why bring me there if someone like Bernard was going to be there?"

He shakes his head. "I needed to see the truth for myself."

"See what?"

When he doesn't answer, I release a sigh. *You should be able to tell me whatever you want. I don't understand what's going on, Stolas.*

He rubs his hand along his jaw. "It's not about me, or what I want to say, Kilian. Giving too much information could result in one or both of us dying, and I can't risk that. I won't."

His admission makes me swallow hard, and there's a long moment of silence between us.

I wish you could.

His otherworldly gaze slides to mine, and he reaches over to grasp my hand. *"I know."*

Chapter 35

We pull into the driveway of the rental, and I climb out of the passenger seat, absently shutting the door. The sound of a car starting nearby catches my attention, and I track the white SUV with dark tinted windows as it passes.

Part of me wonders if it's best for me to stay in the dark about everything, as much as I hate it.

With everything going on at work, Aiden, and my health, it's probably best not to adopt more problems, especially if I can't solve them... but something about how Bernard looked at me makes a boulder of unease settle in my gut.

I pace to where Stolas holds the door open, passing by him with a million unanswered questions that I want to ask, yet I'm too afraid to know the answer to.

Stolas' phone rings, and he puts it to his ear. I watch as he listens to whoever is on the other line until our eyes meet, and he gives me an apologetic look.

I don't wait for him to tell me he needs to speak freely with the person on the other line, and I head straight for the shower. Our flight is in a couple of hours, leaving me with just enough time to clean the paint off and change before we need to go.

My heart sinks into my stomach as I turn on the faucet, and peel my clothes off, glancing in the mirror at Stolas' handiwork.

Without a mirror in the room at the exhibition, I hadn't seen what the finished product looked like, but I can't help but stare at it now.

The gold paint covering my body is a stark contrast to the white feathers that look like they could be real, and tangible, attached to my skin. They cover my arms, intricately painted with golden swirls leading to a spot in the center of my chest. More feathers scatter throughout the rest of my body, but I can see why, standing in front of the golden tree, I might become part of the art piece.

Why bring me to the tree, Stolas? What's so special about it?

When he doesn't answer, I sigh and climb into the shower. It takes a few minutes for the paint to scrub off, with the water turning a pale gold color and flecks circling the drain.

My skin feels raw as I work my way from my chest and down the rest of my body, finally taking turns scrubbing along my arms. Halfway down my forearm, a ribbon of gold won't seem to come off. Rubbing, scraping and running it under the water does nothing, and I give my skin a break to continue to scrub the rest of my hand.

By the time my arms and hands are mostly clear, I bring my arm close, inspecting the ribbon that leads to my palm with more curiosity than anything else. At the base of the ribbon, a black symbol marks where it meets my wrist, and I think back to when my palm touched the tree.

There was no pain, only peace.

Yet the ribbon and symbol make me uneasy, and for a moment, I contemplate telling Stolas. I know he'd understand where it came from, and what it means, but something in the back of my mind gives me pause.

I don't know what he'd do with that information.

He could use it against me for all I know.

I shake my head, shoving the thought from my mind. If Stolas had poor intentions, he would have shown them by now, especially after Bernard's offer. A shudder runs through me as I reflect on being nearly sold like livestock.

Expensive cattle, but cattle.

When I'm finished showering and changed into a comfortable sweater and pants, I haul my carry-on to the front door, feeling the symbol and ribbon on my right arm like a lingering scar.

Stolas turns to me, his expression surprisingly soft as he reaches for the handle of my carry-on. "I'm sorry we can't spend more time. I would have liked to show you more of the city."

He hauls everything out the door, holding it open for me as I follow in close. "I need to prepare for our new round of clinical trials anyway, but maybe we can come back some time."

Our eyes lock, and he laughs softly. "The world is a big place, Kilian. There's much for you to see, but Los Angeles is beautiful. We can return whenever you'd like."

My heart stutters in my chest, and I bite back a smile as I go to the car. The thought of us returning some time is an enticing prospect, and I ignore the quiet nagging doubt as I climb into the passenger's seat.

Stolas settles into his seat to drive us to the airport as I chew the inside of my cheek thoughtfully. "I take it you've traveled a lot?"

He chuckles and gives me a look. "I'm a demon and older than you can count. I don't think there's a place on this earth I haven't been." He says, before tilting his head. "Well, other than the Vatican. They don't take kindly to our kind there, and it's heavily guarded. I'd rather not venture into that place willingly."

I raise a brow. "The Vatican is heavily guarded?"

"Is that so surprising?" His lips twitch as he glances at me.

"Not really, but it's hard to imagine that they know what you are, and picture them doing something about it."

He just shakes his head. "They wouldn't know quickly, but I'd have to be very careful if I didn't want them to know. Without immense power, it's nearly impossible to hide what I am in such a place."

We pull onto the highway, and I glance over at him. "What would happen if they discovered you?"

Part of me knows the answer to this question, but for whatever reason, I want to hear him say it.

"Well, I'd have to kill anyone who got in my way." I swallow hard, and when our eyes meet, he just shrugs. "I said I hadn't gone there for a reason."

We fall silent as we arrive at the airport, and it's another twenty minutes for us to make it to the gate, just in time for boarding to start. Each step onto the plane feels like I'm leaving the quiet bubble we'd made for ourselves, and I replay every moment until we're taking off.

The plane surges higher into the air, the engines loud as my ears pop.

Stolas?

He turns his head to look at me, searching my face, waiting for me to continue.

What did Bernard mean when he offered you a relic from death himself?

He considers my question, and my ears pop as his rich voice echoes in my mind, sounding farther away than normal. I chalk it up to the plane's engines and pressure in my ears.

"Azrael's dagger is a weapon of... incredible destruction. It could send thousands to the afterlife if it gets into the wrong hands."

My heart stutters. *And he has the dagger?*

Stolas blows out a tense breath, and tilts his head to the ceiling of the plane. "According to Bernard, they do. I called my brothers while you were showering, and they confirmed it's going to reappear soon, but to what extent and how, they didn't know."

The realization that they were willing to trade so much money and such a weapon to a demon in exchange for me and maybe the tree makes my heart sink into my stomach.

Stolas' rich voice fills my mind, and my eyes slide shut. *"I never would have agreed, Kilian."*

Why? It seems like their offer was more than generous.

"There would never be an offer worthy of you." My heart thunders. *"My brothers are extremely skilled at finding lost relics. Once they do, I'll recover the dagger from them."*

I know he's saying that to reassure me that this weapon is under control, but a demon holding such a weapon for safe keeping seems like such a hypocritical sentiment.

Why is this weapon so important?

"Because my brothers are at war."

I frown. *But you're not?*

A long moment of silence stretches between us, and I glance over to see him deep in thought.

"Until now, I had not had a stake in their war. I'd always considered the conflict to be... exhausting and pointless. Sure, every now and again I'd helped tip the scales, but not for the purpose of changing the outcome."

It only seems logical that someone would be at war with demons, but to think it would be humans at war with them.

Are angels real, then?

His gaze slides to me, and I see the guarded look in his eyes, telling me this is one of those questions that he can't answer.

"Do you think they are?"

I blink at him. *Well... if demons are... then I'd assume angels are too.*

His lips twitch in my peripheral. *"Why do you ask such questions?"*

I just don't understand why humans are the one fighting demons. Why wouldn't angels be fighting demons unless they aren't real?

The conflict in his expression is clear, and I just nod to myself slightly. *Right. Can't answer that one, I guess.*

"I'm sorry, Kilian."

Inhaling deeply, as he encircles my hand with his, I nod. *I know more than I ever would have... so thank you for sharing what you can.*

Even though my words convey appreciation, there's some part of me that grows increasingly frustrated by whatever stops him.

Clearly, I'm already involved in this entire situation one way or another, so keeping me in the dark just seems unfair.

The seatbelt sign dings off, and I excuse myself from my seat to stretch my legs before squeezing into the restroom. The lock latches shut and I exhale a tense breath.

Rolling up my right sleeve, I stare at the ribbon, its gold now duller than before, a twist of unease tightening in my gut. As if the paint or whatever coloration stained my arm has tarnished, I swallow hard, tracing the dark ribbon all the way to the black symbol on my wrist.

Tugging my sleeve down, the lump in my throat grows, and I flip the latch to return to my seat. My eyes slide shut as the seatbelt sign comes on, and the captain warns everyone of some rough air up ahead.

When my mind wanders to work, Aiden and parting ways with Stolas, an odd note of dread hangs over me, staying there like a thunderous rain cloud for the rest of the flight.

Chapter 36

"Wait, so you just flew to LA with some random hunk and went to an art exhibition where he put you on display naked?" Aiden's voice is shrill, and he clicks his tongue. "You naughty, naughty woman. Who are you, and what have you done with my Kilian?"

I huff a dry laugh, staring at my ceiling before putting my phone on speaker. "Don't get too excited. I haven't seen him since."

"You ghosted him?"

My chest tightens, and I chew the inside of my lip as I tab over to Stolas' messages.

Still nothing.

After getting back from Los Angeles and Stolas dropped me off at home, whatever mental connection Stolas had opened up, seems to have come to an end because he's been radio silent.

I'd thought about meditating this morning, but for whatever reason, I couldn't bring myself to.

"Kil?"

"Ah, no. Not really. We just... haven't talked."

A long moment of silence comes through the phone line, and Aiden yawns. "Well, babe, I gotta go. Our flight is in like ten hours."

"Okay, sleep tight."

"Are you sure you're alright?" Aiden's voice is thick with concern, and I swallow.

Staring at the now black ribbon spanning from my wrist to my elbow, the lump in my throat grows. "Yeah, I'm just tired, I think."

"Alright, if you're sure... Night Kil."

The call ends, and I release a deep sigh, feeling a crackle in my lungs before I cough. The coughing doesn't stop after a minute, and my chest grows tight.

Fuck.

I surge forward as my lungs seize in my chest, and each cough feels as though my lungs are closing entirely. My feet can't carry me to the dresser fast enough, and I fumble for the inhaler, dropping it in my panic.

By the time the cold mouthpiece is against my lips, I can hardly suck enough breath to get the medication.

When the cold spritz is nothing more than a burst of air, a fresh wave of panic washes over me.

I'm out? ... No way.

This was a new inhaler.

My lungs wheeze as air forces through what I presume is a pin-sized hole, and I throw myself down to the garbage next to my bed, rummaging through it as I find the older inhaler I'd thrown out a week ago.

Please work.

God help me, please work.

Pressing the top, I inhale as a faint mist of cold hits the back of my throat with relief that makes me feel like I could pass out.

Or maybe that's the lack of oxygen.

I need help.

This is bad.

The next breath I drag in is barely enough to satisfy my need for air, and I stutter empty gulps to no avail. My head swims as I pull out my phone and panic wells in me as I dial 911.

The ringtone drags on for what feels like an eternity before the operator's voice fills the air.

"Nine-one-one, what's your emergency?"

"H—" My voice is hardly audible over the blood raging in my ears.

"Hello?" The operator's voice fills the air, and tears spring to the corners of my eyes.

By the time I finally tell her I can't breathe, I'm crawling to the hallway on all fours with my phone clutched tight in my hand.

"I've got paramedics on the way."

Even if I wanted to ask how she knew where I was, there's no way I'd be able to.

"Just hold on, ma'am. I'm with you."

The room spins as I collapse to my side in the middle of the hallway, staring at the chipped paint at the base of the wall. My body breaks out in a cold sweat as I think back to that day when Aiden had been over to help move the furniture with me.

He'd freaked out when the chair leg scraped the wall, thinking I was going to be mad.

I couldn't have cared less, though.

The only thing that mattered was having him around.

Stolas comes to the forefront of my mind, and tears well in the corners of my eyes.

I hope this isn't the end for me.

I still have so much to tell him, and so much I wanted to experience.

My vision goes blurry, and I blink slowly to clear it before everything goes black.

Chapter 37

Rhythmic beeping fills the air, and my eyes peel open. The crust pulls at my lashes painfully, and I wince.

It takes a few seconds to recall the moments leading up to this, and it's not until I look at the IV in my arm or the wires connected to my chest that the seriousness of my situation really sets in.

I don't think I need to wonder how they found me or got into the house, but damn, am I glad they did.

The beep that mirrors my heartbeat quickens as I survey the empty room, and the soft light filtering in from the window.

A crinkle echoes in my lungs with each shallow breath, but at least I can breathe. The panic leading up to me calling 911 resurfaces and I squeeze my eyes shut as my pulse hikes.

I was so sure I was going to die.

The rhythmic beeping gets faster, and the door to the room opens as my attention snaps to my left.

Dr. Newlin breezes in, running his hand through his hair. "Ms. Sterling." He adjusts the clipboard in his free hand as he moves to sit on the chair beside me.

Some part of me recognizes the expression on his face is not one that screams good news, but I swallow down my fears as he clears his throat.

"How are you feeling?"

I stare at him for a moment, biting back a handful of sarcastic responses before landing on a more appropriate one. "Like I passed out from lack of oxygen."

He nods his head a few times before running his finger along the clipboard. "Quite the asthma attack it was. Looks like your test results are mostly normal, but there's some buildup of fluid in your lungs from what we can tell. I suspect you have an acute case of pneumonia."

My heart sinks. "How? I just–"

"I'll have a script written up for a round of antibiotics, but I suggest taking it easy for the next week and plenty of rest."

I stare at him with wide eyes as he scribbles something down and tears a paper off the thin pad of paper on his clipboard before holding it between us.

"I just finished a round of antibiotics." I whisper, and he just nods dismissively.

"Yes, yes. It appears that round was rather ineffective. I've ordered an emergency biopsy of your lungs, and until then, I want you to remain here, get your medication, and rest."

He gives me a deadpan look, and I'm about to argue when the memory of drinking during my last night of antibiotics comes to mind.

My retort dies on my lips, my mouth snaps shut, and I just nod.

For whatever reason, some part of me knows I could have done better, and I resign myself to another grueling week of antibiotics. The other part of me wonders how long it'll take before I actually get some actual answers, but I shove that overly negative voice out of my mind with force.

He's the doctor, right? I should just trust in what he's saying.

The flip of paper fills the air as he turns the clipboard toward me.

"You'll have to sign this consent form to have a driver and team of nurses drop you off after the procedure."

I glance between him and the paper, hesitantly taking the pen from his hand as the tip hovers above the paper.

At least it's testing I haven't done before. Maybe now I'll finally get results.

I guess it's never too late to put my faith in the healthcare system.

The pen tip meets the paper, and I scribble my name down before handing the paperwork back.

Dr. Newlin flashes a smile. "Great. The nurses will get you prepped, and we'll have you home in no time."

My heart pounds hard as he breezes from the room, leaving me alone with my thoughts as sunlight crests in from the window. Whether it's a figment of my imagination or not, the room warms, and I sigh deeply before coughing hard.

Damn, I hope this test gives me some kind of answer.

I glance down at the blackened ribbon on my forearm that's doubled in length, stretching halfway up my bicep.

Whatever the tree did when I touched it, it can't have been good.

The irony that it's made my asthma worse after the clinical trials did the same to the volunteers sends a bitter note of regret through me.

Maybe this is what I deserve.

For letting every single person in that trial down, including Aiden.

Flexing my arm, part of me wonders if the movement will usher my illness forward faster, and I shove away the temptation to flex faster.

My eyes slide shut, with shallow breaths making my head feel light. I'd never imagined it would get this bad, and even though it's selfish, some part of me wished I could have just had a normal life.

A life filled with energy and movement without the fear of an impending asthma attack. One where I loved my body… Where doctors didn't blame the extra weight I've gained for my medical issues.

A single tear trails down my cheek, and sleep takes me.

Chapter 38

It feels like I'd only just closed my eyes when the door to my room swings open, clattering against the doorstop with a clatter.

"Sorry to wake you, Ms. Sterling. It's time for your procedure."

My crusted lashes tug open painfully. Three nurses fill the room, bustling about, getting bands, needles and various other things I can't keep track of.

Focusing on any of them proves impossible, with their murmured instructions going in one ear and out the other.

It's hard enough to breathe, nevermind listen to a word they're saying.

The nurse to my right turns my forearm to get access to my vein, and I notice the entirety of my limb has turned black. The nurse doesn't seem to notice it, and he straps something around my bicep.

Another nurse catches my attention as the nurse to my right inserts a needle into my arm and I inhale a sharp lungful between my teeth. The sudden influx of air sends me into another coughing fit, and it's a full minute before I calm down.

I'm half lucid as the nurses continue to bustle around, and before I know it, I'm wheeled into the center of another room.

My gaze lazily bounces between the surgeon and who I assume is the anesthesiologist. They've put me under a couple of times in my life, but each time usually feels just as nerve-wracking as the last.

Oddly enough, I find myself looking forward to the blissful sleep that awaits, regardless of the reason for it. It's not true rest, but it's better than whatever this is.

"Alright, Ms. Sterling. I'll have you count down from ten for me." The anesthesiologist looks at me as I breathe slowly, my body feeling as if it's being sucked into the bed.

"Ten. Nine. Eight."

He glances over at the monitor before his eyes settle on me once more.

"Seven... Six..." I blink once, and it takes a long moment for my eyes to open again.

"Five." I say with a muffled voice, and when I try to say the next word, everything goes dark.

Chapter 39

"Isn't this yet another pleasant surprise."

My heart stutters in my chest as the deep tenor of Stolas' voice fills the air, and I look around the florals of the garden.

It's like I never left.

Each flower, stem and leaf looks just as it did the last time I found myself here. The stars stretching above the tallest trees in the distance paint the most beautiful contrast to the garden.

It's a sight that would make any normal person stare at it in awe.

Yet I feel nothing.

Stolas' eyes trail down my body before his brows pinch together. "Are you alright?"

I follow his gaze down to the hospital robe wrapped around my torso, and nod. "Yeah, just getting something done."

He doesn't look convinced. "What is it, Kilian?"

My mouth drops open and even though part of me instinctively wanted to respond in truth, I hesitate. *What's the point of telling him? He can't help me. No one can.*

This is my burden to bear and mine alone. It would be a cheap excuse and a coward's way out to use his help.

An odd sense of despair and hopelessness takes over as I shake my head, and Stolas' eyes narrow.

"Kilian, you need to tell me what is going on."

He searches my face, and while everything in me gravitates toward him, getting drawn in by the world-like irises fixated on me, I can't help the urge to draw into myself.

The feeling is so odd and out of place that I blink at him.

"I–" *Why the hell **am** I being so negative?* "I'm getting a biopsy."

Surprise flashes across his face. "Why?"

As if he doesn't know? Or maybe he just doesn't care.

Swallowing my sarcastic retorts, my answer remains curt. "Because I'm sick."

"You should be better—" He catches himself and the muscle in his jaw tenses. "You were getting better when I last saw you."

I nearly scoff. *He thinks healing is linear? I guess an inhuman being **would** feel that way.*

"Yeah, well. I got worse again."

He looks at me–really looks at me–and tilts his head. "Where are you? Let me help."

Part of me hates that it feels like he can see straight into my soul. "Stolas, I–"

He steps in close, cupping my jaw as he tilts my head back to look at him. "Kilian, just say the word. Say the word and this could all be done."

The contact feels grounding. Like a beam of light chasing away the shadows in my mind, and I sigh wistfully.

"There are people in this world that need that help more than me, Stolas."

He exhales sharply. "Kilian–"

My heart is nearly in my throat, and I place my palm on his chest as I feel the steady thrum of his pulse in my hand. Pressure builds in the back of my mind, and I frown at him.

"Stolas, I just–" I don't get another word out before the world goes dark.

"Give her one dose. She'll get the rest at the house."

Is that Dr. Newlin?

A chill runs through me from my arm to my spine.

The urge to shiver is strong, but my body stays still, completely unresponsive. I've had numb legs and hands before, but never has my entire body gone completely immobile like this.

A low rumble of air conditioning fills the background, contrasting the shuffling of people moving around me before the cool breeze kisses my skin.

Clearly I can still *feel*.

I try to wiggle my fingers, toes, or any muscle in my face. No response.

An unfamiliar voice a few feet away reverberates in my ears. "The van is ready."

"Angela's ready?" Dr. Newlin asks. My eyes are still too heavy to open, so I do my best to listen. "Great. Let's get going before she wakes up."

Part of me hones in on his words. Something inside me growing increasingly desperate to move, but my body still feels so heavy, and a loud clank sounds out to my right.

Another clatter soon follows, and another just beside the bed. A brief pause extends around me, only broken by the quiet breathing of the medical staff nearby, and within seconds the bed I'm on rocks, making the world feel as if it's spinning.

Or maybe I'm the one spinning.

For a split second I'm airborne, with my arms and head hanging loose, dangling with gravity that threatens to drag the rest of me down with it.

Instinct urges me to move, to raise my head and open my eyes, but no matter how hard I try to mimic the action I've grown so used to, nothing works.

My body collides with a hard and awkward surface, like I've been shoved into an oddly shaped box with how my head teeters over the back. I can only assume it's some sort of chair by the way I've collapsed into it, with someone suddenly grabbing my feet and resting them on a hard surface.

I've only started to really pay closer attention to my surroundings as a rhythmic squeak fills the silence. The breeze shifts my hair against my face, and even though it tickles, I can do nothing to scratch at it.

Something in front of me creaks open, and a sudden rush of cold air hits my skin. Even though my eyes are still closed, it's not hard to tell we've made it outside as goosebumps break out all over my body.

Is this what they meant by triage waiting for me? That they'd bring me home after the procedure?

The cold air rushes into my lungs and I feel my chest tighten painfully, but every part of me feels as if it's weighed down.

"Watch her head." Dr. Newlin's voice fills the air beside me and within seconds, I'm airborne once more. I barely feel the hands gripping my thighs before I'm dropped into what I can only assume is another chair.

"Shut the door, Ang."

I hear a car door slam shut, and another. A third sounds out before the rumble of an engine fills the air.

They're driving me home when I'm still not fully conscious?

Even though the notion is bizarre, I recount the papers I signed to be brought home by a team of nurses with a modicum of relief.

The question is, will they stay until I'm fully awake, or will I be fending for myself?

What if I never go back to normal?

The car moves side to side as whoever is driving presses down on the accelerator, sucking me back into the seat more. I drift in and out of consciousness with the motion of the rocking vehicle until it suddenly lurches to a stop.

"Get her to room three and close the windows."

Room three?

Why would they close the windows? Do they think it's an allergy?

A door opens, and when hands painfully grip my arms and legs, tugging at them before hoisting me into the air, I realize that my mind is much more focused, and I can feel everything, yet I still can't move.

Could I be in a coma?

Is this what locked-in syndrome feels like?

A fresh wave of panic washes over me, but I'm helpless to do anything as the team of nurses plops me into another seat. Someone keeps me upright as I nearly slump over, but the loss of control makes my head swim.

Every move of my body has me instinctively wanting to adjust, but that's where it stops. Not a single muscle twitches or contracts from my mental efforts, and I'm completely at the nurse's mercy as wind hits my face. The bitter chill settles into my skin, and my eyes burn beneath my lids as the sound of a door opening fills the air.

A sudden wave of heat of air hits my face, and after a long moment, I finally come to a stop. Seconds pass before a creak sounds out, and within the same breath, I'm in motion once more.

"Get her settled and give her the next dose. She should be up soon."

Little do they know...

My momentum comes to a stop, and footsteps shuffle on either side of me before I'm in the air once more. I'm only airborne for a breath before I fall limp to the bed, and the springs rattle as the realization sets in.

They didn't bring me home.

This isn't my bed.

There were no stairs to get in the house.

Where did they take me?

A hand grabs my arm, extending it out as some clattering echoes into the room, and within moments my arm goes ice-cold, with the chill travelling all the way to my shoulder.

It's not long before the cold goes away, and a jittery sensation travels over the length of my body. My muscles suddenly warm, but the warmth gives way to more and more heat until every inch of my body is on fire.

The urge to scream, to shout, to cry, to do anything to stop the pain comes to the forefront of my desperate mind, but my body remains motionless as the medication makes its way through it.

Every second I think it can't get any worse, it builds, and finally I cannot take anymore, and the world goes dark.

Chapter 40

I'm gasping as crisp air hits my lungs, and my tear-filled eyes are wide, surveying the garden as I desperately fight to gather my senses. My limbs tremble, and I look down at them, searching for any lingering burns as my stomach flips.

What the hell just happened to me?

Within seconds, bile rises in my throat and I hurl the contents of my stomach up, which isn't much.

"Kilian?" Stolas' deep tenor is like a balm to my soul, and the tears at the corner of my eyes fall in earnest as his hurried footsteps grow closer.

I can't bring myself to move, but when I go to speak and my mouth drops open, only a sob escapes my throat.

What if I'll never be able to move again?

Can someone stay trapped here forever?

My arms fight to keep me upright as Stolas' pristine white pants come into view, kneeling in the dirt path with his hands reaching for me.

"Kilian, what's wrong?" The concern in his voice squeezes my heart in my chest, and I just shake my head.

He wouldn't understand.

There's a small voice at the back of my mind screaming for me to tell him anyway, and I'm internally fighting on both fronts when he pulls me into his arms.

"Kilian, say something."

My eyes flutter as I tilt my head, only for tears to continue streaming down my face. "I don't understand what's happening to me, Stolas."

He lifts me with ease into his lap, and I shudder as his arms encircle my shoulders. It takes everything I have to not break down as I wrap my trembling arms around his large torso, with the relief that I can still move this much crashing into me like a freight train.

"I can't help if you don't let me."

How can he fix this? Fix me? Of all the people in this world, there are others who deserve to feel better so much more than I do. People have suffered so much more than me.

I pull back to look in his eyes, and the sincere look in them has me swallowing hard.

"I couldn't move."

He frowns, tucking a lock of hair behind my ear as he waits.

"They were transporting me and I couldn't move my body, but I was awake. Could something have happened during the biopsy, Stolas? What if I'm in a coma? What if—?"

My words catch in my throat, and Stolas' presses his lips to my forehead. "I've got you, Kilian. Can you tell me where you are?"

Everything feels fuzzy, and a tug makes me feel like I'm being pulled away as a fresh wave of despair washes over me.

"I don't—" I can hardly get the words out when I'm ripped from the garden and everything goes dark once more.

My eyes peel open slowly, taking in the near empty room with my nerves all on edge.

"Oh good, you're awake." My head snaps toward the woman's voice, who I can only assume is Angela, and I groan slightly as the twinge in my neck sends electrical currents down my spine.

Angela laughs. "Easy. We had to give you a couple doses of medication while you were unconscious. You'll probably feel sick, and really stiff."

My mouth drops open, and I'm about to ask how long I've been out when Dr. Newlin breezes through the door.

"Ms. Sterling, great to see you awake." He wheels the chair over and sits down beside the bed with a pensive look etched into his features. "How are you feeling?" Searching his face, I inhale only to cough hard, and he winces. "That about sums it up. Unfortunately, Ms. Sterling, there's no easy way to say this, so I'm just going to. Your biopsy results came back positive for adenocarcinoma."

He continues to talk, but I don't listen to a word as I stare at him with wide eyes.

This can't be.

How did they miss this on all of my other tests?

"... I assure you, this is the best cancer center in the city."

I'm still in a state of shock as he looks at me expectantly.

"We'll have to keep you under observation for the next few days to make sure you're stable, but with our rigorous approach to treatment, your prognosis is favorable."

There's no way in hell, days ago, I was in Los Angeles at an art exhibition and living a dream, only to wind up in a cancer center days later.

My mind goes back to the sensation from the tree and my stomach twists.

It couldn't have been...

"Ms. Sterling?"

My attention comes front and center to Dr. Newlin as he waits expectantly.

"I'm so sorry, I have cancer?"

He nods as if it's the most normal thing. "Lung cancer, yes. Adenocarcinoma is typically slow moving, but we'll have to evaluate your progress to determine how to respond to treatment."

I swallow hard and nod, not trusting my voice.

"Angela here will get you set up for another round of medication over the course of the next few hours. There are some side effects which I'm certain you're already feeling, but it's important to go through the full round of treatment, or we risk your cancer spreading."

There are no words forming on my tongue, no arguments in my mind that I can make as I struggle to reconcile the news.

When I don't respond, Dr. Newlin glances between me and Angela before patting my leg. He pushes to his feet and gives her a single nod before breezing out of the room as quick as he came.

"Alright Ms. Sterling." Angela moves to my side and I watch with apprehension as she plunges a syringe of liquid into the line of my IV. "This is just some nausea medication to keep you from getting sick. I'll get your treatment set up shortly."

Everything in me doesn't want to be here, doesn't want to be sick, doesn't want to be dying, but that's how the world works, isn't it?

Some things are just outside of your control, and to fight it feels exhausting.

"How long will I need treatment?"

She reaches over to the laptop and clicks a few times, answering with her eyes remaining glued to the screen. "We'll need to keep you under observation for the following week–"

"Week?!" My voice is shrill, but it doesn't take her attention away from the laptop as she nods, scrolling and clicking some more.

"Yes, Ms. Sterling. This is an intensive treatment designed specifically to target adenocarcinoma of the lung. Because of the intensive nature of it, we need to monitor your progress and receptiveness to treatment."

A wave of dizziness has my head falling back to the bed, and I stare at the ceiling before my eyes flutter shut.

God. What am I going to do about work?

"I need to tell work–"

"We've already arranged that for you, Ms. Sterling."

My body tingles, and I wiggle my fingers slowly in response. "They were okay with it? How did you contact them?"

The way my body melts into the bed has a yawn creeping from my throat as Angela moves around busily.

"Their contact info was in your emergency contacts section of your visits, which this would qualify for. They didn't say anything about your absence being okay, but we'll keep in regular contact with them to ensure job abandonment doesn't occur."

The sentiment makes me feel somewhat better, but the room is still spinning as I sigh a shallow breath and nod. "Alright. Thank you."

I want to ask more, to understand more of what's happening, but I don't have that luxury when it's hard to breathe.

"Just rest, Ms. Sterling. We'll take good care of you here." Angela's hand rests on my forearm, and she rubs her thumb along my skin soothingly.

The motion grounds the spin of the world around me, and within seconds I fall asleep once more.

Chapter 41

I'm not sure how much time has passed as I drift in and out of sleep.

If I saw Stolas again, I wouldn't know it, as the time between breaths of clarity is few and far in between, with nothing but darkness taking up the rest of the space or time.

There'd be times Angela would come in, and I'd wake up to a bowl of soup, but I'd hardly get any down before feeling ill. Other times I'd wake up coughing, and it wasn't until I'd seen blood in my palm that the severity of my situation really set in.

My eyes peel open, squinting against the fluorescent lights as I glance at the clock.

Every morning, Angela comes in quiet as a mouse, or at least I think she's quiet since I never hear her until she's gently waking me up to have breakfast after a morning prayer.

I haven't been one to know much about religion or have faith in any God, but each morning when she recites it, I can't help but feel the frigid edge of desperation that keeps my attention to her words longer and longer.

With a couple of hours left before she's due to come see me, I shut my eyes once more, welcoming the dark to take me.

"Rise and shine, Ms. Sterling." The gentle coo of Angela's voice is the first thing that catches my attention before the soft shake of my arm, and I slowly open my eyes to look at her.

She's perched beside the bed, with a bowl of something that looks like scrambled eggs, and my stomach churns uncomfortably.

"I don't think I can eat anything right now, Ang." My voice is hoarse from sleep, and each breath feels pained.

She frowns and chews her lip. "You need to at least try."

Pain lances up my neck as I shake my head ever so slightly. "Not a chance."

"Two bites, and I'll leave you alone."

I huff a laugh, throwing myself into a coughing fit as I cover my mouth, feeling the spray of liquid before looking at my hand. The varying shades of red that coat my palm has Angela hurrying over to wipe it down.

"Okay, one bite." She concedes, and I smile weakly.

"One. Small bite."

She beams and spoons some eggs before holding it to my mouth. "Don't make me do the choo choo sound."

My lips twitch, and I open my mouth for her to plop the small portion of food in, and I chew slow. My entire body is stiff because of the medication; chewing is no exception, and it feels completely unnatural.

By the time I swallow, she's already placed the platter of eggs and jello on the table behind her, and she sits back down with a clipboard and pen.

Normally, she grabs my hand and lowers her head to pray, so the sudden change makes my stomach drop.

"We received a call from your health insurance company, Ms. Sterling. It looks like they denied your claim as not medically necessary, and won't cover the costs of care."

Of course.

My mind wanders to what I had to do to pay off my debt last time, and tears spring to my eyes.

"This waiver is to state that if your insurance doesn't pay, you're liable for the cost of treatment." Her voice gets softer, quieter as she continues. "If you don't agree to this, Ms. Sterling, you will not continue treatment at our facility or any facility owned by Ethena Health."

My heart drops. "That's every medical center in the city." I whisper, and she gives me an apologetic look before holding the clipboard and pen between us.

What choice do I have? I can either die fast or die slower?

I stare at the clipboard for a moment before reaching over, stiffly taking the pen and scribbling my signature on the line.

She hurriedly puts it all aside before taking my hands in hers. "Would you pray with me this time, Kilian?"

The thought of putting my life into the hands of an almighty being would have once seemed far-fetched or outlandish, but with the way my life is going right now, I might as well try everything.

If Stolas exists, that must mean that God does too, right?

A deep-seated sense of desperation and despair settles into my bones as I think about the demon who helped show me the beauty in myself.

The demon who I wish was here with me.

A rogue tear falls down my cheek, and I nod. "Sure."

Angela's face lights up, and she leans forward to bow her head. "Almighty God, we ask for Your intervention today. In your presence, nothing is impossible." I murmur along with her, and she squeezes my hands slightly. "Heal Kilian from her illness. Bless her with Your Holy Spirit and drive this illness plaguing her away. Your timing is perfect. Your plan is perfect, and we hold on to the hope You give us to go on. In Jesus' name, amen."

She leans over and strokes my cheek with her thumb, looking much more hopeful than she did when she came in. I can't help but latch onto that hope with everything I have.

Maybe this will be the difference between life and death for me.

Perhaps faith in Him is all I need.

Chapter 42

Treatment isn't working.

It's obvious from the way my breathing has slowly gotten more shallow, and how I'm coughing up blood more often than not.

I've drifted in and out of sleep for another few days, with Angela switching between praying to God and pleading for Archangel Raphael's intervention.

The rapid decline of my health only tells me one thing.

I'm not worthy of their miracles.

As my eyes peel open to the dim light of the room, I survey the area, only to see a handful of candles flickering from where they sit around the room.

Perhaps even the hospital staff knows that I'm near the end.

I think back to Stolas' pleas for me to accept his help, and regret seeps into my bones as I fight the urge to consider how it could have been if I'd only accepted his help.

What if this was a test?

God does that, doesn't he? He tests his faithful servants...

I'd never been faithful, but maybe this is His way of saving me.

Swallowing hard, the door opens, and Dr. Newlin takes long strides into the room.

"Ah, Ms. Sterling. How are you feeling?"

I shake my head weakly, unable to answer more than that.

He seems to understand, and crosses his arms over his chest. "Angela says you've been quite the participant in her prayer sessions. I just want you to know that, I believe you're worth saving."

Tears spring to my eyes, and my chest tightens, constricting what little room I have to breathe as the door to the room opens once more.

Four individuals step inside, their faces obscured in the minimal light, and I can only assume that it's Angela and the rest of the nursing team.

A loud tapping sound hits the window, making it rattle as Dr. Newlin glances back at the others. He walks over as the tapping sounds out again, but when he lifts the blinds, there's nothing.

Blinds lowered, he turns toward me when the tapping sounds out even louder and more urgent, and Dr. Newlin quickly opens the blinds to see nothing there.

"The hell is going on here?" Dr. Newlin growls, the sound unlike anything I've heard from him as he unlocks the window, sliding it open before peering his head outside.

He's withdrawing into the room when something must catch his eye, and he suddenly recoils from the window as a blur of black barrels through the air toward him.

The sound of feathers rustling fills the air until the enormous creature collides with Dr. Newlin, and they fall backward to the floor and out of view.

There's no way that was...

Was that Talon?

The others in the room move toward the window, and that's when the closest face comes into view, illuminated by the low candlelight.

My heart nearly stops in my chest.

Bernard.

Movement in my peripheral catches my eye as I stare at the man from LA, only to see another ghost beside him.

William Rempson.

The third man takes a step forward, and my eyes widen at the visage of the man I'd bumped into at the grocery store weeks ago. My blood runs cold.

Holy shit.

Both men step back and hit the wall as my gaze slides to the middle of the room. Talon's already large body grows in size before a mist of darkness engulfs him, stretching taller until the ominous shadow towers over the men surrounding it. My eyes widen as the smoke starts to take form. What once was long, ebony feathers and mist, solidifies into Stolas' broad shoulders. His hands form fists at his sides, and within seconds I'm staring at his human form, his chest rising and falling hard with an expression of barely contained rage.

His otherworldly irises sweep the room as I gaze at the prince of hell with a mixture of awe and relief. Vines creep in from the window, and ease in from the gap in the door before sprawling over it, effectively shutting us in.

"What the hell–" Dr. Newlin barks from the floor before his shout is muffled, lasting hardly more than a breath of a moment before silence ensues.

"We can negotiate a deal, demon, there's no reason to—" Vines from the window grab Bernard, dragging him to the wall. I watch in horror as the plant forces itself into his mouth, and he suddenly goes limp.

"Negotiate from hell." Stolas' baritone voice carries in the air, vying for my attention as much as the stench of death as I watch Bernard stare at the floor before he convulses.

Oh my God.

"Kilian." Stolas shoves a ruby inlaid golden dagger into his coat before he steps closer, and I notice the other men in the room have suffered the same fate as Bernard as Stolas reaches the side of my bed. "It's okay, we can fix this."

He sounds like he's assuring himself more than me, and my next breath is hardly noticeable.

"Why–?" I cough suddenly, and blood spurts from my mouth, splattering the pristine white bedsheets as I choke.

Stolas moves quick as he leans me on my side, cursing beneath his breath. "It's not too late. We can fix this. You're going to be okay."

After a long moment, I get my cough under control, but the blood pouring from my mouth is a constant stream as my head spins.

I should have listened to him. I should have taken his help.

Why didn't I?

My mind goes back to the distrust and anger I'd felt after touching the tree. After meeting Bernard.

Oh, God. What if it was Bernard the whole time?

"Stolas..." I whisper, the sound almost inaudible as he pulls me into his arms. "I'm so sorry."

He hauls my limp form into his chest, and hurriedly carries me to the door as the vines move out of his way with each step.

"You have nothing to apologize for, Kilian. I should have done more. I should have intervened sooner."

I frown, feeling as if the life force is being drained from my body, and it's all I can do to whisper my response. "Intervened?"

His jaw tenses, and he nods slightly before kicking a door open, and cold air hits us as he quickly reaches his SUV. Within seconds, he's settled me in the driver's seat with him, and he throws the vehicle into drive.

"You were being targeted because of your genetics, Kilian. Your soul contains something they have been searching for, for millennia because of who you descend from. I didn't believe it when my brothers told me that there were daevari on earth, never mind that they'd fallen in love with them."

His otherworldly irises search my face with a heavy note of sadness. "Imagine my surprise to later learn that a daevari—a half-human, half-angel woman—was a researcher for the lab I was funding to find the cure for cancer."

I inhale to ask a question and cough hard, sending another splatter of blood everywhere, including all over Stolas' chest, but he doesn't seem to notice the mess.

"Easy," he whispers, and I don't miss the way his voice wavers. "Don't overdo it. Just hold on a little longer."

It's a constant fight to keep my eyes open, but I try nonetheless, even though the silence makes it nearly impossible to keep them open.

"Tell me," I whisper between shallow breaths, "everything."

His grip on me tightens. "When I first saw you, you'd just uncovered the use of oleander as an effective method for accelerating cancer treatment, but once you discovered that it was an effective cure, I knew they would ramp up their efforts to take you."

Even with my entire body sprinting towards death, I still feel frozen at his words.

Nobody knew I was the researcher who discovered it.

I kept that hidden.

He's entirely oblivious to my internal shock as he barrels onward. "My brothers are at war, Kilian. A war that, for millennia, I'd refused to join. Orobas prophesized that humans and angels would become one before heaven's fall, and I'd assumed it meant we would lose. I'd assumed he had seen a future where humans ceased to exist, and our war would be lost."

"But what if he was wrong? What if my assumptions had been wrong? What if he only prophesized of the existence of the daevari?" He shakes his head. "If the latter is true, then he also saw how they would seek to harvest your souls, like adding natural born generals of immense strength and speed to their ranks." His voice is hardly more than a whisper, as if afraid to speak the fall of heaven into existence.

"Little did I know that I'd have found a young daevari researcher, hidden away, oblivious to who she really is." His grip on me tightens as he steers with the other. "Unfortunately by the time I'd discovered you, they already had started to sink their claws into you, and I've spent the past few years..." He trails off and pauses before sighing, as if resigning himself to something. "I spent years manipulating their plans, but it became near impossible when they tried to use your asthma to make you more sick."

I frown and get a single word out. "How?"

His grip on my arm tightens as he turns off a main road into a parking lot. "Remember the medication you were taking when we first met?"

"Yes." I whisper, and my eyes flutter as I fight to keep them open.

"It was poison, Kilian. They've been poisoning you for years. The tree should have healed you, but Bernard was a step ahead somehow."

That's why I'd felt better when I had stopped taking my medications and went to LA with him.

If I had the strength, I'd have gasped, but all I can do is focus on keeping my breathing even as he hauls me from the driver's seat and carries me into a building.

My lungs hardly move as I try to inhale ever so slightly, and I know I'm close to my end. My fingers and toes tingle, with the tips going numb in a way even the cold weather could never do.

At least Aiden will have Connor. At least I figured out the error with the trials.

My eyes widen.

"The trials." I whisper, and Stolas nods his head.

"They were the ones who swapped the drug during the first trial, too, thinking they could ruin it, which would push you further into their hands."

They... they were the ones who swapped it? And he knew the whole time?

I can't ask the questions I wish to with such few words, and I know my time is running out as my head spins.

"Watch over Aiden?" I whisper, word by word, and his chest shudders as he shakes his head.

"Take care of him yourself, Kilian. You're not going anywhere."

The conviction in his voice is almost convincing, but when a droplet falls to my chest, I know better.

He turns a corner into a well lit room, and I glance around weakly as he moves to the center and sets me down.

Moonlight crests in from the glass ceiling, and even though light pollution would impair this sight anywhere else, I sit and stare at hundreds, maybe thousands of brilliant stars that cover the night sky.

It's breathtaking, and part of me knows it's the perfect sky to be under on the last night of my life.

Stolas looks me over, and his face falls.

I can almost feel the fracture in him as he quickly reaches for the dagger he'd previously taken from Bernard.

I want to ask what he's doing, to tell him it's okay, to stop worrying, but I'm too exhausted. My body too drained to speak up as he drags the blade over his palm.

He smears the blood over his chest before drawing a symbol into it, and the blood looks as if it's alive on his skin as a breeze picks up.

"Brother." Another voice fills the air behind Stolas as he turns around.

"Azrael." Stolas chokes out, his voice filled with relief. "Thank you for answering."

Azrael? Isn't that an angel?

"Duty demands it when one is summoned with such... desperation." Stolas steps aside, and my gaze lands on a man mere feet away. His dark robes flow to the ground, and when he takes a step closer, my breath catches in my lungs at the smoke billowing from his back in the shape of wings.

His dark hair falls forward in front of his blue eyes that look as if they see right through me.

And maybe they do.

"She's dying." He states before his attention turns to Stolas. "Why summon me for a mortal?"

I want to tell him there's no need, but Stolas' next words douse my body with cold.

"Exchange. My life for hers."

Oh, God. He's the angel of death. That has to be why Stolas summoned him.

Azrael's brows pull together. "She's mortal, Stolas. You trade eternity for a breath. This is not–"

"I understand the price, and yet I demand it."

The angel's jaw tenses as he glances between us, and I want to scream and shout for him not to, but before I can, he reaches behind his back, pulling out a black, curved blade that glimmers in the moonlight.

"You understand what this means, yes?" Azrael whispers. "Trading your life for hers will pull you from the cycle. You will not be reborn."

Azrael's golden eyes flick to me for half a second, and my heart stutters in my chest.

He can't do this. I can't do this without him.

There's no way I could go on knowing what he sacrificed.

I don't want to live a life without him.

No.

Stolas nods, moving to kneel between us with his head bowed. "Let it be done."

Every second feels like an eternity as Azrael crosses his arm over his chest. Stolas' eyes close as my body continues to shut down, and whether because of my panic or the poison, my lungs seize.

The angel of death brings his blade down, aimed for Stolas' chest, and I don't think, I just move.

My heavy limbs respond just in time to thrust me from where I sit, and I cover Stolas with my body, wrapping my arms around him as something cold slices through my back from my shoulder to my hip.

Surprisingly, I feel no pain as Stolas rears back with wide eyes, and horror etches his expression as his arms snake around me, and he clutches me to his chest.

"No! Kilian, what in God's name are you doing?"

The numb feeling in my body grows rapidly, spreading to my limbs as my head bobs. Tears stream down his face as he supports my head and glares desperately at Azrael.

"Do something, fix this."

"You know as well as I do that this cannot be undone by me."

The world grows dim, and he presses his forehead to mine with a sob. "You stubborn fool. How can you expect me to simply exist as if you hadn't?"

I vaguely feel his hands against my hair before my soul leaves my body.

Chapter 43

My eyes flutter open as a breeze glides over my skin, and I surge upright, scanning the tall grass that surrounds me.

Doing a full circle, there's nothing else in sight, just a sea of yellow and green grass so tall that from where I sit, the tips are at eye level, only giving way to the deep blue sky above. The sun beats down on me, and I squint before turning the other direction.

"Where the hell am I?"

Pushing to my feet, I turn in a full circle again.

Shouldn't I be dead?

Could Stolas have had something to do with this?

My chest squeezes at the thought of him, and I swallow hard.

Do I leave this spot or stay here?

Chewing the inside of my cheek, I settle on the decision to move forward, and I aimlessly put one foot in front of the other.

I'm not sure how long it's been when I finally see something in the distance, wandering among the tall grasses, and head toward it. At first with the sunlight half blinding me, I think it's the silhouette of a handful of trees and bushes, but when a cloud hovers overhead, blocking the sun's rays, I stop dead in my tracks.

It's a herd of horses.

No. Not horses.

Enormous bodies of white or silver stand off in the distance, with large, folded wings tucked into their sides as they graze. Their manes and tails flow in the breeze, and I find myself frozen in place as I watch them.

Where in the world am I that has winged horses?

Is this some kind of dream?

The winged horses snort at one another before they all turn to look in another direction, with their ears all perked as a note of unease sinks in. Their reaction is reminiscent of a herd of prey animals when a predator is nearby, which is only reinforced when they all gallop away, wings spread wide, and they take into the air.

It's an odd sight, watching horses ascend into the sky until they disappear on the horizon.

They disappear as my eyes sweep the horizon for any movement, and the realization that I truly might be alone sinks in.

What if this is some kind of purgatory?

Resigning myself to continue my search, I put one foot in front of the other, following in the direction I'd seen the winged horses. Clouds come and go, giving merely a breath of reprieve from the sun beating down on my shoulders.

Every so often, the grass rustles in the breeze, and I turn my attention to the sky, where the sun creeps slowly toward the horizon. By the time it's nearly set, just hovering over the line where the sea of grass meets the sky, I'm exhausted, and bordering on hopelessness.

I don't regret dying—assuming that's what happened. I guess part of me had hoped that I'd be able to find a way out of here, or at the very least, find someone else here.

The grass rustles in the breeze, and by the time the sun has nearly set over the horizon where the sky meets the sea of grass, I'm exhausted.

My gaze scans over the rippling grass once more, following the long shadow from the clouds overhead.

Is this really all the afterlife has to offer?

It's just an eternity of nothing except some winged horses?

Is this what Stolas would have been doing? Would he have been stranded, like me?

The thought of him springs tears to my eyes, and I can't help but think back on everything he'd said.

He knew the things I'd kept a secret.

He'd tried to help me, even when he had already decided he wasn't going to get involved like his brothers were.

The urge to see him and find a way out of here makes my limbs electric, and I push to my feet, conceding to the urge to move forward.

I only get a few steps in when a deep yet unfamiliar voice halts me in my footsteps.

"Going somewhere important?"

Whirling around, my gaze lands on the tall form of a man mere feet away. The dress pants and shirt he's wearing wouldn't be out of place on earth, nor would his near-black hair that he runs his fingers through. Something about him screams we are not the same, though, and I keep my guard up.

"Who are you?"

His bright grey irises pin me in place as he shoves his hands in his pockets and grins. "My name is Kane. I assume you're Kilian Sterling?"

My heart beats hard as I contemplate the danger of confirming who I am to this stranger—as if I have any other choice.

What if he was working with Bernard?

"I still don't know who you are."

Kane's lips twitch. "I just told you."

"Right, but that doesn't really answer my question." My eyes narrow on him. "What do you want?"

"Well, I have to assume I've found the right person." He glances around us, as if wordlessly pointing out there's no one else around.

But that's just it. I'm dead, and this place will be my eternity. I'm not just about to trust some random guy I don't know in the afterlife. Not after everything Stolas said about who—and what—I am.

"Where am I?" My voice wavers, but if Kane notices, he doesn't show it.

"You're currently in what we call the barrens." He must notice my confusion as his lips twitch. "The afterlife has multiple levels to it. The closer you are to heaven, the more the levels are inhabited. The barrens are one of the lowest levels where the arionus travel with their herds."

"I'm going to pretend that I understood half of that."

The humor on his face appears genuine. "I wouldn't expect you to. This is not where you belong just yet."

It takes everything not to scoff. "Oh ya? And where do I belong, then?"

"Come with me, and I'll show you."

I level him with a deadpan stare. "I'm not going anywhere with you unless I know what the hell you want from me."

Kane just chuckles to himself. "He really wasn't joking about you being stubborn."

The last word from his mouth sends a wave of relief over me, and he must see it on my face as his expression softens. "Azrael told me everything, including that you sacrificed yourself for Stolas, who would have otherwise lived for an eternity."

My chest tightens, and my gaze drops.

"It was not your time to die, Kilian." His voice is agonizingly soft, and it takes a moment to register his words before my attention drags back to him.

"What is that supposed to mean?"

"There are rules on earth between the forces of heaven and hell, and Azrael should not have reaped your soul. I'm here to restore the balance and escort you back to where you belong."

My brows pinch together. "I don't—I don't understand. My body–"

"Your body has *mostly* been returned to the state it should have been in without interference from either demons or angels." He searches my face for a moment. "God himself wills for you to return to earth, Kilian."

This can't be real. It has to be some sort of trick.

My breath catches, and Kane pulls his hand from his pocket and offers it between us. "Let me take you home."

I swallow hard, struggling to place my trust in this stranger as I reach out to slide my palm into his. His fingers are warm as they encircle mine, and he brings his free hand to his mouth and murmurs.

The air in front of us ripples, and before long an oval shape shimmers, the area widening until it's the same height as me, and I stare at the glimmering image of my bedroom.

My stomach flips as I step up to the portal and pause to look at Kane. He tilts his head curiously, and it makes my nervousness build even further as my palms grow slick.

"Are you hesitating for a reason?"

I turn my attention to the portal again. "Will Stolas live if I return?"

"He will."

"Will he remain unharmed?"

My eyes find Kane again, and he nods. "Unharmed, yes."

"His life span will be unchanged?"

Kane laughs–really laughs–as if he finally realizes my hesitation. "You're concerned this is a trap?"

"He's immortal. He will live far longer than I will, and he should. I don't want to be the reason his life gets cut short."

Kane regards me with a look I can't quite place. "This is not a trick, Kilian. Azrael owes a debt. Taking a life is not something easily repaid."

The look on his face is genuine, and I nod as he releases my hand. "Return to your world, continue your research. Stolas is waiting to live a *very* long life with you."

His last sentence makes my heart soar, and I blow out a breath.

"It was nice meeting you, Kane." He inclines his head, as I go to step into the portal and whisper. "I hope it is the only time."

Chapter 44

Using my momentum to get through the portal, I feel it wash over my face and chest first before travelling along to my back, and when I open my eyes on the other side, I find myself alone in my bedroom.

How Kane knew where to portal me, I guess I'll never know.

"Home sweet home." I whisper. A clatter sounds to my left, and I jolt in the direction.

Before I can make heads or tails of anything, a tall form rushes forward, and a mess of dark hair fills my vision as I'm swept off my feet. The woodsy scent of his cologne fills my senses, and I wrap my arms around Stolas' shoulders as he shudders.

"Thank you, God." He murmurs into my hair, clutching me to his chest as he spins us in a slow circle, peppering my head with kisses.

"What happened, Stolas?" I whisper, and he sets me on my feet, but his kisses don't stop as he walks me to my bed, pressing his lips anywhere he can.

My legs hit the bed, and he eases me back into it, boxing me in with his arms as he continues to turn my entire body flush.

"My price."

I freeze. "Your price?"

Shit. Was Kane lying?

Stolas pauses and searches my face. "It's you. You are the price I'd never pay. I told my brothers I'd never truly join this war in earnest. I told them I held no value in joining their battle, but I was wrong."

I stare at him, and he presses another kiss to my forehead before leveling me with a serious look.

"The false prophets in this world made a mistake when they tried to take the mortal I value above all else from this world, from me. For so long I've sat back and watched, taking small steps when I needed to, but now? Their claim to what is truly my dominion has come to an end."

"What does that mean?"

He grins and kisses down my chest as my pulse spikes. "It means the princes of hell are coming for them all, and their command will crumble."

Kane's words all come rushing back.

God willed for me to return to a prince of hell?

I swallow as Stolas looks up at me from where he hovers above my stomach.

I know I was never well versed on the subject, but...

"I thought God abandoned demons?"

Stolas eases my shirt up, and my breath hitches. "History has been, and will always be, written by those who were victorious, Kilian. We were never abandoned, nor did we fall from heaven. We fled."

My blood runs cold. "Fled?"

"It's a long story, but suffice to say that nothing is what it seems, Kilian. Demons for a long time have accepted the stain of our existence, but to us, it speaks more of our resilience than of any shame." He presses his lips to my skin. "But that is a story for another day."

Chapter 45

Six weeks later

Standing beside the other researchers along the walls, I join in on the loud clapping that roars in the air, watching as all the volunteer participants in the clinical trial form a line at the beginning of the hallway.

Tears stream down their flushed faces as the first person takes a step to the bell hanging near the entrance to the building. The now-cancer-free volunteer takes the last step to the bell, and when the sound echoes through the hallway, half of the researchers wipe at their eyes.

Ron hands a card to the man, barely holding himself together, shaking his hand before Jen gives him a hug.

If you had asked me five years ago if I'd thought it was possible to have found the cure for adenocarcinoma, I'd have said not a chance.

If you had also asked me if I was going to meet a prince of hell, get poisoned and subsequently die all because I found the cure for adenocarcinoma, I'd have said you're crazy.

But now? As I watch every single volunteer in the trial ring the bell announcing their triumphant victory over the disease, I can't help but feel appreciative of the path I was on, even if it meant that I needed to die.

In the end, Aiden's surgery was successful in removing his tumor. Ron gave the entire control group the option to receive the drug once the trial ended, and with no negative side effects, all of them had started their round of treatment this week.

My phone vibrates in my pocket, and I slide the answer button and put it to my ear, dipping into the dark office behind me. "Hello?"

"Is this *the* Kilian Sterling?"

I frown, and suspicion coats my veins. "Who is this?"

I can hear the smile in the stranger's voice as he responds, sounding lighthearted and cheerful in contrast to my wariness. "My name is Vassago. I'm Stolas' brother."

The way he leaves it slightly open-ended with his tone has me swallowing. "Ah, right. What can I do for you?"

He chuckles. "Actually, Stolas called and said my legal services are needed to fight some denied claims from your health insurance?"

My brows shoot up. "Uh, yes, actually. I was literally dying, and they declined them."

"Wonderful. Well, not wonderful, but clearly you're sort of alive now, so all is well, that ends well."

I glance at the closed door to make sure no one's come in. "So you think you can win?"

He laughs. "Not only will we win, Kilian, but this lawsuit will change everything. They won't expect it. I'll stop by on Friday to discuss."

My heart feels like it could beat out of my chest at the confidence in his voice, like he really truly believes we will. "Thank you, Vassago."

The humor in his voice disappears. "You're family now, Kilian. You never need to thank any of us. If anything, we should be the ones thanking you. Two hundred years of asking Stolas to join us fell on deaf ears, but when he found you? Everything changed."

Reflecting on the events leading up to my death, I nod. "I know the feeling."

"See you Friday, Kilian."

"Have a good day, Vassago."

The line clicks as he hangs up, and I hold my phone to my chest, taking a deep breath.

Between curing adenocarcinoma, fighting the insurance industry, and everything in between, these assholes won't know what hit them.

And I have the rest of eternity to enjoy seeing them fail.

... The end

Epilogue

Meanwhile, on the West Coast...

"Hello, this is Ethena Health. How can I direct your call?"

Putting on my most neutral tone, I lean further over my cell phone. "Hi there. My name is Maris Sylvara. I'm a reporter for News Alliance. I'm looking to ask some—"

The line cuts out and I release a tense sigh. It's been weeks of interviews and dead ends trying to figure out the truth behind the disappearances of so many doctors.

Every provider's office I've called for statements or requests to speak directly with staff has been turned away, save a few. The few who spoke to me hardly gave much of an answer.

The most I have to go off of is that they worked at the same facility, saw a handful of the same patients, but all of them saw one patient in particular.

A throbbing headache builds behind my eyes, and I rub my palms into them as the door behind me creaks.

"Babe, are you going to start getting ready?"

I glance at the time and groan. "I lost track of time. Shit."

Robert chuckles behind me. "Tell me something I don't know."

Pushing off the desk with a sigh, I cross the room, cutting right down the hallway as Robert's footsteps trail behind me. It's been a year since we'd moved in together, and he has never been far away since.

Outside of going to church by himself every Sunday now, we're nearly inseparable. We live together, work together, sleep together. It's a decent arrangement for two lonely hearts that somehow found solace in one another.

Robert brushes past me to his side of the bed, opening the drawer and dropping something inside. It's only another few minutes before I've tugged a dress up the length of my body and touched up my makeup.

My gaze flicks to Robert, staring at his phone with a frown. "What is it?"

At the sound of my voice, his attention turns to me. "You know that viral video of the civilians being bombed overseas?"

My eyebrows shoot up. "Yeah. The one half the networks are saying is propaganda?"

He nods. "Channel Five News is covering it." His lip curls and he shakes his head. "I guess they'll cover anything nowadays."

Part of me wants to tell him that Channel Five News just has more freedom than us, but I drop it. News Alliance runs our stories most of the time, but the messaging has to go through several rounds of approvals before it even makes it to the air.

The last story we covered was one we did together, and it nearly got smothered because I accidentally interviewed a woman who spoke poorly about one of our investors. Granted, she wasn't incorrect in anything she'd said, but regardless, it took six revisions and three cuts of content before they'd approved it.

Rob ended up getting all the credit for that story, anyway, and it was a gutted shell of what it could have been.

"Remind me why we need to go to this dinner again? It's not like it has anything to do with us," Rob groans, turning off the light next to his bed and pushing to his feet. He stands half a foot taller than me with my heels on, and I laugh under my breath.

"You mean other than welcoming our new director?" My eyes slide to his, and he bends over to tie his dress shoes. "Apparently, he's passionate about art, and thinks news is art in itself. So if that's true, technically, we will have everything to do with it."

My phone vibrates in my purse as we head out the door, and I pull it out, seeing one of my correspondents in Pennsylvania with a hidden message preview. My heart thrashes.

Geramy: Dr. Newlin and three medical staff died in a murder-suicide three days ago.

I falter, coming to a stop as I stare wide-eyed at the message.

"Maris?" Robert's voice reaches my ears, but I can't bring myself to respond to him as my fingers fly across the screen.

Maris: I'm sorry, what?!

Robert steps in close and reads the messages over my shoulder. "You're still obsessing over that damn string of deaths?"

Anger rises in me, and it takes everything I have not to snap at him as my mind runs a mile per minute. Weeks ago, I'd spent nearly eighty hours per week researching, gathering intel, doing interviews, and following leads on the deaths of these doctors. Robert had finally had enough after one night when he'd overheard me call Ms. Sterling to see if she had anything come up.

I knew at that point I was hitting a dead end, but now with Dr. Newlin dying in a murder-suicide...

Maris: Who was the suspect?

Geramy: Dr. Newlin's nurse, Angela Thomas.

A pit forms in my stomach. I'd interviewed her right off the bat, since she worked under most of the doctors who'd died.

Geramy: Police are saying she was having an affair with Dr. Newlin, and it was a crime of passion. She murdered the nurses on staff with her and the doctor before taking her own.

Maris: How do they know all this for certain?

"Maris, let's go." Robert says more forcefully, his tone curt with his growing frustration as he gestures to the car. I mindlessly close the distance to the passenger side and climb in as my phone vibrates again.

Geramy: One of the nurses Angela worked with had screenshots showing Angela confessing everything, including her intent to murder them just hours before their death.

Something about this still doesn't sit right with me, and I chew the inside of my cheek as Robert navigates out of our neighborhood.

Maris: What was the method she used?

Geramy: Cyanide poisoning.

My hand covers my mouth as I connect the dots to the rest of the doctor's deaths. How is it possible that one nurse could have murdered so many medical professionals?

What purpose would that serve?

"Maris, what is it?" Robert's voice is tight, and I glance over to see his jaw tensing. His hand grips the wheel hard enough that his knuckles turn white, and I shake my head.

"There was a murder-suicide in PA." I whisper, and his brow twitches up ever so slightly.

"Is this related to—?"

I nod. "Yeah. Another doctor was murdered, and the suspect confessed before taking their own life."

He sighs. "Well, at least you can stop obsessing now that you know who the murderer was."

The pit in my stomach grows, and I nod, staring out the window as buildings pass by. "Yeah, maybe."

It's the best answer I can give him after spending weeks chasing leads. Part of me suspects that there's more to it, but Rob made it clear a week ago that he didn't want to entertain any other fantasies about what could be happening there.

My mind wanders to Kilian Sterling as Rob puts the radio on, blaring the local news, but not loud enough to drown out my thoughts.

"... we cannot allow this propaganda to be spread further. Foreign entities are investing money into sowing discord among our population aimed at creating political and socio-economical duress."

I glance at the GPS, seeing that we have five minutes left until we get there.

"Government officials have put in place a Kharidian travel ban for all civilians after a reporter for Channel Five News was caught in the crossfire between local authorities and rebel factions."

Rob reaches over and turns the volume up more.

"The Kharidian parliament is working closely with government officials to find a solution and work toward a ceasefire in the region, but the question is, will the rebellion leaders agree to peace?"

Another voice chimes in to answer. *"That's a great question, Mark, and I think that while our government works to support the Kharidian people, we need to tend to more matters at home, not involve ourselves in a foreign country's war and politics."*

We pull into the near-full parking lot in silence, and Rob finds a space closest to the doors. The guests filing into the building are all dressed impressively, putting my meager cocktail dress to shame with their extravagance.

Swallowing my nerves for a first introduction to our new boss, I climb out of the car and follow the crowd with Rob at my side. Chatter and laughter fill the air, and I spent my time searching the crowd for anyone I might know.

Rob leans in to my ear. "Want a drink?"

My gaze flicks at the line building at the bar, and I nod. "Two, please."

He just gives me an exasperated look, but stalks toward the bar, leaving me to my thoughts. Tearing my focus from him, I scan over the crowd, half people-watching and half keeping an eye out for people I know.

Someone bumps my shoulder from behind and I twist to see a gorgeous, but familiar face of a woman who should, by all reason, be in Pennsylvania right now.

"Oh! I'm so sorry!" She says in a shrill voice, her eyes wide as she covers her mouth. "I wasn't paying attention. Please forgive me."

I release a quiet laugh, noticing the mountain of a man beside her. "Kilian Sterling, is that really you?"

Her eyes widen, but not enough to show she's overly surprised. "It is, and who might you be?"

The man next to her brushes her hair over her shoulder, his fingertips brushing her skin as a flush crawls up her neck. I can't say part of me isn't jealous to see such a tender act between who I'm assuming are lovers.

"Maris Sylvara." I state, seeing the recognition flash across her expression as she gasps.

"Oh! Wow, what a small world. What are you doing here?" Her gaze shifts to her male counterpart, and if I didn't know better, I'd think she's nervous.

I glance around the room and gesture to the crowd. "My new boss wanted to host a company-wide art-meets-news convention and dinner for his entrance into News Alliance Network, it seems. What about you?"

She grins at my tone and choice of words. "Ah, we had an invitation. I suppose we're the art in the equation of your bosses grandiose entrance."

I catch a glimpse of Rob stepping up to the bar finally as Kilian gestures to the man beside her. "Maris Sylvara, this is Stolas, my boyfriend."

The way she says it is almost hesitant, but before I can raise a brow, Stolas steps over and extends his hand between us. I shake it gently, returning my attention to Kilian as her mouth drops open.

"Did you ever find out anything more about that story you were researching?" Again, she looks so hesitant to ask that I'm borderline suspicious.

"Uh, well... Since Angela confessed to the murder before it happened, I'm assuming she was involved in all the others, too, and she just got caught this time." I say, and Kilian's eyes widen into saucers.

"Angela!?" she squeaks.

I nod. "Yeah, apparently she texted a friend her confession before it all happened." I pause as Stolas squeezes Kilian's hand for a moment. "Since the other deaths all had the same sequence of events, I can only imagine she was responsible." I murmur, seeing Rob picking up our drinks... or struggling to.

"So, are you still investigating?" Kilian asks quietly, and I shake my head.

"I've been told it's a waste of resources, so no. I need to go, though. It was nice to see you," I say to Kilian before turning my gaze to Stolas. "And meet you."

They both smile, murmuring goodbyes before I head over to Rob. He hands me my drinks, and I spill a little of one, so I take a sip of both. My eyes trail the crowd, still looking for someone but for the life of me, I can't figure out who.

We make our way from the reception to the dinner over the next thirty minutes, and my mind wanders to the radio station news earlier. Without having a story to focus on, I might go insane, but if I could get a unique story or perspective that hasn't gone viral...

Perhaps that will be the key to my success in this damn company.

As long as Rob doesn't overtake or steal my thunder.

Kharidian war, prepare yourselves for Maris Sylvara.

To be continued in Syndicated...

Acknowledgements

I have to first, again, say a huge thank you to Amanda Dumky for the insanely gorgeous cover. I will forever appreciate your immense talent more than you will ever possibly know.

A huge thank you to my husband, who supports all my chaotic hobbies, endeavors and passions without a second thought. I love you to the moon and back. In all the romances I write, there's always so many layers of the devotion and undying love that you surround me with that inspires these connections, and I will never take that for granted.

Thank you to my street team for being so supportive, hyping me up even when I was lost in the sauce, and always bringing excitement to my life. You are all beautiful humans and I cannot tell you how thankful I am to have you all in my life.

Lastly, much like with my Unbroken series, thank you to all the readers who decided to give this new series a chance. I can't promise it's the most well written, or well written at all... but I, as with many authors, put a piece of myself into my work, and taking the time to read it... well that may be the best gift of all.

It's just my hope that you enjoyed it, even if only for a moment before you move on to your next adventure.

Other Works by Aella C Grey

- 252 -

The Unbroken Series

> Shadows of Dusk (Unbroken Book 1)
>
> Light of Dawn (Unbroken Book 2)

Prince of Hell Series

> Summoned (Prince of Hell Book 1)
>
> Barred (Prince of Hell Book 2)
>
> Convalesced (Prince of Hell Book 3)
>
> Syndicated (Prince of Hell Book 4)
>
> Classified (Prince of Hell Book 5)

Eclipsed Souls Series

> Wings of Doubt (Eclipsed Souls Book 1)
>
> Obsidian Flames (Eclipsed Souls Book 2)
>
> Ascent of the Fallen (Eclipsed Souls Book 3)